I0760972

The Manifestation

Black Spiral, Book 2

Rob Tucker

Black Spiral Series, Book 2

Tell-Tale Publishing Group, LLC
Swartz Creek, MI 48737

Printed in The United States of America

Energy, such as light, is given off and absorbed in tiny definite units called quanta or photons. Light appears to be in a steady stream or continuous flow, but is a series of many small actions. Radiant energy is transmitted in waves in ranges of certain frequencies called spectrums. When the atoms of a substance are disturbed, such as in a metal or in a biological form, the death of an animal or a human, all the atoms of that substance begin to vibrate and the energy radiates outward and escapes just as a vapor dissipates into the medium of air from boiling water. It becomes dark energy. Spirits reside in these dark spaces of the universe.

Avatar - *The descent of a deity of earth in an incarnate form or some manifest shape, the incarnation of a god. An embodiment or concrete manifestation of a principle, attitude, view of life, or the like.*

I

The Manifestation

Prologue

"The last time I saw him alive, he was walking toward the elevator," said Bernadette. "I was some distance away down the hall. He gave me a little wave and stepped inside the elevator."

"Was he alone?" FBI Agent Leon Safullo and Bernadette walked beside a line of yellow crime scene investigation tape from the glass-fronted office along a row of insulated partitioned cubicles, toward the elevator bay on the fourteenth floor. CSI forensic specialists finished swabbing for prints in Gale Walsh's office and checking the elevator. Leon would soon discover that both were devoid of evidence.

"I couldn't see from where I was."

"Do you know if he was leaving the building?"

"His laptop was still on his desk. He always took it with him if he was leaving for the day. He didn't have any meetings scheduled and it was past lunch time. I thought he might be going to see someone in another department."

"When he didn't returned by the end of the day, did you call anyone?"

"I did call some of the other managers he might have been likely to visit, but no one else had seen him."

"How about security?"

"I checked with parking security to see if he had left. His car is still in its reserved space."

"The building has surveillance cameras in every hall. My partner, Agent Berzinsky, looked at the electronic backup covering the week Mr. Walsh was gone."

"I don't know anything about that. It's strange. It seems like he just walked into the elevator and vanished."

"I'm sure there's a logical explanation," said Leon. "We just have to find it. Would you give me directions to the security department. Agent Berzinsky will continue examining records in Mr. Walsh's office. He'll have more questions for you."

"Of course, I'll go back. Security is on the main floor to the right of the entrance lobby. Any one of the guards can help you."

"Thank you, Miss Garcetti." Leon walked away to the elevators. Bernadette returned to the glass office.

"Maybe he had a heart attack or a stroke," she commented to Ed Berzinski, the second investigating agent.

"He's been missing for a week," said Berzinski. "No one has heard from him or seen him again until now."

"How do you suppose he died?"

"We won't know until we have an autopsy report."

Curious employees gathered and stared through the glass wall. Three were rapidly taking photos using their iPhones until a police officer ordered them to leave and another officer widened the cordoned off area with yellow tape.

"It seems like he just wandered away somewhere and then suddenly came back," said Bernadette. "I walked into his office at the start of the business day and discovered Gale Walsh dead, sitting upright in his chair. At first, I thought he was sleeping, but upon a closer look at his lack of response, I realized I was talking to his corpse. He was fully clothed in the gray stripped business suit and red tie he was wearing at the time of his disappearance one week ago."

"Either someone brought him back dead and planted him here, or they killed him when he returned," said Berzinski.

"How do you know he was murdered?"

"I don't. The condition of his corpse would indicate that he was. He's been gone a week, then shows up sitting at his desk, and no one knows of his whereabouts and how he got here. He had to be carried in, but there isn't any sign in the video surveillance."

Bernadette's professional composure suddenly unraveled. Her face turned white and she began to tremble. Berzinski grabbed her arm and tall slender body and supported her into a chair. Notwithstanding her beauty and expensive light blue business suit, she looked like a frightened child. Her manicured hands tentatively crept upward to clutch and interrupt the coiffed strands of her dark hair.

"This is so chilling."

"Do you recall anyone threatening Mr. Walsh or making a negative comment to you about him?"

"No, not that I can remember. He was always well-liked."

"Any enemies or adversaries in the business world? Any lawsuits?" Berzinski knew the company was hounded by the liberal media for engaging in questionable Government contracts and funding lobbyists with conservative agendas.

"He never mentioned any?"

"Did you screen his calls?"

"Yes."

"What about his Emails," asked Berzinsky, craning his thick neck.

Had he not arrived with his graying late middle-age partner, she would have taken Berzinsky for a bodyguard or a wrestler. Leon's younger muscle-charged partner leant the pair a threatening aura of force that the slender gentle-looking Leon did not possess.

"Only his business Emails, not his personal ones."

"Did he give you his password to access personal emails?"

"No, he was very private about that. I did not get involved in his personal life other than in a superficial way, usually related to his social agenda, birthdays and anniversaries, theater tickets, vacation reservations, and the like."

"We'll be taking his hard drive, laptop, and cell phone. You mentioned anniversaries. How long was he married to June Walsh?"

"Twenty-seven years."

"From what you know about them, would you say they were compatible?"

"They had their differences, like most couples, and there were problems."

Berzinski shifted in his chair. "What can you tell me about their differences."

"They had arguments."

"Arguments."

"Yes."

"So you must have overheard some of these arguments."

"I didn't spy on them, if that's what you mean."

"I'm not accusing you of anything," said Berzinsky. "I'm just searching for information."

"Sometimes June would come into the office and I couldn't help overhear them."

"Did Mr. Walsh ever discuss their differences with you? Confide in you?"

"I'm always a polite and sympathetic listener when Gale had a need to share his problems."

"I can see you are a sympathetic person. How long have you been Gale's, Mr. Walsh's secretary?"

"Going on ten years."

"So you know a few things about their relationship."

Bernadette nodded.

"Were you a friend of his wife?"

"Yes."

"Did you talk to each other, confide in each other. Go out and have lunch. You must have been invited to the Walsh's parties."

"A few times."

"Did she ever ask you about her husband's mistress?"

Bernadette did not respond.

"You know about his mistress."

Bernadette nodded.

"Did his wife know?"

"Yes."

"Is it something you heard them argue about?"

Bernadette nodded.

"Did June Walsh rely on you for information?"

"She did."

"For instance."

"When he would go to see her and take her out on the town."

"You kept Mrs. Walsh informed."

"Yes, I sympathized with her. Despite all the money she and Gale had, she was an angry sad woman."

"So you didn't approve of what your boss was doing."

"No, I didn't approve. I don't approve of men who are dishonest and cheat on their wives."

"Is that something you've experienced?"

"No, I'm not married. I've never been married."

"We tried to contact June. She's not here in New York."

Bernadette nodded. "She went back to Ireland. She and Gale have a second home there."

"How recently?"

"About a month ago."

"Does she know her husband is dead?"

"How would she? I just found out myself."

"Do you maintain contact with her? Talk to her on the phone? Exchange Emails?"

"Not since she left. She didn't have anything to do with this. She just wanted to get away from him, change her life. Like I said, she was not a happy woman."

"You were friends."

"She was a lonely person. We became friends."

"Because of his mistress."

"No, we were friends before that. We genuinely liked each other. We shared a few common interests."

"What interests?"

Bernadette folded her arms across her chest and sat upright in her chair. "We like classical music, opera, dance and theater. She always had tickets available and asked me to go with her, since Gale didn't care about any of that."

"So you went to concerts and the theater. Anything else?"

"We both liked art. We'd go to museum exhibitions. Her sister, Keira, is an art historian and collector and works in public relations. We attended her exhibits."

Berzinsky continued his line of questioning. "Working here ten years you've been privileged to know the operations of the company and, in particular, the details of Mr. Walsh's business."

"What has been shared with me is confidential."

"I can appreciate that. However, the FBI has the authority to investigate and review all information, regardless of its confidentiality. There's at least circumstantial evidence that he was kidnapped. What you know might lead to the cause of how and why he died."

Bernadette looked over at Walsh's corpse. "I'm not withholding anything from you, but I do want to be sensitive to his wife's feelings about all this."

"Did you ever sleep with Mr. Walsh?"

She flushed. "Never. I feel insulted that you ask. Mr. Walsh and I had only a professional business relationship."

"You're an attractive woman. Do you have a relationship with another male, or female?"

"I know you have to ask these things, but do I have to answer?"

"Yes, you do."

"I date other men, and I am not a lesbian."

"Thank you."

"You're welcome. Unless you have more questions, I have to take care of some matters at my desk."

"You may return to your desk, but all electronic communications to and from this company have been placed under immediate surveillance."

"Does that mean I can't do my work?"

"You can do whatever work you usually do. It's just being closely watched."

"What about him?" The corpse's head was thrown back and his gaping eyes stared at the ceiling.

"Mr. Walsh's corpse will be removed by the coroner."

Bernadette nodded, rose from the chair near the door and walked unsteadily to her desk in the office directly across the hall. Placing the cursor at the Internet browser, she keyed in the letters EVOL. A moment passed and she experienced a strange sensation of light-headedness and some level of energy evaporating from her.

She wondered if she were ill.

***

Gale Walsh's final thought as he entered the elevator was a vision of himself lying naked and alone on a remote island beach. Simonetta materialized like a water nymph out of a clear azure lagoon. He focused on her perfectly arched bare feet stepping with long, graceful strides across the warm white sand. His gaze moved up her lean muscled legs to her hips and flat abdomen and further to her swinging arms and swaying breasts glistening with droplets and further to the magnificent beauty of her face and cascade of wet golden hair.

She spread her legs and lowered herself to consume his intense painful erection and moved rhythmically up and down, taking him deep inside her. He came with an enormous gasp but the flow of his semen did not cease and his erection did not abate.

As she gazed into his eyes, he sensed his life fluids ebbing out of him and into her and he knew that he was dying and could do nothing to prevent his death.

Within a short time, his body was reduced to a dried out wraithlike creature in rigor mortis, much like the remaining chitin shell of a dead grasshopper.

Chapter 1
The Beginning

"How do we investigate this?" asked Berzinsky. "It's more bizarre than the last one. And we never really solved that."

"That was the beginning of a trail," said Leon. "I had hoped we would see the end of it, but now this."

"We have nothing to attach it to. The DNA analysis Amy Jacobi gave us last time doesn't take us anywhere. There isn't any link to anything."

"At least nothing tangible."

"I still don't buy into that dark energy Satanist crap," said Berzinsky. "Someone had to put up that website as an Internet hoax."

"The unknown suspect behind it isn't a joke. He was obviously playing with us. Gale Walsh's murder has the appearance of the same kind of otherworld killer."

"That's the point. The operative word here is appearance," said Berzinsky. "He's hiding behind this persona like a mask or disguise."

"There is a difference between what happened last time to Paul Evans and now, to Gale Walsh," said Leon. "Evans was only persecuted. He wasn't murdered."

"They were both high-ranking globalist CEOs running billion dollar companies."

"We can explain what happened to Paul Evans as a form of psychological terrorism," said Leon. "We don't know enough about Gale Walsh to even make an assumption."

"I can't imagine any explanation for how this was done."

"We'll take it one step at a time. Find out who knew him and had any interaction with him."

"I have a friend who's a magician, an illusionist," said Berzinsky. "Maybe there's a way this was pulled off as some kind of trick."

"A good place to start. Something that's real."

"Max can make illusion look real." Berzinsky auto-dialed Maximilian Schultz on his cell phone and set up an appointment for that afternoon.

Usually Leon and Ed would wait to receive the medical examiner's report, but in the case of Gale Walsh, as a year ago with the bloodless murder of Reverend Lawrence Livingston, Leon and Ed attended the autopsy.

They followed the balding bespectacled medical examiner into his lab and focused their attention on the corpse on the stainless steel examining table. Leon nodded to begin. The pathologist pulled on blue latex gloves.

"On an initial exterior examination of the body, I have not discovered any puncture wounds or bruises from blunt trauma. I will later draw fluid from the heart, lungs, and brain to determine whether a chemical injection occurred," he spoke into an overhanging microphone describing in detail each step of the procedure.

The pathologist made two incisions from the shoulders to the sternum to connect with the vertical cut and then pried open the body cavity. He carefully lifted the viscera from Gale Walsh's torso and arranged the mucous coated coils in a sterile white plastic tub. He made a second incision across the head continuing below and behind the ears to provide access to the skull which he opened using a vibrating saw. He severed and removed the brain from its attachments.

Using a long hypodermic needle and syringe, he extracted fluid from the heart for chemical analysis. A lab technician in the histology department later confirmed that the victim had not been injected with drugs that could cause heart failure.

As each organ was individually removed and examined and the smaller parts weighed, portions were saved in a preservative fluid and the remainder deposited into a biohazard bag and container to be cremated.

"There is no evidence of physical force or a chemically induced death," said the pathologist, "only that the victim's heart ceased to function. My conclusion is that he suffered a heart attack."

"That doesn't explain or account for his disappearance and then return one week later," said Leon.

"I don't have any answer for that."

"Would you send me your report."

"Of course. It will be in your Email within an hour."

"Thank you."

Leon and Berzinsky departed.

Chapter 2
The Magician

Leon was surprised when they left Broadway and made several turns along commercial and industrial side streets that brought them to an old brown brick warehouse.

"Here?" asked Leon.

"This is the place he stores his stage props."

"Does he live here too?"

"Actually, he does. He's had the second story designed and decorated like you'd find in an upscale architectural magazine. Beautiful inside, walls, furniture, the works."

"Does he live here alone?"

"He has a girlfriend. She's his assistant in his acts, a very talented contortionist. She's the one gets sawed in half inside the box, supposedly has swords stuck in her and emerges without a scratch, and levitates. All the gory and spooky stuff."

"I've always been curious how magicians do that."

"He'll never tell you. So don't ask. Professional magicians take an oath that they won't reveal to the rest of us how they do their tricks. Want to keep the mystery in what they do and how they do it. He told me people don't really want to know." They got out of the car. "He said if they find out, it spoils the experience for them and – they're less likely to come back."

They went up the concrete steps and walked along the empty loading dock to a single closed door at the far end.

"Does he just do local gigs?" Leon asked.

"He's a bit older now, but he used to be a headliner in Vegas."

"How long?"

"Twenty years."

"Must have done well."

"He had a following and he was creative. Very innovative. Always coming up with fresh new acts that were relevant to the ages of his audience. Got great reviews."

"How did you come to know him?"

"Interesting story," said Berzinsky. "Max needed a strong man for his act. Since I was a body builder and looking for some way to break into entertainment, I auditioned and got the job. Lasted for one year. That was before I became a cop."

"You ever tell our boss about that?"

"Hell no, it would just add fuel to his thinking I'm gay. He thinks all body builders are gay."

"He ever come right out and say anything?"

"No, he's such a wimp. He's afraid I'd throw him out his office window."

"Probably more afraid you'd take him to court on a discrimination charge."

"Now that's a good idea. Only neither of us would have a case. I'm not gay and he's just prejudiced against body builders. His biggest issue with me is that I don't respect him. He doesn't deserve his position. He never earned it."

"Most of the staff agrees with you on that."

"Except the ass-kissers." Berzinsky's rapid knock did not bring anyone to the door. He pressed the button on an intercom attached to the wall next to the wooden frame. A disembodied deep male voice responded. "Who is it?"

"Ed Berzinsky and my partner, Leon Safullo. We're a little early. Hope you don't mind. You can see us through your surveillance camera."

"I see you through my cosmic eye."

"Same old bullshit, Max. Let us in. We need to pick your brain."

The door opened by remote control.

"Come in," said the voice.

They entered the dimly lit interior of the thirty-thousand square foot warehouse and peered down the aisles of steel racks stacked with clearly-labeled bar-coded boxes containing twenty years of archived paraphernalia used in performances. A skein of dust coated the scene background drops and theatrical sets stored in slots along one wall.

As Leon and Berzinsky approached a set of steel steps next to an elevator, Leon asked, “We walking up?”

The opening elevator door answered him.

“Max hears all and sees all, at least in this building,” said Berzinsky. “He has the latest in surveillance technology. He’s pretty nerdy for an old guy.”

“Why his interest?”

They stepped into the elevator. The door slid closed with a soft cushioned sound.

“He says the digital world has created new forms of magic and illusion. He doesn’t use it himself, because he stopped performing. But he’s interested in following the developments as personal entertainment, a kind of hobby. He’s become a hacker. Says it keeps his brain active. He hasn’t done anything illegal. Just for fun. Says it allows him to explore the cyber world.”

Without experiencing a sense of movement and elevation, they arrived at the second floor. The door whispered open and they walked into a massive living room overlooked by a raised heavy wood beam ceiling and the same brick walls of the warehouse below. Comfortable contemporary designer furniture was curiously accented by several vintage antique pieces, four eighteenth century hand carved chairs, an Italian Renaissance desk, a heavy wooden serving sideboard that merged the juncture of the living and dining rooms centered by an oak dining table that seated twelve, overlooked by a tall crystal cabinet display of cut glass and fine china. Explosive bold vibrant colors of a few over-size modern paintings adorned the walls.

As they crossed the teakwood floor to meet the smiling elderly gentleman coming forward to greet them, Leon noticed there were no table lamps. Strategically located overhead mini flood lights and recessed lighting hidden behind the crown molding of book-filled shelves of a small library illuminated the rooms. The delicate aroma of lavender scented candles permeated the air.

"Ed, you haven't changed a bit. You still look like a strong man."

"I have to work harder to keep the weight down." He gently shook Max's deft hand. Prominent veins pushed at translucent skin. From a nest of bushy white brows, Max's clear blue eyes assessed Leon as though reading his mind and sizing him up for a trick. Leon caught a twinkle of recognition between two old men. Although Max was in his eighties and ahead of Leon by thirty years, he had a magnificent crown of silver hair, more than Leon who took pride in his graying curls with a tempered vanity.

"It's a pleasure to meet you, Mr. Schultz."

"My pleasure, as well, Agent Safullo. And please call me Max."

Leon nodded. "Leon."

"Where's Lia?" asked Ed. "I hoped to see her again."

Leon followed Max's gaze to a three by five foot silver framed portrait photograph of an acrobatic dancer who stared down at them with an expression of exquisite dark-eyed Asian beauty. Her brunette hair draped in a long cascade over her right shoulder. She wore only a plain black leotard.

"I have only photographs of her, but this is the most memorable."

"What happened to her?"

"She moved on, three years ago."

"What do you mean moved on?" asked Berzinsky. "Did she leave you?"

"Yes, in a manner of speaking. She crossed over."

"Crossed over?"

"She died," he said in exasperation. "She's gone, at least from here."

"I'm so sorry, Max. I know how much you meant to each other. How did she die?"

"A stroke. It was sudden."

"How are you doing?"

"She visits me from time to time."

"You mean you dream about her?"

"No, she actually appears."

Berzinsky offered a non-offending grin. "You told me you never believed in that stuff."

"I have real contact with her, not imaginary, real."

"Do you take medication?" asked Leon.

"Only for cholesterol and blood pressure. No symptoms of schizophrenia or dementia." Max smiled. "At least not yet, if that's what you're thinking. You are a psychiatrist, after all."

Leon nodded.

"Drug induced hallucinations might be your first diagnosis, but I've never taken drugs. Lia and I led a clean and healthy life. There was no accounting for the stroke."

"There's nothing unusual about talking to people you love and remember in any form, imaginary or in dreams," said Leon. "Our minds can handle reality and imagination in the same moment."

"I couldn't agree more." Max motioned for them to follow him out of the dining room and down a long hallway to his office. "That's the point of cross-over, the gateway. It's the mechanism that creates the illusion, makes us believe in something that doesn't really exist. Only in our minds," said Max. "Even if she is only in my mind, I see her because I want to see her."

They paused to take in the sweep of six flat screen computer terminals and three work station terminals. One was linked to the security system that provided real-time images of the warehouse exterior and interior.

"Please have a seat, gentlemen. Stage magic is a form of theater. It plays on psychological perception and awareness of the viewer. Illusions and distractions are created to keep the mechanisms of the trick hidden. It's basically stagecraft and you're here to ask my help in your investigation. Given today's technology using electronic imagery and gadgetry, it's possible that the killer or an accomplice, a programmer perhaps, hacked into the company's security system, shut it down so he could get inside, and substituted visuals that showed an empty fortieth floor while the CEO's body was being returned to his office."

"That's a plausible explanation," said Leon, "but his body didn't show any evidence of how he was murdered."

"I have no explanation for that," said Max. "I'm just an entertainer. That's medical and forensic science."

"That hasn't given us any answers either," said Berzinsky.

Max shrugged. "What about his secretary?"

"I questioned her," said Berzinsky. "It's highly unlikely she could have or would have killed him. She's spooked, terrified by what happened. Doesn't understand how or why any more than we do."

"Considering the way he was found, it's easy to jump to the conclusion that some paranormal influence is behind it, but like you said, we believe the illusion of a paranormal existence is nothing more than computer programmed theater stagecraft. But what do you make of this?" Leon pulled up a message on his laptop computer. "It was sent to me by the news anchor, John Morley, when we began the investigation into the murder of Reverend Lawrence Livingston a year ago."

Max put on a pair of glasses and read the message.

Spirit is a process that begins with pure thought or logic, goes on into other beings and pictorial presentation or nature, and returns from nature to complete self-consciousness or the spirit proper. I do not believe that what I think and do is evil. To be evil, one must be conscious of the norms one rebels against and will ultimately obey. I do not recognize norms. Self-consciousness is the true reality. I provide the means for that future consummation and it is nothing like you and others might imagine. It is the realm of darkness, the ultimate reality.

Cultures and societies can maintain their organization and activities for varying lengths of time by capturing energy and expending it according to needs in the maintenance of its ordered state. I know that life, in any form, adjusts its structure and behavior in such a way as to remain adaptive to environmental conditions and that the persistence of life on earth in the face of death's certainty depends on the ability of organisms to reproduce themselves. But they can repair and adjust for only so long before they inevitably pass into death. I do not exist in your reality but I have the power to create and to destroy life. This fact further reinforces the insignificance of mortality and the nature of souls.

When the atoms of a substance are disturbed, such as in the death of an animal or a human, all the atoms of that substance begin to vibrate. The energy radiates outward and escapes just as a vapor dissipates into the medium of air from boiling water. It becomes dark energy. We spirits reside in the dark spaces of the universe.

By putting the biological life form to death, we cause the vibration of energy. The atoms, and the soul are set free. The former Reverend Lawrence Livingston is now one of us.

"I think this is the work of a hacker," said Berzinsky.

"Most likely," Max nodded in agreement. "This sort of thing is easy enough to pull off, but it was sent to you for some reason other than information. It's deliberately intended to make a connection."

"The psychological manifestation is what's disturbing," said Leon. "Despite the unusual circumstances of these murders, I don't believe in this hocus pocus."

"Someone is trying to convince you otherwise. I would call this a form of paranormal or ritual magic," said Max. "Whoever is behind it is creating the illusion of his existence or maybe it's a group, a new age cult of some sort. A lot of charlatans and scams have proliferated all over the Internet. I've made a study of them. Online channelers and alternative religions have replaced the local palm readers and fortune tellers. They have all the special effects software available to them that film and television have. They can interchange the sounds and images of the real and surreal worlds with a few keystrokes and create the illusion of miracles and other worldly existence."

"You're not saying it's actually possible to move into that reality."

"That message on your computer could be only a prank, but it's clearly tied to the evidence of the two murders. I would say the killer is playing a game with you or trying to lure you in."

"Lure me in where?" Leon's voice dropped to a disgruntled tone.

"In there, what it describes."

"That's impossible," said Berzinsky. "We can't move in and out of our bodies."'

"There are some who believe it's possible."

"Bullshit!" blurted Berzinsky. "They're full of shit. Who? Maybe they're the ones we're looking for."

"You said this came from a website," said Max. "A website has to be created and exists in cyberspace. It's located in a tangible electronic platform."

"Are you suggesting whoever created the site could be other than real people?"

"I'm saying there's a possibility, if only because you have two murders that appear to have the same paranormal source and are unexplainable in our conditions of reality."

"Once we have evidence, there won't be anything paranormal about them," said Berzinsky.

"But what if you reach the point where you can't find traditional evidence, evidence in our reality?" asked Max.

"We'll find it. There has to be some explanation, some way someone is pulling off this crap," said Berzinsky.

"You mentioned there are people who believe it's possible," said Leon. "You've been doing research. Who are they?"

Max spun his ergonomic chair into position and rapidly tapped out a sequence of letters and numbers on the keyboard that brought the system to a series of on-line choices. He positioned the cursor and clicked on domain names that described out-of-body experiences.

"A consistent observation that I used in performing magic and illusions is that we individually create and see the world we want to see with ourselves at the center. So our construction of our self and the world we see we call reality. Our other perceptions are dreams and fantasies. The studies of near death experiences have shown them to have a physiological cause in neurochemistry. People who are dying see what they expect to see. But what they see is a hallucination, an illusion of their own making. There are case studies about these experiences and there are common physiological explanations.

"What's different about what you've brought to me is that some other source, calling itself the dark energy source, is creating the illusion and displacing the model we have created of our world according to our perception. How it is able to achieve that is the point of your investigation. That's what you have to discover. That's your evidence."

Berzinsky and Leon remained silent.

"So what you're saying is we have to allow that source to inhabit us and create our perception of the world according to what they or it wants us to see and live," said Leon.

"That's how I interpret what you're dealing with," said Max.

Berzinsky looked at Leon. "What do you think?"

Leon shook his head. "I don't think it's possible."

"I agree. We'll find another way."

"Well, keep an open mind," said Max. "Keep an open mind."

Chapter 3
The Error

"Gale Walsh was not supposed to be taken." Hiram Bean barely contained his anger. "We support and encourage people like him. We don't annihilate them."

Hieronoymous Blum looked up from his work station. "Is there a probability of error in Simonetta's DNA program?"

"How is that possible? The black spiral helix is impervious to mutation. There's no trace in our system that a gene transfer has been introduced to attack it, not by microinjection or a delivery vector. Our Unicell Laboratory has captured and maintains all the most recent gene therapy trials research, on biological viral DNA delivery systems, and chemical non-viral delivery systems. Black Spiral DNA is unknown to human genetic research. Even if it is discovered, their genetic scientists won't be able to unlock the genetic code. No entity is able to do that, human or spirit. Our opposition with humans is not biochemical. It's intangible, their values and belief systems."

"Looking at the map, we've made progress."

"What we see is only the beginning. When the entire world is red, we will have succeeded. Do you have an update yet on our food chain strategy?"

"It's too early to have any results. When we start seeing green dots appear on the map, we'll know the introduction is taking effect. Our laboratory experiments on primates have been successful. After nine months, the black spiral helix appeared in blood and tissue samples taken for DNA analysis. We can only estimate when it might appear in human populations."

"Why haven't any of our agents found Bram Vernon?"

"They're still trying. They report he has effectively disappeared, vanished. There doesn't seem to be any trace of his existence. They say all potential evidence has been erased."

"If word of black spiral crops up, then we know he's out there. Then we have a starting point to find him."

The First World Corporation couldn't ask for a better arrangement. Their front was to masquerade as a diverse multinational company. No one would suspect their position and investigate their real objective.

The momentum was accelerating exponentially with the competitive surge in the global economy and wars in the Middle East. North Korea needed to be tipped further over the edge. The First World Corporation now manipulated both sides of the equation. All the more reason to put on the pressure for increasing the war. War was profitable. Eventually First World would become the center of economic power and world government in the Middle East. Soon the U.S. Government would collapse as planned as long as First World kept the war going through missionary politicians strategically placed inside the Government. Keeping the war going would not be difficult given the ignorance and blind faith of zealot Jihadists. They would wreak havoc as though Satan himself were wielding the sword of the apocalypse. The societies of man would implode and dark energy would move in to replace them.

Hiram turned away from the digital message to gaze at the floor to ceiling fourth dimensional screen on the wall displaying a proliferation of locations of operative cells and targets on a white lined digital world map. Millions of luminescent red dots populated the black screen, many of them in dense clusters of activity in China, North Korea, the Middle East, Mexico, Central and South America, Africa, and in major capitols, preeminently Moscow and Washington, D.C..

The smaller screen was the only item on his expansive curved black ebony desk. He briefly touched his clean-shaved head with the palm of his right hand as though sealing in a cosmic acknowledgement. The news of the murder caused a flush of anxiety to rise in his chest. His deep black leather executive chair rotated with a quiet swish, as he turned to address his staff.

One of the immortals of darkness, Hiram Bean's human persona was as a billionaire executive. He possessed the charisma and physical appearance of a leader, tall, a full but lean face with prominent features and a patient, benign expression.

Among his diversified holdings, Unicell, a medical research and development division, had made the discovery of an unusual black spiral DNA structure that Hiram held in secrecy. The black spiral DNA was man's link to the origin of the dark energy of the universe. He believed that no one outside the evolutionary scientist, Bram Vernon, who had uncovered its source, and himself knew of the structure. There had been no announcements and no papers published. All evidence was kept locked in a secret vault.

"Simonetta is the first female we've introduced into the mix. Perhaps that was a mistake. She might have assimilated psychological influences from human female characteristics, of the nurturing and compassionate kind."

"That shouldn't happen," said Hieronymous Blum, a clone of his master. "We've built filters into our DNA programming to block any such impulses."

"Nevertheless," said Hiram, "she's active."

Chapter 4
The Shadow

Sigmund Safullo popped awake from his snooze. He had just returned from a late afternoon walk in a nearby park with his master's wife, Julie. He had barked loudly and chased a frightened squirrel up an elm tree. He had a healthy bowel movement and enjoyed watching Julie pick it up in one of her plastic blue bags. A series of investigatory pee stops along a familiar path and two dog biscuits for a treat had culminated the satisfying outing.

The sound of his master's car pulling into the driveway signaled to him that dinner would soon appear in his bowl, and, equally important, Leon might drop another stress ball on the desk top in his study, or even on the dining room table. Sigmund looked forward to adding to his stash of a dozen stress balls hoarded in a far corner of the back yard. Life was good. He barked to announce his master's arrival.

Leon entered through the front door. "Hi, Sig. Have a nice day." He patted the retriever's golden head and gently tugged his long silken ears. Sigmund liked the feeling of having his ears gently tugged. The sensation gave him a sense of well-being and belonging.

"Where's your mom?"

Sigmund delicately mouthed Leon's wrist and escorted him across the living room through the dining room to the family room adjoining the spacious kitchen.

Julie looked up from working her crossword puzzle. "Hello, dear. I heard Sigmund bark. Knew you were home."

"Hello, how was your day?"

"Same O, same O, perfect. Yours?"

"Enigmatic."

"Well, that's got to be different. What's an enigmatic day like?"

"There's been another murder similar to the one a year ago."

"The paranormal killer?"

Leon nodded.

"That's creepy. I thought he burned up in a car crash."

"He's not the only killer."

"Then there is a cult."

"A cult would simplify things. There was no blood this time either."

"I'm not sure I want to hear about this. Who was it?"

"Gale Walsh."

"The Wall Street billionaire?"

"The same. He was missing for a week, then suddenly turned up dead in his office chair."

"I'm sorry. I wish there were something I could do."

He grinned his appreciation for her blonde blue-eyed enthusiasm and snug suggestive T-shirt and tight tan slacks and sandals. He had the perception he was married to a younger woman than one his own age.

"I met a retired magician today."

Julie put her crossword puzzle aside. "Really, how did that happen?"

"Start of our investigation. Berzinsky introduced us. An old friend from Ed's pre-cop days. What we came away with is a better understanding of perception, how based on our influences, we create the world we perceive. We believe our illusions."

"He's got that right."

"It's a psychological principal he used in performing stage magic. He said it applies to these murder cases and I have to agree. We see what we expect to see."

Julie laughed. "Well, after forty years of marriage, I'm glad we're seeing what we expect to see."

Leon recalled his discussion with Roland Pogue, an IT forensic specialist, when he was investigating the murder of Reverend Lawrence Livingston a year ago. "I'm dealing with a classic psychopath," said Leon. "Some deranged new age schizophrenic. The question is how he can be sending messages over the Internet and not be traced. He has all the symptoms of living in an imagined sordid dream world. Based on the fact there was no blood or identifiable cause of death, I have to assume whoever killed Gale Walsh is a similar killer to who murdered Reverend Livingston."

He paced the living room while he talked. Julie recognized the pacing as his method for working through investigative issues. She had witnessed it many times during their married life and appreciated her inclusion in the process.

" In Jungian psychology, the Shadow is the archetype that represents all that individuals consciously are not aware of. A person's daytime persona or mask is normally polite and sociable, but aspects of the self are consciously hidden from other people. The hidden aspects are called the Shadow. They function outside a person's conscious awareness and control."

Leon was familiar with the Shadow. It was the aspect of a personality from which a killer's profile emerged, once Leon had determined the characteristics by reading and interpreting the behavioral indicators and signs. The Shadow was a psychological component of every man, woman, and child. It often appeared as a sinister threatening presence in dreams. For individuals who became aberrant, they succumbed to the Shadow and allowed it to govern their lives. For a healthy psyche, acceptance of the Shadow as an aspect of the self was essential. Repressing the Shadow within a person's conscious self kept it mentally captive and hidden.

In the prior murder one year ago, Leon had immediately catalogued the identifiable personality characteristics in the context, message, and manner of communication he had received directly from the man who had left Reverend Livingston dead at the altar of St. Stephen's Cathedral.

"The killer doesn't perceive that anything is wrong with him," he continued explaining to Julie. "He seems to take a secretive authoritarian position. Sociopaths often assume a double or perhaps triple identity to hide or repress their sense of paranoia. His goal is to enslave victims and exercise despotic control over every aspect of their lives until he can destroy them. The killer's pattern, assuming they're the same, seems to be of selecting model individuals who can be shamed and humiliated once they're conquered. The killer is so out of touch with reality that by degrading his victims, the killer seeks to eliminate the very same presence he is struggling with in his own mind."

He stopped thinking out loud and conjectured that the killer clearly expressed an emotional need to justify his crimes and desired his victims' respect, gratitude, and even love. By his act of murder, he cuts himself off from human attachment.

Leon wondered if, after so many years of analyzing the shadows of others, he was now being forced to confront his own. The investigation of the murder of Gale Walsh engaged his mind with a surreal phenomenon. This shadow was speaking to him directly through his conscious self.

There were clues in The Beginning.Com website that unexpectedly appeared on his computer to which he would respond. The shadow often did not give reliable information. What was stated could not be literally interpreted

The next morning, following the discovery of Gale Walsh's corpse, Leon had met with Roland Pogue, the staff physicist he had consulted during his investigation into the death of Reverend Livingston one year ago. The bespectacled blonde bushy headed scientist from Great Britain clarified the nature and existence of dark energy from a scientific perspective to counteract the paranormal references Leon was experiencing on his personal computer. They now revisited the similar phenomenon in the Gary Walsh murder. They attempted to access the earlier beginning.com website and view it together, but the site was gone, as though it had never existed except in Leon's imagination. He wondered if he had been dreaming and walking in his sleep the night he saw the website on his personal home computer.

Roland shared another observation.

"There is a theory called the fifth essence in dark energy which proposes the existence of a repulsive field embedded in space, not unlike a gravitational or a magnetic field. Under that hypothesis, the field was created in the beginning moments of the universe along with the other forces in nature, and now stretches across the universe like a spider web. As the universe expanded and cooled, gravity and quintessence or the fifth essence were competitive forces. Both fields weakened as the universe expanded, but ultimately quintessence became stronger than gravity and pushed the galaxies apart."

"This happened in the beginning of earth's formation?" Leon keyed on the word.

"Within the laws of physics in geologic time, yes."

"Which accounts for the name of the website, Thebeginning.com."

"It's unusual that a website would be selective, but as you have described the situation, the killer or killers continue to make themselves known to you."

"They are intending for me to follow them in some manner by exposure to the created dreams of someone other than myself, perhaps their next victim."

"Maybe they're using the website as a medium."

Leon nodded.

"There is another aspect of dark energy related to dreams that has come out of the research."

"What is it?"

"It's rather involved in terms of the latest in quantum analysis, but its premise is that humans are part of dark matter or dark energy as dreams or memory. The physiological process of mental activity involves mass and energy. The distribution of mass and energy can reach a significant gravitational threshold causing changes in the neurological structure of the brain.

"There are some who believe that the universe is itself a phenomenon that has as its goal self-consciousness and that humans are its mechanism. The structure of the universe may not be only physical. In the context of the mind in the structure of the brain, dark energy could be manifested as intangible attitude, simply how and what we think, rather than something we do physically, and it can be linked to dark energy."

"So on the basis of what you've described, it's possible for my subconscious to be channeled and merged with another being."

"Based on mathematical models, it is possible."

"I have a hard time accepting that."

"Most of us in scientific fields do," said Roland. "We work with theories, but you seem to be experiencing a phenomenon that goes beyond theory and becomes a kind of surreal reality."

"People sharing the same dreams."

Roland shook his head. "More than sharing dreams, the merging and commingling of physical existence with non-physical existence."

"How is that even possible? It just makes me wonder where this investigation is going to lead. For the time being, the murders are real, but the circumstances that seem to define the killer are not. They aren't logical. The profile doesn't seem human."

"Well, as the investigation proceeds, if I can be of further assistance, please don't hesitate to call on me."

***

That a second occult style murder had been committed incensed Roy Waterman. The Special Agent In Charge thought the case had been put to bed at the conclusion of the Paul Evans' and Reverend Lawrence Livingston incident. Now they had the death of Gale Walsh, and it was far too similar to be a coincidence.

Roy couldn't believe what he had just read in the coroner's autopsy report of the Wall Street billionaire. No blood. No evident cause of death.

"What the hell is this? No evident cause of death. There's always a cause. Having no blood is a pretty obvious cause of death. Something or someone made it happen." He hit the intercom button to his secretary. "Did Safullo and Berinsky call in yet?"

"No, sir. No message."

"They were supposed to be here ten minutes ago. Call Safullo's cell phone and tell him I'm waiting. And Berzinsky better not be working out at Gold's Gym."

"Sir, John Morley called again. He requested an appointment to interview you. He said the media has a right to know what happened?"

"The media, especially Morley, doesn't have a right to know shit. He'll hear what I have to say when I issue a statement and have a press conference. When he calls again, tell him that. There's nothing to god damn tell. We're going to look like a bunch of incompetent boobs. That is not meant to be a sexist remark."

"I know, Roy. I understand. You don't have to qualify it."

"Thanks, Lola. I think of you as one of the guys. Don't have to worry about what I say in front of you."

"That makes me feel so privileged, Roy. I'm taking another call."

"It better be Safullo."

Safullo and Berzinsky arrived thirty minutes later. Roy said nothing when they entered his office.

"We apologize for being late," said Leon. "Uptown traffic." He and Berzinsky took the two chairs lined up in front of Waterman's desk.

"Gentlemen, I can't believe what I'm reading in this report. What have you got?"

"The pattern is the same as with the Lawrence Livingston and Paul Evans case," said Leon, "only with a slight variation."

"A different killer?"

"It's possible. We have no way of knowing until we proceed further with the investigation."

"I've got John Morley and the rest of the media monkeys breathing down my neck. Anything I can give them?"

"Too early."

"I want to know you're pursuing real evidence, not some hoodoo black magic crap," said Waterman.

"Walsh is a prominent public figure in the banking industry with ties to questionable international corporate business and war profiteering. He's already been in the news on that score. Media journalists and pundits have been doing their own investigation for the past six months. He was supposed to appear before a Senate panel the day after he disappeared. That should give you a starting point. Someone didn't want him talking. Have you contacted his attorney?"

"We'll see him this afternoon and, later, his mistress," said Leon.

"Don't forget his wife. She has more of a reason to see him dead than his mistress."

"She's out of the country. Walsh owned a half dozen houses and a small Caribbean island. According to the State Department, she's been living in France and Ireland for the past year."

"Was she notified about his death?" asked Berzinsky.

"Not by our office," said Waterman. "What about his secretary or his attorney?"

Berzinsky shook his head. "Nothing from her. We'll ask his attorney."

"As soon as you have actual evidence of any kind, even a suspicion, let me know immediately. You're awfully quiet, Leon."

"Nothing to say at the moment."

"Enjoy your cruise?"

"Very nice, peaceful, restful."

"Not anymore. You and Berzinsky have got your work cut out. Hope you weren't planning on taking a vacation, Berzinsky."

"Never gave it a thought. Work is my life and my life is my work."

"Good. Keep it that way. That's all. Stay in touch."

Leon and Berzinsky stood and left the office.

"Why does he always have to be such a prick?" said Berzinsky.

"That's how he sees the world," said Leon.

"That's how the world sees him."

Chapter 5
Jubal Stroud

The law offices of Heizinger, Stroud, Ferris, and Monahan occupied the top three floors of the Stroud building in downtown Manhattan. When Leon and Berzinsky entered Jubal Stroud's suite, the secretary showed them into his private office and closed the door on her way out. Following mutual introductions, the tall accommodating Stroud led the two agents into an adjoining glass-walled conference room.

"Gale had his fingers in a lot of pies." The relaxed vowels and southern cadence of Stroud's speech seemed out of place in a New York office tower. "And I know you're going to ask, yes, he had enemies. Anyone who works on Wall Street and in a law office does. That's where I get my gray hair or what's left of it." His mouth broadened into a self-deprecating grin. "But his death is unfathomable. How do you explain it?"

"We don't have an explanation," said Leon. "One of the reasons we're here is to learn more about him, about his business involvement that caught the attention of the Senate. His disappearance the day before the hearing leads us to believe he was abducted and murdered."

"Do you have any suspects?"

"Not as yet. That's why we're here. We're hoping you can help us."

"Did you determine the cause of death?"

"We're still working on it," said Berzinsky.

"Was there an autopsy?"

"Yes, for the time being, the results are confidential."

"Understandable. We've had to ban the media from getting into our building. My secretary has had to block calls and dump Emails ever since the hearing was announced."

"The press reported the sums of money being solicited from city and county funds for investments in high risk equities is a starting point," said Berzinsky. "Tax payers aren't happy when they're being ripped off."

"Other than negotiating contracts, I wasn't personally involved in the firm's stock transactions. Nothing was done outside of SEC regulations. City and county treasurers decided where they wanted to invest. Walsh Capital was just the middleman. Certainly tax payers are going to be disgruntled, but they're directing their anger at the wrong party. Their district attorneys need to be pursuing that end of this."

"As well they are," said Leon. "Did Walsh Capital solicit investors?"

"Of course, obviously. Walsh is a resource to a wide range of capital. Now before we get too far down this road, gentlemen, I may exercise the right of client attorney privilege depending on your line of questioning."

"We respect that," said Leon. "We're not trying to determine guilt or innocence. We're just looking for a motive or the potential source of one. The media has also published allegations of his wartime profiteering, participating in Government defense contracts in the Middle-East and profiting from disaster relief money in the South."

"Admittedly, Gale had political connections and a strong business presence in the South. Have you talked with Gale's secretary, Bernadette Garcetti? She's as close as anybody regarding his communications and transactions."

"We've had an initial conversation with her," said Berzinsky.

"Mr. Stroud, were you a close friend of Mr. Walsh?" Leon asked.

"Yes, we've known each other for over twenty years. Gale's originally from Ireland where he met his wife, but he grew up in Atlanta. We're both alumni of Auburn University. Belonged to the same fraternity. We're southern boys. I came north by way of Virginia Law and he worked his way through the ranks on Wall Street."

"Did you socialize with Mr. Walsh and his wife?"

"We each had our circle of friends, but we got together from time to time, when he became one of our major clients."

"How about family?" asked Berzinsky.

"His or mine?"

"His."

"There is some separation, but our families are related. My wife is June Walsh's sister. I met her through Gale and June. Her name's Keira. You may know Gale and June were divorced."

Leon nodded.

"Their kids and ours grew up together. We lived in the same neighborhood in the Hamptons." Jubal grinned. "Not my idea of small town life in Alabama when I was a kid. But we change with the times, don't we."

"In your opinion, did change have something to do with what happened to Gale Walsh?"

"I'm not sure where you're heading."

"Other than the Senate hearing, did anything else happen recently or in the past that might relate to his murder?"

"I think he panicked at growing older. The thought of mortality comes down hard on some people. He was only fifty-five. His money bought him a lot of things, five mansions, a yacht, a fleet of high end cars, two private jets, an island in the Caribbean. You name it. He had it all, but he told me he was never satisfied. It was never enough. He once told me he thought his purpose in life was to get as much as he could and then get more."

Jubal's now familiar grin irritated Leon. "He was not what you'd call a humanitarian or a spiritual kind of guy," said Jubal.

"That doesn't answer the question," said Leon, "but does provide some insight. So in his pursuit of more, who did he push too far who might have pushed back?"

"I don't have an answer, because he pushed everybody, his wife, his three children, his friends and colleagues, even me. But he paid me well. I extracted my highest client fees from him."

"It sounds like there were others who weren't compensated for subjecting themselves to him," said Berzinsky.

"That was Gale. That was how he operated. If you did business with him, you did it his way. If he could get away with cheating you, he would. People who did business with him had to fight in court to get their money. He didn't like to pay anybody but himself. To put it bluntly, he was an obnoxious son-of-a-bitch. People reached a point where they just didn't want to have to deal with him anymore, so they capitulated. Gale's father moved the family over here from Ireland when Gale was still a boy. His father was elected to the state Senate for fifteen years in Alabama until someone assassinated him on the steps of the capitol. Like father like son, except his father's killer was arrested and hung outside the courthouse. He was a Black, of course. They didn't hang white men down there in those days or any time for that matter." Jubal grinned. "Maybe a chicken thief or two out in the back woods or clans feuding with each other. They weren't newsworthy enough to make the New York Times."

"So it sounds like he was generally disliked," said Leon.

"Hated is more accurate," said Jubal. "And by a lot of people."

"Were charges of any kind ever brought against him?" asked Leon.

"Threatened charges by the IRS for tax evasion. He had connections with Irish banks and other offshore tax havens, a common practice these days. The IRS never had evidence to make a case against him or bring him to trial. As you might be aware, the tax laws are friendly to corporations and CEOs."

"But he operated on the fringes of those possibilities."

"He had a really good attorney looking out for him," said Jubal with a smile. Seeing that Leon and Berzinsky didn't appreciate his little joke, he exchanged his smile for a serious expression.

"I don't consider corporate and financial felonies and crimes are unusual," said Jubal. "They are the norm. That's why I have a job. People and companies are always pushing around the edge of the law for one reason. They want a fast track to easy money and lots of it. That's reality. That's just the way people are. Gale was no different, no better or worse. There are thousands of Gale Walshs, not just on Wall Street, but in cities and towns all over the country, all over the world. A few get picked off in the news every once in a while. That's just how people are and how companies operate. It's all about politics in one form or another. It's not about people wanting the same things. It's about the differences. Like Gale, people who have more want more. At a lower economic level, people who have less want more. It's a natural instinct, a drive.

"Just because laws are on the books doesn't mean everyone agrees to follow them. That's where you come in – the police, the FBI. We're in this together, gentlemen, not always on the same side of the table, but together. I worked for the District Attorney as a prosecutor for eight years before moving into private practice."

"I see the building is named after you," said Berzinsky. "What happened to Heizinger?"

"He retired five years ago. We keep his name on the door as a senior partner for branding purposes. It's well recognized. He successfully led this company for thirty-five years. I bought him out when he retired."

Chapter 6

Keira Stroud

Keira Cavendish Stroud struggled with an internal conflict of moving between the Renaissance art exhibit public relations campaign and having to support the Gun Rights Association (GRA) lobby in their strategy to block and crush opposition to the existing gun laws. Their diametrically opposed cultural values challenged her worldly perspective of professional neutrality.

She occasionally discussed this requirement of her occupation with her husband, Jubal, who was an expert in subverting any emotional capital he might have in representing corporate felons. "The secret," he told her, "is to focus on the letter of the law and not let prosecutorial interpretation overshadow it. Laws are written in such a way to allow for creative opportunities to circumvent them, because they rarely cover every contingency. And the bottom line is it's your job to make your clients look good and for you to make lots of money doing it."

Keira recalled how she and June and Bernadette Garcetti had spent two hours one day viewing and discussing the depiction of *The Birth of Venus* in the Botticelli Renaissance paintings, *Allegory of Spring*. They agreed that *The Birth of Venus* had a special symbolic significance for them.

June had told Bernadette that as young girls growing up in Derry, Ireland, she and Keira had ambitions to become glamorous and worldly. Their grandmother told them stories of knights and beautiful ladies and mythical dragons and legendary stories of fairies who used their magical beauty, their glam, to charm and allure mortals into their world. She said that glam was a trick of the eye. Fairies created something you might see, but was not actually there, did not exist but in your mind. It was a trick that fairies used to control reality. Glam gave them their mystery.

As children, although they had strived unsuccessfully to become beautiful and to be glamorous according to the images of movie stars and fashion magazine models, June and Keira understood the link between glam and the mystique it created. Since they had no money, they would sneak into movie theaters and steal fashion magazines from newsstands. They poured over the glossy photographs of the elegantly dressed, bejeweled, beautifully coiffed woman staring out at them with alluring expressions and imagined themselves wearing such elegant clothing instead of their tawdry dresses hand sewn by their mother who made side money as a seamstress.

June hated her flaming red hair, flushed complexion and emerald green eyes and thought she would be ugly for the rest of her life. She envied her older sister's, Keira's, smooth alabaster skin and petite features topped with scintillating deep blue eyes and framed by luxurious dark hair, said to be inherited from their mother, who had been a real looker during her younger days.

June physically favored their father's side of the family, the Cavendish side. Although she loved him despite his irascible nature, especially when he came home from the pub, she preferred not to look like him and her three brothers.

The two sisters would fasten up their unwashed straggly hair into a French twist with clothes pins and, enduring the derision and laughter of their dirty-faced brothers, practice their strut and glide up and down the hall between the bedroom and the lue they shared with them and their little sister and their mum and da'.

June and Keira told Bernadette stories of their childhood in an Irish ghetto neighborhood of wall to wall red brick three story tenements. They lived near the bottom of a steep hill overshadowed by a massive Medieval stone wall that segregated the protestant sector of the city behind it.

Occasionally they heard a bomb explode and the pop and rattle of gunfire as British soldiers made house to house searches for members of the Irish Republican Army. During gun battles that raged through the streets, they would lie flat on the kitchen floor to escape stray bullets that shattered the windows.

Keira became the worldly one. As children, they thought that being worldly meant you traveled around the world, which Keira later did as an art collector and public relations director for a major New York art museum. She also became more knowledgeable and intellectually informed than her sister, who focused on wealth by marrying a banker. Keira understood accepting differences in cultures and their values without being judgmental. She was analytical and derived informed personal conclusions not influenced by her family or background and the Catholic school and church teachings that had been drilled into them from the time they were old enough to speak. Their mother called Keira a heretic, but remained proud of her scholarly achievements.

June was passionate about everything. Her mother called her wild and unmanageable. June wanted to become a dancer, an entertainer, an actress. Her school did put on plays other than Christmas and Easter pageants in which she portrayed The Virgin Mary in one and an over acting sobbing mother of Jesus at his crucifixion in the other. The nuns told her to knock it off. They said Jesus' mother did not carry on like that when he was crucified. She challenged them with "How do you know? You weren't there," at which they removed her from the cast and replaced her with a prayerful looking fourteen year old who had soulful deep brown eyes. The nuns ordered her not to "ham it up."

Gifted with a natural soprano voice, she sang lead solos in the church choir and was always invited to sing Irish ballads and folk songs at Peter O'Malley's pub, her father's favorite watering hole. She continued the tradition well into her teens and as a young woman waiting on tables.

When she turned sixteen, she worked as an usherette at a local theater where she witnessed live productions of plays by John Millington Synge, Oscar Wilde, George Bernard Shaw, Samuel Beckett, and Anton Chekhov. Although she begged to audition, the producers didn't think she was mature enough and told her she needed to go to a school to be trained as an actress. They admired her singing voice, but they didn't produce musicals.

From time to time, O'Malley's Rovers, a quintet (guitar, fiddler, bagpipes, flute, and drums) who played at local pubs, would get a booking at the upscale end of town at a hotel banquet or a wedding. June was their lead singer. To her own surprise, outgrowing her awkward childhood and teenage features, she had blossomed into a svelt beautiful redhead. Keira told her she finally had glam. At one of those events, she had met the successful young banker, Gale Walsh, who had brought her to America.

At June's and Gale's wedding, her grandmother told her that her husband was a leprechaun in disguise. She warned that he hoarded vast sums of other people's money and, as soon as they took their eyes off him, their money disappeared and their wealth. Since he took his profession quite seriously, she and Gale did not get along.

The night after being visited by the FBI, Jubal went home and told his wife, Keira, that Gale Walsh had been murdered. He asked Keira to get in touch with her sister, June. "Rather than me going across the pond, I'd prefer she come here. There are legal documents for her to sign. The estate is complex."

"It's that tax evasion thing again, isn't it," said Keira. "Is the FBI going to want to talk to her about Gale?"

"I'm sure."

"Even though she's been in France and Ireland for the past year?"

"They're looking for information, evidence."

"Does she have anything to do with his putting his majority of tax free profit in Irish banks?"

"She's not involved, but the FBI considers all potential sources are important. And Gale never broke any laws. What he did was perfectly legal."

"That's why the IRS couldn't touch him."

"Exactly. He also paid taxes on profit here in the U.S."

"Not enough, obviously."

"He paid his share."

"June won't have anything positive to tell them," said Keira. "Will they talk to his mistress?"

"You mean his girlfriend? Unquestionably."

"No, I mean his mistress. A girlfriend is one thing. A mistress is quite another. Why do you think June left him?"

"His mistress then. All the same to me."

"How would you know? You've never had one, have you?"

"No, I have no need or interest in a mistress."

"Need is not a factor, Jubal. Nobody needs a mistress. She's an indulgence for someone who has wealth and no sense of ethics, loyalty, and morality."

Jubal grinned. "I'm relieved to know I have all those traits and meet with your approval."

"You wouldn't be married to me if you didn't."

"How well I know. Courting you was not easy."

"Courting? Is that what you called it? Isn't that a little old fashion?"

"Not for me. I'm a southern boy, a country boy. My mama was as hard as a hickory stick and my pa was worse. My middle initial D doesn't stand for David. It stands for Disciplined. Talk about strict parents, even though my pa was a landowner and had money, I had to work starting at an early age. I was out picking cotton with the hired help during summers when I was ten. I had to learn the value of a dollar. I had to pay my way."

"The hired help. You didn't call them niggers?"

"Not me. Not like my old man. Working side by side with 'em, I came to know them. We came to know each other."

"But one of them killed Gale's father."

"Yes, an unfortunate misunderstanding."

"Didn't you tell me the man was lynched?"

"After a fair trial."

Keira smirked. "Was there any such thing in those days?"

"Depends on whose point of view, the defendant's or the jury's."

"I think your pa taught you how to be a bull-shitter. That's why you became an attorney."

"A successful one. Required of the job."

"Lucky for you I came along."

"Have to admit, you did temper my enthusiasm for exaggeration."

"Hardly. That's what makes you fun and engaging at parties. You're an entertainer. That's what attracted me to you in the first place. You reminded me of my father telling stories in the local pub."

"That's what law practice is, dear, entertainment."

"Unless you lose."

"I've had my share of losses. They were still entertaining."

"Not for your clients."

"Losing gave them a different perspective, a learning experience that helped them grow."

Keira snorted. "That is bull shit and you know it."

"I'm serious. I've always believed that win or lose, a person learns and grows."

"Or makes money or loses money."

"That's just a side effect."

"I think the learning and growth are the side effects. What about the downside? Look what happened to Gale. He turned out to be a miserable excuse for a human being and look what it got him."

"I was just his legal representative, dear, not his priest."

"You were his good buddy since college. That's what you said."

"That's southern slang for friend."

"My sister fell in love with him and married him. What happened?"

"Time. Change. We don't stay young forever."

"That's an excuse?" Keira removed her dress.

"No, we're just better suited for each other."

"A match made in heaven," Keira quipped.

"Better heaven than hell."

"You ever heard of a match made in hell?"

"I've had clients who fit that description."

"Gale Walsh must have been one of them."

"Don't be too hard on Gale. He just did what successful bankers do," said Jubal, admiring her gradually revealed body. He always enjoyed their bedroom conversations. They ended up in bed.

"Make lots of money."

"That was the point. And we were friends."

"Good buddies."

"You liked him in the beginning," said Jubal.

"That's because June was in love with him. I didn't want my sister to be disillusioned by my prejudices."

"It's a good thing. Otherwise, I'd never have met you."

"And you'd never have gotten me my great job."

"I thought you liked your job."

"For the most part," said Keira, "but there are aspects lately that rub me the wrong way."

"You've always been good at handling office politics."

"This is more than politics."

"You can always quit. Go somewhere else."

"It's not that simple and I'm not a quitter going all the way back to when June and I were growing up in Derry. This has a certain feeling about it I can't seem to shake."

"What kind of feeling?"

"You'll laugh if I tell you."

"I never laugh at you, only with you. Come on. Spit it out."

"When June and I were small girls, our grandmother told us stories about fairies."

"And that gives you a bad feeling now?"

"I can't put a finger on it. I can't describe it. Maybe it's intuition, but there seems to be something happening. I don't know where it's coming from. Given the corruption that's going on centered around Gale and the push from the right that he represented, the gun related murders I have to refute in the media. I had enough of that when I was a child."

"What does that have to do with fairies?"

"Something that Bernadette Garcetti told me and June once."

"What's that."

"She thought she had a spirit that inhabited her."

"You're joking."

"She said it related to a painting in the museum, The Birth of Venus. Obviously, she felt self-conscious even bringing it up and wouldn't say any more."

"Sounds like she has an active imagination."

"I get a sense that it's more than that."

"Well, if you find out, let me know. Let's make our own magic."

Keira nestled her nude body in close to his.

Chapter 7
Marietta Bloom

Since Marietta Bloom had met Gale Walsh, the name of her business was John, Inc., which served a twofold purpose. One, she possessed a sense of humor and, two, she could call herself a company. Her articles of incorporation described her business as "executive support services." Such a generic category allowed her a wide range of options as to what services she provided, but were primarily those of a "social consultant" and "adviser of fine art." These included "travel guide and companion." Although the last item was listed on her website, the term "escort" was never associated with her.

She kept her own books and punctually filed quarterly and annual taxes on dividends which, through Gale's recommendations, had become her primary source of income. She earned a reasonable annual six figures from stock and real estate transactions and had never been audited by the IRS.

The knock at the door gave her a start, as she was removing a blended carrot, spinach, kale, apple, and honey smoothie made that morning with her juicer. She had just returned from her daily workout at a nearby health club and wasn't expecting any visitors. She quickly checked her iPad calendar. None of her friends were scheduled to drop in and this wasn't the day for the house cleaning service. The property manager would always call before taking the lift to her penthouse, and security would clear any other visitors. She thought whoever the caller was might go away if she didn't answer. The second more insistent knock gave her a stab of apprehension. She set her smoothie on the black quartz kitchen counter and waited. At the third knock, now louder, she crossed the living room in four long-legged strides to peer out through the eyehole on the door. Her bare feet left imprints in the deep pile of the white carpet. She saw the two men, one elderly, one built like a personal trainer, wearing dark suits.

When she opened the door, they showed her their badges and explained who they were.

Berzinsky was instantly impressed by the tall, statuesque blue-eyed brunette. Her pixie style cut framed flawless proportioned features that could grace the cover of a high fashion magazine.

"I saw what happened on the news," she said. "Unfortunately, considering my relationship with Gale, there wasn't anybody I could call or write to express my condolences."

A slight guffaw escaped Berzinsky at her remark.

"It's true, Agent Berzinski, and not all that amusing. Gale and I were quite close. And I can see from your expression that your thoughts gravitate toward a gutter mentality only, but there was more to it than that. We shared common interests in art, music, film and theater, since we live in the heart of it. Not in books and literature, however. He preferred financial and political non-fiction. I enjoy thrillers. So it's interesting to be included in your investigation."

"You say you and Mr. Walsh were close, but you don't seem particularly disturbed by his death," said Leon.

"I'm a practical woman," agent Safullo. "I've had to be all my life. I acknowledge that whatever situation in which we may find ourselves is not going to last. I enjoy what I have without regrets. Am I saddened by his death? Yes, absolutely. But I'm not going to wear black and go into mourning, except at his funeral."

"You're attending his funeral?"

"It is my prerogative. We were as close as a husband and wife can be without being married. In some ways, relationships between men and women are better off without the constraints and obligations of marriage."

"Where did you graduate?"

Marietta's eyebrows raised at the unexpected question. "Why do you ask?"

"Your use of language, your vocabulary. You don't get that from reading pulp fiction thrillers."

"I have a degree in English from New York University."

"This seems an unlikely profession you've chosen."

Marietta smiled. "It's the oldest profession, Agent Safullo. I'm a business woman. I did spend a year as a reader for a publisher, but it was too static and just made me aware of how desperate neophyte authors are to become successful and I was either hindering them or helping them along the way."

"Pick any best sellers?" asked Berzinsky.

"No, anything I recommended my senior editor turned down. I decided I needed to work in a," she paused a moment, "profession that was more vital, that had a reality beyond what someone had imagined on the printed page."

"How long have you known Walsh?"

"Five years."

"During those five years, did you date other men?"

"No, Gale and I hit it off from the beginning. We fulfilled each other's lives. There wasn't a need for other relationships."

"Monetarily speaking."

"And emotionally. Both. I believe he would have eventually asked me to marry him. It wasn't just an illusion."

"Did you date other men before you met Gale?"

"A few. Nothing that lasted."

"How did you meet them?"

"In singles bars."

"Were you hustling then?" asked Berinsky.

Marietta scowled. "I never hustled, Agent Berzinsky. They were legitimate dates. No financial transactions were involved."

"Did you pursue Walsh?" asked Berzinsky.

"I don't pursue men, Agent. Men pursue me."

"You advertise. You have a website."

"Naughty man. Are you married?"

Berzinsky blushed.

"To desire sex is the strongest force in life. It creates a demand market. The website was Gale's idea. His sense of humor matched my own and he made me a corporation with all the tax advantages. And why not, with one of Wall Street's top financial advisors."

"That still doesn't answer the question," said Leon. "How you met."

"Oh yes, you must investigate for the cause of the crime."

"I'm just asking how you met. If you know something about the cause, we're interested."

"I was a docent at the Metropolitan Museum. Gale came in to see an exhibit. He was a collector of fine art. He asked me to dinner. That was five years ago. I have since traveled with him to select and buy various works."

"Gale's sister-in-law, Keira Stroud, also dabbles in art."

"Yes, Keira and I are acquainted and we don't dabble. We collect. Keira is more knowledgeable than I am, of course. She studied art. It's her career. For me, collecting is just a hobby. Something I fell in to after I met Keira."

Leon had noticed her expensive crystal sculptures, and porcelain and glassware collection of Lalique and Waterford pieces as he and Ed entered the penthouse.

"Do you know of anyone in the art world who held any animosity for him?" asked Leon.

"It's possible. Gale was very competitive and he could afford to be. Like many wealthy people, he had a driving need to possess things. If he wanted a painting or a sculpture badly enough, he never walked away from an auction without the closing bid."

"So it sounds like he was a gambler."

"He took risks, if that's what you mean."

"Yes, so taking a particular risk might have fostered an enemy, someone pushed enough to want to see him dead."

"That's possible. How did he die?"

"He was murdered."

"I understand that, but how was he murdered?"

"That's what we're trying to determine," said Leon. "There's a lack of physical evidence, so we have to approach how it happened or what actually happened in an indirect way. We have to learn as much as we can about Gale. We're looking for influences, connections, associations."

"He was missing for an entire week," said Berzinsky, "then someone brought him back and propped him up in his office. There's no evidence as to how he left and how he was returned. Were you with him or did you see or talk to him prior to the week of May twelfth?"

"No, I was out of town and he told me he was going to Atlanta to visit his mother. May twelfth was Mother's Day."

"According to his secretary, he was reported missing on May ninth, one day before his Senate hearing. Did he mention the Senate hearing to you?"

"He was only mildly concerned. He said the Senators had to demonstrate due diligence, whatever that means."

"They had questions about Gale's financial business."

"I've always known Gale to be ethical and honest."

"We're not here on behalf of the Senators," said Berzinsky. "There's a missing piece regarding his murder. We're trying to find it."

"I'll answer your questions and help you any way I can."

"We know in the business world he had enemies, some extreme enough to want to see him dead. Your bringing in the art world casts a different light, but it still doesn't address the nature of the murder," said Leon.

"How do you mean?"

"No sign of blood," said Ed. "No evidence of how the killing was done, nothing."

"I guess I don't find that hard to believe."

Leon and Ed stared at her.

"What makes you say that?" asked Leon.

"Gale wasn't what you would call a spiritual person, not in the sense of the religion in which he was raised. He was a Catholic, as you probably know, but not a practicing Catholic. He told me he hadn't attended a service or mass in over twenty years. He said he had discovered something better, something that delivered. That was the word he used, delivered. He said any other religion was just ritual claptrap that pandered to people's faith-based beliefs."

"So what was this something better, something that delivered?" posed Leon.

"He kept it a secret. He wouldn't share it with me. No matter how I prodded him, he wouldn't tell me."

"You lived on and off with the man for five years and presumably came to know him quite well. If you were to take a guess, what would your supposition be?"

"About his secret?"

Leon nodded. "About his secret."

"It had something to do with money. There was no end to it."

"The criminal underworld?" asked Berzinsky. "Insider trading, foreign politics, drug cartels?"

"I don't know. I really don't know. To be honest, I preferred not to know, if he was involved with something illegal. And perhaps he was protecting me by not telling me. If that's the case, I'm grateful. I wouldn't want to be an accomplice. I admired him for the man he was and I was glad to be part of his life. He was not the kind of man who encouraged or even wanted long term relationships. I think he used people and then dropped them when he got tired of them and had no further use for them. He believed he had a gift, some special power that he could control people and situations, hold sway over them. And he did."

"Until someone killed him," said Leon.

"Until someone killed him."

Chapter 8

The Influence of Venus

For Bernadette Garcetti, the influence of Venus originated when she was a young school girl and became a secret obsession in her adult life that she did not fully understand.

Bernadette was among a small group on the docent led tour of the National Art Gallery. The articulate art history major from a local university had presented an overview of the special Renaissance exhibit featuring some of the replicated sculptures and paintings representing the Uffizi in Florence, Italy.

Bernadette watched and listened closely to the tall lithe young woman whose pristine youthful face and rust-colored curls draping her shoulders created the impression she had stepped out from among the characters in the paintings.

"As you can see, the early Renaissance artists were heavily influenced by gothic religious motifs and symbolism. Keep in mind that during the fourteen and fifteen hundreds, most of the people were illiterate and the function of religious art was to convey the stories and mysticism of saints and Biblical figures, which accounts for the extensive use of golden auras around their heads, denoting their holiness or state of grace.

"As we move into the High Renaissance period, the style changes radically to a poetic lyricism represented here by the prominent works of Sandro Botticelli, who lived from 1444 to 1510. His *Allegory of Spring* introduces a life flow and rhythm that has broken away from the friezes and sculptures on the walls of churches and cathedrals. Botticelli introduced a secular style in his work used to decorate the palaces and villas of the ruling class. Lorenzo the Magnificent of the Medicis was a patron of artists and scholars. Venus is the central focus in this painting and carries over to Botticelli's thematic imagery and allegory of his related second work, *Birth of Venus.*

"The wind of two zephyrs are blowing her toward land. The interpretation by some art critics is that Venus symbolizes the merging of spirit and matter or idea and nature. It is interesting and noteworthy that the model for many of Botticelli's women was Simonetta Cattaneo Vespucci, among the most beautiful and highly desired women of that period and loved and coveted by Giuliano dei Medici."

The pure beauty of Venus tinged with a gentle expression of sadness impressed the five women in the tour group with varying degrees of intensity and significance.

Bernadette's appreciation for art had begun as a small child during Sunday services in the Catholic church she and her family attended. The soaring blue and green and red stained glass windows held her in thrall as she tried to decipher the shapes and figures they contained. Her awareness reinforced her emotional capitulation to the crushing echoes of organ and choral music, and to the gilded ritual robes worn by the priests. Those first impressions were religious associations that had brought her to the gallery. A confusing dream stimulated by a television commercial announcing the exhibit merged with a shocking confession made to her and their mother by Bernadette's younger brother.

In her dream, Bernadette watched her brother as a young altar boy wearing a white alb assisting the parish priest during a service. The church was empty and the dream was silent. Her brother was carrying the sacramentary to the priest, who took the book to read. The dream morphed to her brother taking a wafer from the priest's hand into his mouth, then drinking wine from a golden chalice. The wine spilled from his lips and gushed down staining the boy's white alb red. The scene swirled away in a cyclonic mix of stain glass images with the painting of Venus swooping forward to dominate the churning vortex.

Bernadette jerked awake and bolted out of bed expecting to see the priest and her brother at the tabernacle. The only light in the room was the green luminescent glow from her clock radio.

She didn't understand the dream or even why it appeared in her sleep. Her brother had been young then, ten years old. She had been thirteen at the time he was an altar boy. The incident had never been clear to her, never explained. She knew something bad had happened by the way they were acting, her mother's uncontrolled weeping and her father's vituperative rage. Yet, when she asked what was wrong, they wouldn't explain, as though they were shielding her from knowing. When she tried to get her brother alone to talk to him, he would shake and tremble and struggle to get away as she grabbed his shoulders. She remembered the first time he ran crying from the house. Her mother stopped her from pursuing him.

"What did you say to him? What do you think you're doing?"

"I'm not doing anything," said Bernadette. "I just want to know what's going on. You and Dad won't tell me. He won't tell me."

"This doesn't concern you."

"I'm his sister. I'm your daughter. I have a right to know." Bernadette could not fathom the change that had come over her mother, trying to cope with her emotion. She stood backed against the kitchen sink. Anger streaked her milky blue eyes and spilled over with pain and sorrow dragging down her sagging face that Bernadette had known since childhood to be uplifted with laughter and love. Her shoulders hunched and her thin body crumpled inward. Her knuckles whitened from the intensity with which she clutched the counter. Her chestnut hair in which she took pride hung in unwashed ringlets over her ears and crept down her forehead like spiraled worms.

"I love Timothy, Mom. That's why I want to know."

"I know you love him, but there's nothing you can do. There's nothing anyone can do. Your father is taking care of it."

"What's he doing? What's he taking care of?"

"Stop asking questions. Just stop asking questions. We were told not to discuss it, not with anybody."

"Who told you?"

"The bishop."

"The bishop? Who's the bishop?"

"I've said enough. I've said enough. Just please don't bother your brother about this again."

"I don't know what 'this' is."

"You're not intended to know. We'll live through this. Timothy will live through this. It will be in the past as though it never happened."

Bernadette wanted to scream in frustration at her mother, but intuitively understood an attack would only add to her mother's stress and sadness. Anna Garcetti would never tell her daughter of the shame and degradation that had been visited on her family. Bernadette determined she would learn of what happened by other means.

The jangling bell resounded throughout the old wooden walls of the school on both floors and was echoed from the boys school next to the church across the blacktop playground.

Bernadette closed the faded green cover of her math book, gathered it up along with the spiral binder tablet in which she had been doing her homework, and stuffed them into the open backpack on the floor next to her desk. She folded her hands neatly and looked expectantly at the Catholic sister standing at the front of the room. Her hands raised to orchestrate the departure of the girls. They were not allowed to leap up and rush out at the sound of the bell. They had to depart by rows in an orderly fashion. Discipline and control governed every aspect of their young lives from the blue skirt and white blouse uniforms they wore to the communal morning prayer each day before classes began.

Bernadette would normally meet her younger brother, Timothy, at the playground gate and they would walk home together. But since the incident, their parents had decided to keep him home for a week to recover. She merged with the jostling crowd of shouting laughing students hyper-excited about their impending weekend. Their number diminished along the city blocks, as they turned off on side streets, until Bernadette found herself walking alone among a changed demographic of working and shopping adults. By not having her brother with her, she would be able to follow her plan.

Going to and from school every day, she and her brother passed an old bookstore. Its shabby nondescript front did not encourage her to stop and peruse the window display of hardcover and paperback books of various sizes, kinds, and conditions with unfamiliar fiction, nonfiction, and historical titles dating back to the early and middle 1900s. One unusual book had caught her eye and, now that she was alone, brought her back for a closer look. She knew the title related in some way to the second sign posted under the 'Used Books' sign, 'Psychic Spiritual Readings'.

The title of the book was *The Dark Arts.* The cover featured a black and white photograph of a demonic gargoyle similar to those she had seen on the corners and fascia of a cathedral in the heart of the city.

She had not known what psychic meant until she looked up the definition in the school library dictionary. *Of or pertaining to the human soul or mind, noting mental phenomena that cannot be explained, spiritual as opposed to the physiological.*

She had heard the priest talk about the spirit of the Lord during church services, and had never been quite clear about that. She had always wondered what a spirit looked like and, from religious paintings, stories and cartoons and Halloween costumes, thought it was a ghost. But the sign promised something more than her limited imagination.

She did not know how much the book would cost, or of greater concern, what the price would be for her to have a reading. She had transferred her accumulated savings allowance from the jar hidden in the top drawer of her dresser to her narrow pink plastic purse hung diagonally from a long thin strap across her chest and left shoulder.

Now that the moment had come, she hesitated with mounting trepidation that she was about to commit an act that would cast her into hell. She forced her right hand to touch, grasp, and turn the dull brass knob. The musical tinkling of small bells on a leather strap hung on the door announced her entry.

The odor of must and mold laced with the jasmine scent of smoldering joss sticks flowed from several rows of books and tightly packed shelves along the brick walls. The wooden floor creaked under her weight as she approached the counter behind which a middle-aged man sitting on a high stool watched her with curiosity.

Bernadette noticed a tarnished silver pendant nesting among his curly dark chest hair at the open apex of his denim shirt with maroon flowered embroidery over the left pocket. A thick silver chain disappeared under a fall of shoulder-length gray hair. Wire-rimmed glasses accentuated his bony ascetic features giving him an academic countenance. Looking up from the book he was reading, his soft brown eyes missed nothing about her.

"Good afternoon, Miss. May I help you?"

Bernadette stopped just short of the counter, fearful of its proximity, as though she had ventured too far. "Yes, there's a book I'd like to buy." Her voice trembled.

"Do you know the title?"

"It's in the window. The one with the black cover."

The man smiled. "The one with the picture of the gargoyle."

Bernadette nodded. "The demon."

"Oh, yes, the demon. He does draw your attention, doesn't he?"

"I haven't seen a book like that before. I'd like to buy it."

The man stepped down from his stool. "Would you like to look through it before you buy it."

"No, I'll just take it and read it at home."

"Of course." He walked over to the low staging platform of the front window and plucked the book from its display stand. He returned and placed the book on the top of the glass counter with the title directly in front of her. She stared at the book, but didn't touch it. "How much is it?"

"Five dollars."

Bernadette nodded and opened her purse. The man was amused at the wad of one dollar bills she withdrew."

"Your allowance money?"

"Yes, I get a dollar a week. My dad gives it to me."

"Do you do the dishes, help clean the house?"

"Yes, and I take care of my brother when they go out. He's ten."

"I'll bet he's glad you're his older sister."

Bernadettte nodded and counted out five dollars from the roll. She watched him ring up the sale on his cash register. "Is there any tax?"

"It's included in the five dollars."

"Oh." She returned the remaining bills to her purse and snapped it shut.

"Are you going to share the book with your brother?"

"I don't know yet. I have to read it first."

"I understand. Want to be careful what he's exposed to. That's very grown up and responsible. How old are you?"

"Thirteen."

"Nice age, right in between twelve and fourteen." The man chuckled. Bernadette didn't understand why.

He inserted the book along with the receipt into a paper bag and handed it to her across the counter. She didn't leave as he expected, but looked about the store interior as though searching for something.

"Anything else, Miss?"

"What's a spiritual reading? I saw the sign in the window."

The corners of the man's mouth wrinkled down. There was something more happening with this girl than he had thought.

"Do you do the reading?" she asked.

"No, my wife does readings. She's a psychic."

"I looked up that word in the dictionary at the school library."

"So, the sign made you interested."

Bernadette nodded.

"Would you like to meet Lorraine? She does the readings."

Bernadette nodded.

"If you'll wait, I'll go and get her. She does the readings in the back room."

"Okay."

"By the way, my name is Dan. And you are?"

"Bernadette Garcetti. My brother and I go to the Catholic school down the street from here."

"Of course, I've seen you and your brother walk by the store. I'm glad you stopped in. I'll get Lorraine and be right back."

"Okay."

At the gentle touch of his hand on her shoulder, Lorraine awakened from her doze. Her head remained nodded downward, her chin resting slightly to the side against her collar bone as though attached and resisting a return to the world of the apartment above the book store.

"Dear, sorry to wake you. You must have been having a pleasant dream."

She looked up at him from her stuffed armchair. The book she had been reading had fallen shut on her lap. "It was pleasant."

"There's a young person, a teenage girl, downstairs who came into the store to buy a book and would like for you to do a reading."

"A young girl? How old?"

"Thirteen she said. Seems quite bright. Not sophisticated, but definitely interesting. Has an innocence about her."

"What book did she buy?"

"The one in the window, The Dark Arts."

"Did she tell you her name?"

"Bernadette."

"An impressionable young girl. What would she be wanting with The Dark Arts?" A small smile expanded the edges of Lorraine's dry lips. "I'm not fully awake yet. Give me five minutes. Brew some tea for Bernadette. We'll have a cup when I come down."

Dan nodded and left the apartment. He found Bernadette slowly paging through her book as he returned to the front of the store. "Lorraine will be down in a few minutes. I'm going to brew some tea for the two of you. Lorraine always likes to have tea when she does a reading."

"Okay."

"I'll be in the back. I'll come and get you when she's ready."

"Okay."

Dan smiled and walked to the rear section of the store.

Upstairs, Lorraine rinsed her face at the bathroom sink and peered at herself in the cabinet mirror. With the onset of age, tiny wrinkles were beginning to appear as hair-like fractures at the corners of her pale blue eyes. Her fingers stroked the slight softening of her jaw line. She tugged her long lavender floral skirt upwards about her once slender waist beginning to widen from her hips.

She pushed at her salt and pepper hair twisted and swirled up like a nest secured with a wooden comb. Arranging the black knit shawl about her shoulders, she crossed through the bedroom out to the living room door. The aroma of jasmine tea rose to greet her as she came down the wooden stairs. She paused to watch

Dan pouring two cups of tea at the small table covered with a plain red cloth that served as her *mise en scene*.

The girl looked up startled to see her standing there as though Lorraine had materialized out of thin air. Holding the jade green ceramic tea pot, Dan straightened from pouring and motioned Lorraine to come forward.

"Bernadette, this is Lorraine. Dear, Bernadette just bought a book on the dark arts and would like you to do a reading."

"Hello, Bernadette. It is my pleasure to meet you. Please sit down."

Bernadette placed the book next to her cup and saucer and lowered herself onto the straight back cushion chair. As they faced each other across the table, Bernadette asked, "Where is your crystal ball?"

"I don't use a crystal ball."

"How can you see the future without one?"

"Do you want to see the future?"

"I want something to happen."

"A crystal ball is a stage prop. It gives the impression of seeing into the future, but that doesn't really happen."

"What do you do?"

"I ask questions. We talk."

Dan moved away. "I'll be at the front counter."

Lorraine nodded. Her attention remained focused on Bernadette, whose eyes did not leave Lorraine's.

"What do we talk about?" Bernadette sat rigidly upright in her chair.

"You. We talk about you."

"I thought we talked to spirits."

"Do you want to talk to spirits?"

"Yes."

"Do you know who they are?"

"No, I've never met any."

"What do you want to say to them?"

"I want to talk to them about my brother."

"What is your brother's name?"

"Timothy Garcetti."

"Do you love Timothy?"

"Yes."

"Do you protect him?"

"Yes."

"How old is he?"

"He just turned ten last month."

"Did something happen to him that you weren't able to protect him?"

"Something happened, but I don't know what. It made him afraid of everything."

"Did you ask your mother and father?"

"They won't tell me. They don't want me to know."

"And that's why you're here. You want me to tell you."

"Can you ask the dark spirits?"

"There are more questions to be answered."

"What questions?"

"Do you have erotic fantasies? Do you think about sex?"

Bernadette stared at Lorraine in shock. "Why are you asking me that?"

"Part of what draws you to the dark arts is the increase of your adolescent hormones. I imagine from your upbringing that sex is talked about as something dirty, evil, something from the Devil. Something that is forbidden. You're told that to keep you fearful about it. Keep you away from it. And therein lies the attraction. We're always drawn to what is forbidden, essentially when it insists on not being ignored."

"The sisters tell us, me and the other girls, it's a sin to touch ourselves. But I did once, accidentally."

"Accidentally. Did you like how it felt?"

Bernadette's face reddened. Her eyes cast down. She nodded.

"Sex is a normal bodily function. You're just beginning to become aware of your sexuality. Have you started menstruating?"

"Yes."

"And did your mother explain what that's about or your doctor."

"My mother, but she was embarrassed. She had a hard time telling me. She gave me a pamphlet to read she got from the doctor."

"Did you understand it?

"Yes, I'm not stupid. Some of the girls at school talk about it."

"Do you look at boys?"

"Sometimes."

"Do you like them? Do you talk to them and get along with them?"

"I go to a school for girls. The boys have their own. We don't see them much. Sometimes on the playground."

"How unfortunate. Have you ever seen a picture of a naked man?"

"Why are you asking me these things? No!"

"Do you know what a naked man looks like? Do you know what a penis is?"

"I accidentally saw my father naked once. The bathroom door was open. He didn't see me."

"So what did you think about seeing your father naked?"

"He had a lot of hair. I was eight years old. I thought I had sinned."

"I hope you got over it. Seeing a naked man is not a sin."

"When he saw me, he slammed the door shut."

"Do your mother and father hug and kiss each other in front of you and your brother?"

"They did when we were little kids. My Dad used to call my Mom Irish. But he doesn't anymore. Can you tell me what happened to my brother? That's what I came to ask you."

"The truth of the matter is that your mother and father should tell you."

"But they won't and I need to know so I can help Timothy."

"Do you attend church with your mother and father?"

"Yes, my Dad takes Timothy early, because he's an altar boy and helps Father O'Herlihy get ready for the mass."

"Are there other altar boys?" asked Lorraine.

"Sometimes. Mostly Timothy is the only one."

Does your father stay with him when they go early?"

"No, he comes home and gets me and my Mom and we go back."

"When did your brother start being afraid?"

"About a week ago."

"I think I'm beginning to understand what might have happened to him, but I have no way to prove it," said Lorraine.

"Prove what?"

"It's possible that the priest molested your brother."

Bernadette stared at her.

"Do you know what that is?"

"He touched Timothy."

"Judging from your brother's reaction, the priest might have done more than touch him."

"More?"

"Yes, but we'll leave that topic alone for now. It's up to your parents to do something about it."

"If I can call the spirits, I can ask them," said Bernadette.

"Calling the spirits might help you feel better, but there's nothing they can do. They only exist in your imagination."

"So I can do that."

"Your book tells you about it," said Lorraine.

"I'll read the book."

"I know you will."

"After I talk to them, I'll come back and see you."

"I would love to see you again, Bernadette."

"I forgot to drink my tea."

"Let's both drink our tea."

Chapter 9

Dark Arts

From the moment she opened the book and read the first paragraph, Bernadette was hooked under the spell of the dark arts. The belief that she could possess the power to shape reality using the forces of the spirit world awakened her to a new perspective.

Sitting alone in her room, she believed she could see what others could not. She envisioned her room as a private sanctum in which she could commune with spirits from the dark world who would give her special powers to influence others and destroy those she identified as evil. She envisioned herself as a protector and hero of the weak and oppressed victims. In her adolescent imagination, she wanted desperately to believe that by her thoughts alone, she could take vengeance against perpetrators of criminal acts.

When she walked through her neighborhood and along the city streets, her mind transformed the sights and sounds and smells and throngs into an amalgam of otherworldly existence. She viewed people as transparent auras and conjured otherworldly spirits lurking in doorways and riding on the subway and in downtown buses.

She shared none of her discovery with others, and especially kept her newfound knowledge from her parents, who would accuse her of daydreaming or taking drugs. The book told her that those who did not acknowledge the spirit world would call her weird and demented and subject her to the false diagnoses of medical practitioners. She knew she must keep her gift private, a secret to herself and use her powers with discretion.

To call the spirits, you must open up your mind and heart and pray to them. It may not happen immediately. It requires practice. Eventually, they will come.

She closed the book, shut her eyes tightly and whispered so that her parents would not hear her through the thin walls. "I am praying to you, oh spirits. My name is Bernadette Garcetti. I open my heart and mind to you like it says in the book. Please come to me." She opened her eyes and looked about her room expecting at any moment to see an ominous dark shape emerge. She waited and tried again.

"I am praying to you, oh spirits. My name is Bernadette Garcetti. I open my heart and mind to you like it says in the book. Please come to me."

She allayed her disappointment by reminding herself that the book said calling forth spirits required practice. So she would practice. She did night after night for one week with no expected results. On the seventh night, seething with frustration, she slammed the book shut.

The next morning, she told her mother she was going to the drug store to buy school supplies. She needed another note pad and pencils with good erasers. Her first stop was the used bookstore.

Dan greeted her as the tinkling of the bells faded with the closing door. "Hello, Bernadette. Welcome back. I didn't expect to see you so soon. I see you brought your book."

"I need to talk to Lorraine." Bernadette's harsh angry tone made him study her a moment.

"I'll let her know you're here." He left the counter and walked to the back room of the store. A moment later, he returned. "She's waiting to talk to you. You can go on back."

Bernadette quickly slid onto her chair across from Lorraine and dropped the book on the table. "It doesn't work. I couldn't call the spirits. I did what the book told me. I opened my heart and my mind and I prayed. I tried every night for a week and none of them came to see me."

"When you're in church and pray to God and Jesus, do they come and see you?"

"No."

"But you had an image of them in your mind from sculptures and paintings."

"I knew what they looked like."

"But they weren't real. Any more than the dark spirits are real. You see them in your thoughts and dreams. That's where they live. They're not going to appear in your bedroom."

"Oh, I didn't know that. The book doesn't say that."

"Well, Bernadette, I'm telling you and I know that."

"But I need them to do something."

"They don't really take orders from us. What is it you want them to do?"

"Take revenge against Father O'Herlihy for what he did to my little brother."

"Take revenge. I can understand that. My father raped me when I was a little girl."

Bernadette's shocked expression lasted several moments. "Did you take revenge?"

"No."

"What happened to him?"

"He was arrested and put in prison for many years. But he was killed for what he did, by other inmates. I didn't know enough to wish for that. But wishing is what you're doing. You're wishing that something bad will happen to Father O'Herlihy."

"Yes, I want something terribly bad to happen to him. I want him to die. My mother says that what he did to Timothy is the will of God."

"So your mother finally told you what happened."

"I figured it out from something my father said. My mother was there."

"Your mother is wrong. What happened to Timothy is not the will of God. It was the will of a sick priest. Do you know what the word manifest means?" asked Lorraine. "Have you ever heard it?"

"No."

"It means to make something out of nothing. You make wishes, don't you?"

"Yes."

"Did any of them come true?"

Bernadette thought for a moment. "No, I don't think so. I don't remember."

"A wish comes true only if you do something to make it happen. You have to do the grunt work. You can't pass a test in school unless you study and do the work, can you? You can't just wish you'll pass it and get an A."

"I study hard. I do my homework."

"You can't punish Father O'Herlihy, but you can manifest it. You can wish for something to be done to him. Somewhere along the way, he will be caught and he will be punished. Would that satisfy you?"

"Yes, me, but not my brother."

"It will. Trust me, as he grows up, it will."

Bernadette opened her purse. "You never asked me for money. Do I pay you some money now?"

"For what? We're friends. Friends don't pay each other for sharing confidences."

"Okay." Bernadette closed her purse. "Are you a mother?"

"No, I don't have children."

"You would make a good one."

Lorraine's eyes momentarily clouded over. "Thank you, dear. That's a very nice compliment."

"Are you and the man in the store married?"

Lorraine grinned. “My you are curious. But friends should know about each other. Yes, we are married. Not legally. We performed our own wedding ceremony with friends.”

“In a church?”

“No, a forest meadow. We lived out in the country. The woods and fields were our church. There were ten of us, including four children. We lived in a big farm house. We were a family. We grew our own food. Any animals we had we raised as pets. We didn’t kill and eat them. We got milk from three cows and the chickens gave us eggs.”

“Did you talk to spirits?”

“We believed spirits lived in nature, the woods, the trees, the crops we grew, the flowers, the stream that ran through our land. It came from a freshwater spring.”

“Do you still have the farm?”

“No, the man who owned it had some problems with his partner and they separated. The husband was offered a great deal of money for the land for residential development. Once he sold it, the rest of us had to move.”

“I’ve never been on a farm. I’ve only been in the city.”

“It’s an experience you should have someday, just taking a trip out into the country.”

After Bernadette departed from the store, Dan asked Lorraine, “Is there anything we can do to help her?”

“Not from us. She and her parents need legal help. But in time, I believe she’s capable of doing what needs to be done herself.”

“She keeps coming back.”

“Yes, isn’t she delightful.”

Chapter 10

The Predator

Life changed dramatically for the Garcetti family the Sunday Tony Garcetti told his wife they would no longer be going to mass at the Church of Angels they had attended since years before Bernadette's baptism.

The image of Father O'Herlihy's predatory act with his son haunted him. He found it hard to concentrate on the plumbing repair jobs the company dispatcher sent him to cover. He stopped joining his friends for an after work beer in a favorite local pub. He could not quell a pressing need to do something. Even though his son was the victim, he felt violated.

Tony's father established the family plumbing business thirty years ago. Tony and Anna graduated as high school sweethearts in 1972 and immediately got married. Anna gave birth to a daughter seven months later. One of Tony's older brothers had been killed in Viet Nam in 1968. Tony, his father, and another older brother, Lorenzo, who had survived the war with a medical discharge, ran the company. Tony and Anna had a second daughter two years later, then no children until Bernadette in 1980.

During a Sunday morning mass, Tony stood up and stepped to the center aisle. In the middle of Father O'Herlihy's sermon, Tony's voice thundered and echoed his words of rage from the vaulted ceiling and stone walls.

"Shut your fucking mouth, Priest! You have no right to be preaching to us! You molested my son! You fucked my son!"

He heard and sensed the congregation gasping and leaning away. A few at the outer edges of the rows of pews staggered up and moved rapidly toward the exits.

"You're a fraud and a disgrace to your profession! You're not holy! You're dirty! Obscene in the worst way!"

Clutching at his robe, horrified, an assistant priest hurried down from the tabernacle to try to calm him. Tony's violent thrust sent him sprawling onto the laps of a man and his wife gawking at this spectacle.

"How many other children have you touched! Have you forced to do the unthinkable! To have sex with you! You God damn pervert!"

A woman screamed and fainted.

"Everyone here should know what kind of man you are! You should be excommunicated! Thrown out! You should be in prison!"

At that point, Father O'Herlihy turned and rushed away to the sacristy. The congregation erupted in a babbling turmoil and pushed and shoved at each other clamoring like fear-crazed sheep to get out.

The next day, Bernadette and her brother were removed from the parochial school and enrolled in the nearest public middle school.

With the exception of two of her closest friends, Anna was avoided by the neighborhood mothers as though the taint of what had happened to her son might attach itself to their sons. Timothy lost his best friend whose mother believed Timothy seduced the priest. Sick with depression and despair, Timothy feared to leave the house.

Bernadette observed all that was happening and consulted her dark book to bring an evil spell against the priest.

Despite her husband's insistence that they disavow and leave the Catholic religion, so entrenched was his wife's belief, she took the bus every Sunday to another church in a different parish.

After Tony ended his family's attendance at the Church of Angels, a new priest came to see them at their apartment. Tony refused to admit him, shouted at him to "Go to hell!" and ordered him to leave.

Bernadette, Timothy, and their mother watched the altercation at the door.

Not wanting to lose track of Father O'Herlihy, Bernadette sneaked back to the Church of Angels one day on her own and entered the confessional. When she was settled inside and the priest prompted her, she said,

"Father, is it all right if I ask you a question?"

"Of course."

"Are you Father O'Herlihy?"

"No, my dear. Father O'Herlihy moved to a different parish a month ago." The priest heard the slam of the confessional door and Bernadette's running footsteps leaving the church.

Over time, Bernadette nurtured her delusion of possessing dark spiritual powers. At best, her belief gave her a feeling of superiority over her peers. The Dark Arts replaced her religious teachings.

Her mother continued to attend a different Catholic church. Her brother, Timothy, readjusted making new friends in a public school environment. Bernadette continued her strange secretive behavior until Anna discovered her book and demanded to know where she bought it. Bernadette told her, "From my friends, Lorraine and Dan."

"Who are Lorraine and Dan?"

"They own the bookstore. They live upstairs."

"How do you know this about them?"

"I told you. They're my friends."

"We'll see about that." Her mother grabbed the book away.

"That's my book. I bought it with my own money."

"Not anymore it isn't."

Her mother went to the bookstore and confronted Dan.

"My daughter says you sold her this book."

"Is your daughter Bernadette?"

"Yes, how do you know her name?"

"She comes in here from time to time to browse and visit."

"Visit? What do you do when she visits?"

"Mrs. Garcetti, your daughter is a very bright young person. We talk about people, culture, art, philosophy, what's happening in the world."

"Your sign out there says Psychic Spiritual Readings. Do you do that with her?"

"The first time she came in to the store, she asked about it. My wife ended up just having a conversation with her. There wasn't any reading."

"This book you sold her tells her how to talk to the devil. She doesn't believe in God anymore because of that book." She suddenly noticed Lorraine standing quietly near a shelf at the center of the store. "Are you the psychic?"

Lorraine remained silent.

"I don't like the way you're staring at me. You're both staring at me." She suddenly crossed herself. "Lord God protect me. I'm in the presence of Satanists." She left the book on the counter and ran out the door.

***

Bernadette's first view of the countryside was from the window of a fast-moving train. She had promised herself that one day she would make the trip to envision what Lorraine had described to her about spirits in nature.

She recalled how her mother had caused Dan and Lorraine to close down their bookstore and move out of fear of being prosecuted. A detective had come to question them about a complaint from a Mrs. Anna Garcetti that they were cultists trying to brainwash her impressionable teenage daughter. As an adult, Bernadette still carried a grudge against her mother for driving them away.

The trip was her first planned event since her graduation from college two days ago. Her parents, brother, two older sisters, and Uncle Lorenzo had attended the lengthy ceremony. She had achieved straight 'A's all through high school and now college, graduating with honors in business and accounting.

Her younger brother, Timothy, dubbed her "the genius."

Bernadette's father treated them all to dinner at a noisy Italian restaurant redolent with the dense aroma of garlic and tomato sauce. Everyone toasted her with raised glasses of red wine. Although she smiled and laughed and ate a hearty helping of lasagna and a tiramisu dessert, she felt depressed, an apprehension of not knowing what the future might hold for her. She had given up on trying to predict events. Whatever happened would happen. Her evidence sat facing her around the table.

Her brother had suffered from learning disabilities and entered the family plumbing business right after high school.

Her uncle Lorenzo was divorced from his wife who was squeamish about having sex with her one-legged amputee husband. His stump pushing against her naked thigh sickened her.

Her father barely tolerated her mother mired in a trough of religious fanaticism to compensate for her husband and children turning their backs on the church.

Her first roommate, an evangelical Christian, had requested to be relocated to another dorm room within a day after Bernadette revealed to her that she was a spiritualist. The maneuver was Bernadette's strategy to rid herself of the girl, who reminded her of her mother.

Her second roommate had been more to her liking. Antonia Mazarek was nineteen years old, a brunette with a brooding, glamorous face, heavy arched eyebrows and large dark dramatic eyes with a slight upward slant at the outer edges accentuating the lines of uplifted rosebud cheeks. An expressive mouth fully accentuated her words, making the mundane sound important and causing the listener to focus on what she said.

When she first met Bernadette, her sensuous lips slipped up in a slow provocative smile revealing perfect gleaming white teeth. She reminded Bernadette of a panther, her long legs and arched feet moving in a sleek rhythm when she crossed the room.

Antonia was unlike any other woman that Bernadette had known. She envisioned her stepping out of an epic story of gods and goddesses and becoming entrapped in the mundane affairs of humans groveling to survive. Her beauty prompted immediate curiosity and caused onlookers to imagine her identity. They wondered if she were a princess or a European movie star. Her flagrant sexuality appealed to Bernadette's sense of otherworldly freedom.

When Antonia brought her dates to the room to have sex, Bernadette would leave and go to the campus library to study. She recalled that after several such occasions, Antonia asked Bernadette why she wasn't dating.

So she had decided to seduce Oliver Reynolds in her philosophy class who she considered intellectually arrogant and full of himself. She knew of his old Boston family pedigree, because he never failed to interject it into a conversation. So she pretended interest and acted impressed by his family history, wealth and his academic achievements. He strutted and primped and complimented his wavy blonde locks by wearing collegiate clothes that gave him the appearance of a model stepping out of a young men's fashion magazine.

Bernadette worked her way up to the event by engaging him in scholarly tete-a-tetes.

"So what do you think of Heidegger?" he asked her one day as they were leaving a class and walking across the commons.

"He's overrated."

"Meaning?"

"He just rambles. He can't get closure on anything."

"That's what philosophy is all about, the question of being. There is only the question," said Oliver. "There are no answers."

"Of course there are answers. How else do people and societies function?"

"I would say people and societies don't function," said Oliver. "They are dysfunctional, which brings us around to the conclusion that there are no answers. There is only experience and being. Here we are walking along together and our existence is defined by what we see hear, smell, feel, and everything that has gone before to create who we are. I believe it would be fascinating to discover who we are, to learn about each other. Don't you agree? Think of it as philosophical inquiry."

"If that's your original pick-up pitch, what makes you think I'd be interested?"

"Intuition and the possibility. We live in a world in which there are no absolutes, only possibilities. What is possible is dependent on who is seeking the experience."

"Back to people and societies. There are rules, guidelines, laws," said Bernadette.

"So you think human existence is rational. Rules are just illusions, deceptions to be broken. Nobody follows rules and laws. Nobody really wants to. They just give people a false sense of security and a way to relate to whoever they are wherever they are. That's what makes law a wide open career field for me."

"You're going to law school?"

"After I graduate. What about you? You're obviously intelligent. Are you a philosophy major or just taking this class?"

"I wouldn't touch philosophy other than it's required for undergraduates. Are you?"

"Sure, I want to learn all the mind-bending tricks. You play chess?"

"No."

"Playing people is like playing chess. You're always a move or two or three ahead to win."

"Is winning your point?"

"Winning is always the point without letting your opponent know what your plan is."

"Sounds underhanded and devious."

Oliver laughed. "You're being moralistic? I'm realistic. You have to be realistic, otherwise you're the one who loses."

When she finally agreed to go with him to his room, he asked, "Are you a virgin?"

"Yes, why do you ask? Is that important to you?"

"No, but it obviously is to you."

"Am I that obvious?"

"Oh, yes."

"What if I told you I've slept with more men than you have women," said Bernadette.

"I wouldn't believe you. So, you want to change that?"

"Change what?"

"Being a virgin."

"You haven't convinced me that I should."

"Well, allow me, my dear."

"I won't allow you anything. You think I'm remotely interested in being another one of your conquests?"

"Conquests?"

"Scores, isn't that what you call us? How many of us have you scored?"

"You should play chess. I think you'd be good at it."

"How about I challenge you to a game of strip chess?"

"You become more challenging and exciting by the moment. Strip chess?"

"Every time I take one of your pieces, you have to remove an article of clothing."

"And you?"

"The same. But you're the one who'll end up with no clothes," she said.

"What are you, some sort of covert chess champion? Most of the girls I date aren't as smart as you."

"Why do you suppose that is? Easier to get them into bed with your superior intellect?"

"Sex and intellect normally don't mix."

"So you just like your sex stupid and down and dirty," said Bernadette.

"No, but I don't like it to be weighed down with extraneous baggage."

"So that's how you see me, extraneous baggage? "

"Not you, but you're coming at this in a way I never anticipated."

"And you're the one who told me playing people is like playing chess. You're always a move or two or three ahead to win. Are you ahead or am I?"

After sex, he said, "I'm really in love with you, Bernadette."

"You are? I don't believe you. How can you be sure?"

"You're the real thing. I swear it."

"Like Coca-Cola?"

"Like you. Like Bernadette."

"What if I'm not the real thing? What if I'm one of your illusions?"

"You're not an illusion. You're real for me. You're real. I'm not just talking about your body. Your mind. Everything about you."

"You don't think maybe I'm a move or two or three ahead of you to win?"

"You have me. What else is there to win?"

Bernadette burst out laughing and rolled off him.

"What the hell are you laughing at?"

"I'm so far ahead of you, you'll never figure it out." She grabbed up her clothes and raced out of his room and down the hall followed by the hoots of Oliver's fraternity brothers.

"Wait!" he shouted after her. "Come back! We're not finished! I don't understand!"

Once outside, she quickly pulled on her sweatshirt and shorts. Stuffing her panties into a pocket, she walked sedately away from the frat house back to her campus dorm.

Later that day, he went to her dorm to return her sandals to her.

"You forgot these?"

"I left them intentionally, for you to remember me by, like Cinderella." She took the sandals.

"You, Cinderella?"

"Not even remotely."

"So, what's your game? I was being serious."

"So was I. Now that I'm ahead, why would I tell you?"

"Are you saying you won't go out with me anymore?"

"I don't have to say it," her mouth curled in a wicked smile. "You just did."

"You're a strange chick. You know that?"

"Peep peep."

"Maybe you should see a psychiatrist."

"So you think if a woman rejects you, she should see a psychiatrist. You're an egomaniac."

"I take that as a compliment. I've been called worst."

"By women you rejected?"

"Yes."

"So how does it feel, wonderboy?"

"Nada, there are lots of fish in the sea."

"Good thing. I'm a fan of fish."

"I believe it. You lied to me about being a virgin. How many men have you had?"

"You'll never know."

"I know. I'm the first real man. I could tell from your reaction. When you had your orgasm, you were all over the place. No one else has ever done that to you," said Oliver.

"That's quite an assumption on your part. I might have been faking," she said. "I'm not telling and you'll never know."

"You weren't faking. I know you weren't faking. I can tell faking and you definitely were not faking."

"That's because you believe only what you want to believe."

He stared at her. "What's the point of all this, trying to out-game each other?"

"You set it up. It's your game," said Bernadette. "Not mine. I'm just playing along."

"Then you're not serious about what you said. We can be friends."

She brushed back a wisp of hair from her forehead. "I get the feeling you don't have friends, at least not what I think of as friends."

"I do have friends. That's one of the reasons I joined a fraternity."

"For drinking buddies, maybe networking for a job when you graduate."

"The networking becomes more important in law school."

"Okay, how about a casual friendship, coffee and conversation."

"No sex?" His eyebrows lifted.

"No sex."

"But we're really good together, Bern. I mean, are you going to go without?"

"Probably not. Just not with you. I like variety. People interest me."

"People interest me too."

"I'm sure you have plenty of variety," she smirked.

"I guess I have to accept what you're telling me."

"You do."

"Coffee and conversation."

Coffee and conversation."

***

Bernadette got off the train in Montpelier, Vermont, rented a car, and drove out into the countryside along narrow back roads through rolling maple tree forested hills and fields punctuated by occasional farms and signature landmark white church steeples of small towns. With no particular destination in mind, only her intuition, she arrived at the Ryerson Bed and Breakfast Inn adjacent to a dairy farm.

Her car headlights caught a blue neon vacancy sign posted on a stone wall at the driveway entrance. She pulled into the outermost available slot of the parking lot crowded with RV campers, family vans, station wagons, and a few sedans. Her immediate thought was why her parents had never taken her and her brother on a vacation to a place like this. They had never gone anywhere but Coney Island.

The smell of the sea, the keening of gulls coasting on air currents over the milling crowds on the beach and descending to squabble over remote discarded food scraps, the sticky sweetness of cotton candy clinging to her cheeks like pink spider webs, rides on the carousel and Ferris wheel, their voices joining the high-pitched screams of other children, her father spending nickels for her and Timothy to play ring toss for a cheap prize, the ping and clang of the shooting gallery, the tantalizing aroma of hot dogs smothered with mustard, her mother and father wearing tee-shirts, knee-length shorts, and sandals, the only time she saw her mother and father holding hands like young lovers eating ice cream cones – these impressions stayed with her, overshadowing her search for dark spirits even in the house of mirrors that rendered grotesque distortions of the people who ventured through. Only in the house of horrors did the sights and sounds of devils and demons connect with her book, The Dark Arts, until she stepped out again into the brilliant summer sun and the stream of human life surging along the boardwalk.

The next morning, she followed a small group of chattering children down the wooden stairs from the second floor to the dining room. After a breakfast of hotcakes, eggs, and country sausage she studied a tourist guide road map to learn what state parks were in the local region.

In the parking lot, she saw families loading their vehicles and setting out for the day. A winding road enticed her past a young man and a woman departing from the inn on bicycles. She thought that would have been a better way to see the countryside.

After an hour, she came to a marked trail head and parked next to a blue van. A triad of directional signs indicated distances to destinations along the trail.

Following the worn dirt path, she heard voices ahead of unseen children laughing and calling to each other that merged with a bubbling stream through the woods and sounded like they could have been spirits.

As an adult, Bernadette understood that the spirits of nature that Lorraine had described to her only existed in imagination just as she had come to believe the dark spirits she envisioned were the result of her reading her book and that they did not exist at all and could not be conjured up in her present day reality.

She followed the stream to where it flowed into a clear lake that caught the refractory rays of the mid-morning sun. She paused to sit for a while among a field of wildflowers along a bank that bordered the lake. The voices of the children had faded as they moved on accompanied by their mother and father. She spotted them briefly coming into view and passing from sight among the dense forest on the curve of the opposite shore.

A medley of bird song rippled from the tall meadow grass and surrounded her with cadenzas of warbling notes. "They could be spirits," she thought, "if I want them to be."

She leaned forward to tighten a tennis shoe lace and let her chin remain resting on her raised knee. She could see a school of trout feeding among flat rocks visible in the shallow transparent blue and green water near the shore.

The warm sun touching her face and bare arms and legs lulled her into a meditative lethargy. She listened to the bird calls and steady hum of bees and watched the fish and the blue and red and yellow wildflowers swaying in the breeze. She slipped into a doze.

An hour later, submerged in a smothering inertia, she struggled awake. Soft grass shaped an imprint of her relaxed body. She brushed away a ladybug tickling the bridge of her nose and slowly sat up. A few wisps of wheat chafe clung to her hair. The sun was at high noon. The fish were gone. She stood, stretched and yawned, rubbed an insect bite on her left arm, and began the mile trek back to where she had parked her car.

Her stomach tightened with hunger. She wished she had thought to bring along a sandwich and an apple from the inn, or at least a nutrition bar. She chugged the bottled water she left in the car.

The light blue van was still parked at the trail head. She assumed it belonged to the family hiking at the lake.

The fuel indicator of her Honda Accord dipped toward empty. She didn't want to run out of gas on an isolated back country road, so decided she would drive directly to the gas station and mini-mart near the Ryerson Inn until she came over a low rise and dropped down into a hollow and saw the farm set back from the narrow road.

The house was a warm solid place built of stone near a faded red barn and silo and a few sheds bordered by fenced enclosures containing pigs and chickens.

An elderly woman and her dog, a black and white border collie, were sitting on the veranda overlooking the gravel driveway coming up a slight incline through an open pasture dotted with a small herd of grazing sheep.

Feeling as though she were trespassing, Bernadette stopped the car several yards short of the house and left the engine running. The dog stood up on the alert. The woman didn't move. Bernadette peered at her through the front windshield, hoping for a welcoming gesture. The dog trotted down the steps and came over to her open side window.

"He's friendly," Bernadette heard the woman's crackling voice. "Why don't you stay awhile."

Bernadette turned off the engine, opened the door and stepped out onto the gravel. The dog sniffed her extended hand.

"His name's Jasper."

"Hello, Jasper." Bernadette touched his bisected black and white colored head.

"He herds the sheep."

Bernadette glanced back at the flock in the pasture.

"Not often a tourist pulls in here," said the woman.

Bernadette looked back at her. "I just happened to notice your farm. It's a beautiful place. It made me want to stop."

"It does have its charm." The woman's gentle rasp carried a tone of amusement. "You up from the city?"

"Yes."

"You sound like city folk."

"This is my first time in farm country."

"We can't all be so fortunate. I went to the city once and never went back. You're welcome to set a while. And if you want, I can show you around."

"That's very nice of you." With the dog at her heels, Bernadette went up the stone steps onto the porch. "My name's Bernadette Garcetti." She extended her hand and felt the cool dry touch of the woman's skin.

"Maggie Bischoff."

"Pleased to meet you, Maggie. I don't want to intrude."

"Not at all, miss. Always good to share a nice afternoon. Have a seat."

Bernadette settled onto the flower embroidered cushion of a second wooden rocker. "You have a great view."

"Peaceful."

"I'm staying at the Ryerson Inn. It's very nice. Much nicer than a hotel."

"Known the Ryersons for many years. Good people."

"Have you had this farm for a long time?" Bernadette noticed her narrow nose and thin face lined with a network of wrinkles.

"Been in the family since 1905."

"That is a long time."

"Three generations. I'm the last of the baby boomers. Six children grown up and gone. Families of their own. Husband died seven years ago."

"I'm sorry."

"Nothin' to be sorry about. It's a natural conclusion for all of us."

"Do your children come to visit?"

"From time to time. I enjoy seeing my grandchildren."

"Does it get lonely? You don't have any neighbors."

"Me and Jasper keep good company. The air is clean. The hills are quiet. Darkness can't find me here."

Maggie's comment shocked Bernadette into silence. She tried to avoid a conspicuous look at her tarnished silver bracelets and hoop earrings that reminded Bernadette of a gypsy.

After a brief inner struggle, Bernadette managed to say, "You'll probably laugh, but I came out here looking for spirits."

"Not a laughing matter," said Maggie, "except what tickles your fancy. The kind you drink or the kind that are ghosts?"

"So you believe in their existence?" Bernadette skittishly glanced at Maggie's unflinching luminous blue eyes.

"I know they exist. They're all around us. I'm in touch with 'em daily."

Bernadette looked down at Jasper, then out at the sheep. "I tried out in the woods, but I didn't see any."

"Depends on what spirits yer lookin' for."

"I met a woman once who said there are spirits in nature. She used to live on a farm somewhere around here. I met her in a bookstore when I was thirteen. She was a psychic. Are you a psychic?"

"No, my mind is just open to a lot of things. I can see and hear things that most people can't. I was born that way. What city are you from?"

"New York."

Maggie nodded. "Umm."

"What did you mean when you said the darkness can't find you here?"

"The dark spirits hunt for those of us who live in the light. They inhabit humans who never know they are there."

"And you truly believe that."

"I do."

"I wanted to believe that, but I was told it's just my imagination. They don't really exist except in my mind."

"It's not just imagination. They are there. The evidence is what you see, how they

turn people and manipulate them to perform acts large and small that will bring about our downfall. We have to be vigilant to stop them."

"How do you mean vigilant?"

"We have to stop them from the destruction they bring to life."

"You mean when they break the law."

"Then and to stop them from continuing."

"How do we do that?"

"You see signs of it with young people and others who've suffered loss, the violent sacrifice in the name of hate, greed, and corruption committed by those with twisted minds who lead twisted lives."

"There are people trying to change things. They're in the news every day."

"They meet with resistance," said Maggie. "Those who resist the betterment of lives stop the efforts to change, because they have power. They have money. Money is their god."

"I'm only one person. What can I possibly do against them?"

"You have to discover that in yourself, in who you are. That is where your spirit lies."

"In who I am?"

"Yes."

"I gave up on spirits a long time ago."

"You gave up on dark spirits. That's a good thing. Now you are open to what you came here on your search to find."

"But I haven't really found anything," Bernadette pouted.

"She will come to you."

"She?"

"You are a woman."

"But I'm not a spirit. I'm flesh and blood."

"Your spirit lives in you," said Maggie. "She has not yet come fully alive. You will know when she does."

"I don't understand. How will I know?"

"By your deeds, the acts you perform."

"I'm just going back to New York and try to find a job."

"That is a step along the way. Your journey began when you were a child."

"You mean going to the bookstore?"

"What did you find in the bookstore? You talked to a woman there. You said she was a psychic."

"It was about a book I bought, The Dark Arts."

"That was the beginning. Until you recognize the dark spirits, you will not recognize the spirit in you that will fight against them."

"Are you saying I should join some protest movement?"

“You already have, Dear. You already have.”

Chapter 11
Arrival of Spring

The museum brochure about the art exhibit had gone unnoticed on her dining room table for the past month. She had no reason to pick it up and stare into the soothing eyes of the photographed Venus in the *Arrival of Spring* painting. For the second time since the death of Gale Walsh, a subliminal synergetic impulse compelled her to reach for it. She sensed a revival and restoration of the energy that had drained from her a few days ago. She knew the surge was something more than a caffeine hit from the Starbucks she purchased in the office tower lobby. It was something more than stress joining the flow of expensively-suited men and women striding with intense purpose or hailing cabs along the bustling business artery of Wall Street.

The advent of spring clutched the city. Bernadette noticed that most people had shed their long wool overcoats in favor of light weight raincoats and arsenals of umbrellas against intermittent showers and storms.

She passed quickly among the cliffs of tall buildings and dodged down subway steps among a jostling mob to crowd aboard a train that sped through the bowels of Manhattan. She emerged on a quieter street of wall-to-wall multi-story town homes and apartments and escaped up the elevator to her modestly furnished tenth floor flat overlooking a city park.

She normally enjoyed social outings and excursions in the city (dinner and a movie or an off-Broadway play or a musical) with a limited circle of four female friends from a non-profit volunteer group which provided financial assistance and free counseling services to abused women and children. Three of them were licensed psychologists who specialized in family issues. The fourth was Luna Romero, who managed Federal funding proposals campaigns for their nonprofit organization. Bernadette had met Luna as a staff accountant in Gale Walsh's company.

NOTE: ON YOUR RECOMMENDATION, I AM CHANGING ETHNIC CHARACTERS FROM BLACK TO HISPANIC WITH APPROPRIATE MODIFICATIONS INDICATED IN MARGIN COMMENTS.

Luna had approached her one day while Bernadette was eating lunch alone in a crowded deli down the street from the office tower. Bernadette stopped in mid-bite of her pastrami and Swiss on rye and looked up at the generous smile that accompanied the deep mellow voice.

"Hello. I recognized you from Walsh Capital. I'm Luna Romero. Work in a different department. Different floor. You work for the big boss, right?"

Bernadette nodded.

"Mind if I join you? Standing room only in here."

Bernadette moved her sandwich wrap aside and gestured to the opposite wooden chair. "Sorry it's not bigger."

Luna settled her middle-age frame into the chair. "Thank you. I'll make do. Hate to have to carry this back to the office."

Bernadette watched her lithe brown fingers open and spread the red imprinted wax paper.

"I even know your name," Luna grinned and thrust a straw through the cover slit of her iced tea. "Bernadette Garcetti."

"Where do you work?"

"Number cruncher, accounting. There's about two hundred of us." She lifted the top slice of mustard and mayo smothered wheat bread to inspect the contents of her sandwich. "Sure don't skimp on the meat here, do they. Turkey and provolone. What's yours?"

"Pastrami and swiss."

"Gotta try that next time. Looks good." Her curvaceous lips clamped over a healthy bite of her sandwich. She wiped an errant drool of mustard from her chin and clutched the napkin in a loose fist on the table. "Mmmhh," she hummed through her chewing.

Caught up in the energy from Luna's stunning brown eyes, Bernadette continued her bite. "Mmmhh is right." She chewed and swallowed. "I've tried every one they make here."

"I love roast beef, but have to stay away from it," said Luna. "Doctor's recommendation. Cholesterol and cancer in the family history. I listen to her. Do what she says. She's a good doc. Knows her stuff. Reminds me of my daughter. Bossy as hell. Just like me. Moved to California to get away from me. Not really. That's where her husband works. You have children?"

Bernadette shook her head. "I'm not married."

"Wait for mister right. I found him the second time around." She shook her head. "Been married now for thirty-one years."

"That speaks for itself," said Bernadette. "You must be very compatible."

"Long as he does what I tell him," Luna grinned and took a sip of iced tea. "I like your dress. Didn't buy that on line, I'll bet."

"SAKs."

"I don't have the body for clothes like that. Full figure. Know what I mean?" She wrinkled her narrow nose. "Don't watch my diet like I should. Could drop a neck size if I lost twenty pounds. Waist size too. My husband says he likes me this way. Doesn't care for skinny minnies, he says." She chuckled. "Likes somethin' to grab on to," she laughed. "Should've seen me when I was your age, a knockout. Three children have a way of reshaping how you look. You belong to a health club?"

Bernadette nodded.

"That's what I should do. Our kids are all married and off on their own. But I still don't seem to find time for myself what with work and volunteering."

"What kind of volunteering?"

"Fund raising for the poor. It's a nonprofit. Times are so hard for a lot of my people. I didn't see that side of it growing up. I'm a military brat. Air Force. My dad was a flight mechanic. Went to work for U.S. Air when he retired. We moved around a lot. Got to see some of the world. He supported us well. Two brothers and two sisters. Put us all through college."

"What did you major in?"

"Math and accounting. I was a whiz at math. My pop tried to talk me into becoming an engineer." She shook her head. "Not for me. Liked crunching numbers, not drawing lines and spaces. Brothers both joined the Air Force. Followed the old man. Sister always had her nose in a book. She became a librarian. Go figure. Now you know about me. What about you?"

"Nothing special. Grew up in the Bronx. My father was a plumber. My mother was a mother."

They both laughed. "Lotta truth in that," Luna snorted. "All Italian?"

"My mother's Irish. Always said that was the best part of me."

Luna laughed. "My mother said bein' Hispanic was the best part of me."

Bernadette smiled. "Sounds like you had savvy parents."

"Still have 'em. Both retired. Doin' well in North Carolina. "Any brothers and sisters?"

Bernadette nodded. "One each."

"What do they do?"

"My sister's an elementary school teacher. My brother's a plumber in the family business."

"Nice. Still close?"

"On holidays. My mother calls to gossip most weekends, mainly to see what I'm up to. I was her problem child."

"That was because you're smart, I'll bet. My son was a problem child, always in trouble with his teachers. But they didn't realize he was bored and fidgety. Today he's a successful marketing manager. Very social. Good with people. California suits him."

"I've never been there."

"My husband, Leo, and I flew out there to visit him and see our grandkids only twice in the last ten years. They all came here only once. Del's and Mikaela's little girls had a good time. We took in all the sights. His wife, Mikaela, didn't care much for New York, and where Leo and I live. She's a California girl, born and raised. She said here she felt claustrophobic. Can you beat that? But she and Del don't live in the city. Del was kind of embarrassed by what she said, but he prefers California too. It has its ghettoes, but he's nowhere near one of 'em. He's upscale, nice big home in a nearly all white suburb in Orange Country, *Yerbe Verde*, Spanish name. I say nearly, because when I went walking around, I saw an Iranian, an East Indian, and some Asian neighbors. His family's the only Hispanic one. He has a big yard, landscaped and all that. Even has a swimming pool and a spa. I liked sittin' in that spa sippin' my cocktail of choice, rum and Coke, heavy on the rum. Leo and I have an okay house and we don't live downtown, but," Her mouth twisted in a derogatory grin, "we're not upscale."

"My parents still live in the neighborhood where I grew up," said Bernadette. They're not upscale and proud of it, although they could be. They're neighborhood villagers. Members of the tribe. They can afford it, but they never wanted to move out of the city. They wouldn't be comfortable living in a suburb. They couldn't shout at their neighbors and it's easier to be nosy when you're living wall to wall. I think of them as creatures of the hood."

"Creatures of the hood – I like that. I deal with creatures of the hood all the time. Never thought of 'em that way. You sound like one of those creative types."

"I like art and music and books, but I'm not an artist and I don't play an instrument, never had music lessons except junior high school choir. But I do read a lot. My mother still harasses me about reading too much. Says it will only get me into trouble. Make me think too much. She was never one to fight back. God will take care of us, she always said. She was a brainwashed Catholic."

Luna laughed. "Imagine that. Bet she's proud of you though."

"Oh, sure, she cried at my graduation."

"Bet you were at the top of your class."

"I made good grades."

"How good?"

"Summa cum laude."

"I knew it. I could tell just by lookin' at you. You're a summa cum laude." Luna's contagious laugh caused Bernadette to join her.

"I should call you Summa," Luna chortled.

"Sounds like a porn star."

"You know, I read that's a multi-billion dollar industry."

Bernadette's voice flattened. "Sex always has a demand market."

Luna shook her head. "It does at that. Times have changed. Everything's so out in the open, what with the Internet. Nothing sacred anymore. My son keeps trying to convince me I should have a Facebook account so he can send pictures of my grandkids. I told him just send pictures the way Leo and I did when we were young, regular old mail. Don't want any part of that Facebook stuff, all the hackers and such. The only emails I send are at work and the center. Leo and I don't have email at home. We want to talk to someone, we pick up the phone. We don't even have cell phones. Well, Leo does, but he hardly ever uses it. You have Facebook?"

Bernadette shook her head. "I don't need to tell the world what I had for breakfast."

Luna burst out laughing. "Is that what people do?"

"From what I've read, some describe the details of their daily routine and send it out like it's late breaking news."

"Well, it's not my generation."

"It gives people a way to express their opinions they never had before."

"Who in the world wants to hear everybody else's opinions?"

"People get excited about opinions," said Bernadette. They share them. They pass them around and try to convince everybody else to believe what they do."

"My Leo says that's how wars get started. No one can get along. Speaking of which I have to get back to the office." Luna balled up her sandwich wrapper and pushed back her chair to stand. "It's nice talking to you, Bernadettte. Maybe we can get together again sometime."

"We know where to find each other."

Luna's wavy dark hair shook with her vigorous nod. "See you later."

Bernadette raised her hand.

Bernadette liked and respected Luna. They often had lunch together. Bernadette was the only one among the volunteer group who was unmarried and without a family. Occasionally helping them at the counseling center filled lonely weekend hours.

Bernadette was unable to establish a sense of professional objectivity. She could not distance herself from the cases she and Luna and the others encountered. She internalized the conditions of clients, an extension of the conversion disorder she experienced about her brother when she was a child. Their misfortunes and dysfunctional lives constantly invaded her thoughts and dreams.

A news feature about pedophile priests and how the Catholic diocese removed and protected them from prosecution reignited the childhood memory of her brother and how she had so desperately wanted to avenge him by summoning dark spirits. She saw the name of Father Francis O'Herlihy mentioned in the article. He was still out there. He was still active. He was still alive.

She was addicted to watching television news and reading in the newspaper about the endless stream of accidental deaths and domestic and mass murders and body counts from military conflicts, and the social clash of citizens and politicians financially fed by their lobbies.

She rationalized that the assault of the media exploding with the sounds and images of catastrophic carnage were the cause of her agitation.

Chapter 12
Bernadette's Brother

It was not until her brother, Timothy, had just turned twenty-one and was working as a journeyman plumber in his father's business that he told her bluntly what Father O'Herlihy had done to him.

"He made me give him a blow job while he rammed his finger up my ass and rubbed my dick and balls with his other hand. I didn't know what the hell was happening, but I knew it wasn't right. He told me he was a vessel of Jesus Christ and what he was doing was between us and Jesus and I must never tell anybody about it. He said that if I did, I would never go to heaven and God and Jesus would send me to hell for eternity. Can you beat that, Sis? For eternity. I was so scared after that, I nearly shit my pants every time I saw him. Mom and Dad finally figured out what happened with my nightmares and screaming and crying and being afraid to leave the house. When she wanted to take me to see Father O'Herlihy, that did it for me. I told them everything and said I was going to hell." Tim laughed. "I'm still here."

"What happened to Father O'Herlihy?"

"Who knows? Maybe the Pope. They just keep moving those freaks around to keep 'em hidden so the Catholic church won't be embarrassed. But you read the news, they're comin' out of the woodwork left and right, hundreds, thousands. They can't keep 'em hidden anymore."

The conversation stuck in Bernadette's mind as she left the urban sprawl of Manhattan behind and drove through the small towns and villages of upstate New York.

Bernadette did not know her destination. She followed an impulse that had seized her after her brother told her what had happened to him and she had read news articles about abusive priests. She more than imagined that Simonetta invaded her mind and body when she experienced a tingling sensation, an insulin rush that heightened her senses like a narcotic drug. Simonetta blocked Bernadette's rational objectivity and possessed her thoughts and directed her actions. Bernadette surrendered to the fact she was no longer in control of herself and succumbed to Simonetta using her as a refuge, a place of concealment.

Edmund O'Herlihy snugged the red cassock down the length of his tall frame, then pulled the white chasuble over his balding head and watched the pressed white folds flutter to rest at his ankles. When he donned the vestments, he saw the chasuble as a costume for his role as the virtuous and charitable leader of his congregation in his unselfish service for the Lord. The irony of the white garment symbolizing the innocence and purity of his soul at the altar did not escape him. He acknowledged there was nothing innocent and pure about him. Although in the beginning, he had attempted to live the religious mythology of the church, he had never actually believed any of it as it was intended.

He believed that he and the other priests were elite beings in the service of their Lord. This vision of the legion of priests as knights and interpreters and prophets was what had drawn him to the clergy. The religious robes and crowns and scepters were the costumes of their creed.

When he was five, Aunt Budge, as he came to call her after the nickname given her by her parents and brothers and sisters, made a pact with him to keep what they were doing a secret only between them. He was not to tell anyone else, not any of his friends, and not any other adult. He never questioned the pleasure she gave him.

After each sexual episode, they would kneel on the carpet at the side of the bed they shared and say the Lord's prayer together. Edmund mumbled his prayers so he could more easily understand the words being uttered through his aunt's denasal twang.

Budge kept various sex paraphernalia on their bedside table along with prayer beads she told Edmund had been blessed by the Jesus Christ figure hanging on the wall above their heads. She said Jesus gazed down upon them and blessed them for the love they showed one another. The association was burned into his psyche and later, as a young man, influenced his decision to become a priest.

Budge O'Herlihy never thought she would become the guardian of her young nephew, especially since she struggled with what best to do with her own life as a single unattractive woman. She had barely known her nephew until the news of his parents' death in a head-on collision on a narrow two lane country road.

After Budge heard of the accident from one of her other five sisters, a social worker had contacted her with the information regarding her new and unwanted responsibility.

Despite a few attempts at altering her physical appearance, different hair styles and makeovers did little to change her perspective of herself as being a slug.

Her nearly constant sullenness and self-pitying expression in her pinched brown eyes did not invite intimacy to the extent she drove a UPS delivery truck that did not require any more social exchange than a brief electronic signature.

What bound them together in another social context was watching the television program *Star Trek*. Budge had been an ardent fan from the first time she saw the distorted facial features of Vulcans and Klingons. She immediately identified with the weird leprous faces of Klingon characters and ascribed an alien personality to herself. She had not been born beautiful and, to explain the cause of her looks, believed she could actually be an alien, especially after consuming a six pack of beer. She shared her belief with her nephew, Edmund, who didn't want to be a Klingon. He identified with Captain Kirk, a Star Trek hero.

One day, the boy asked her why they didn't go to church.

"We don't need church. We have church in our home. We have our bedroom and we have *Star Trek*."

From that moment on, he saw religion as a manifestation of science fiction. After graduation from high school, he entered a seminary to join the alien legion of priests. He never doubted or questioned the doctrine of the Roman church, but could not help himself fixating on the beauty of young boys.

The young woman in the front row pew had arrived early and taken a seat on the aisle. Familiar with most of the people who attended mass on a regular basis, he did not recognize the woman and assumed she was either a newcomer or a visitor. As he commenced with the service, a feeling of discomfort at her intense scrutiny unsettled his composure despite his years of delivering the repetitive Latin liturgy interspersed with English translation.

He noticed her black tailored business suit and carefully coiffed brunette hair. Her attractiveness distinguished her from the mostly middle-aged and elderly parishioners and more casually dressed family clusters scattered throughout the congregation.

At the conclusion of the service, she merged with the crowd shuffling along the central aisle toward the hand-carved front door standing open to allow for their departure. Disturbed by her presence, but not knowing why, he left the altar before everyone had filed out and did not see her move off to a side alcove and return to the front of the nave.

When Bernadette cornered him alone in the church office, he said, "These are private quarters. If you want to make a confession or seek counseling, the hours are posted."

At her lack of response and unwavering stare, his aggressive tone filled the room. "You have no business coming in here. What is it you want?"

"You know why I'm here. My brother was one of your victims."

"Who are you?" He grabbed a crucifix from his desk top and held it as a weapon.

Bernadette watched him shake and tremble. His eyes rolled back into his head. His skin quivered and shriveled, falling away in red flakes until his muscles and tendons and veins and arteries were exposed. His vibrations steadily increased and his physical presence began to fade, then accelerated to a high-pitched hum. Then he was gone.

One week later, Leon Saffulo and Ed Berzinsky led the investigation of Father O'Herlihy's bloodless murder when his corpse appeared standing frozen at the church altar.

Chapter 13
The Racist

Mikaela Romero entered the deposit amount into the bank's computer system, time-stamped the printed receipt and handed it over the counter with a wide smile to the short elderly woman clutching her purse.

"Have a nice evening, Mrs. Brecht. Thank you for your business."

"You're welcome, dear. You have a nice evening too."

"Thank you."

Mikaela watched the woman walk away and noticed no one else was waiting and her three associates were signing off their work stations. Her white tipped polished nails chattered across the keyboard.

She glanced at her jeweled Movado watch, a moment that cued her thoughts for her evening schedule, avoid taking the freeway home, change her business suit for shorts, T-shirt, and sandals, then drive her daughter, Shana, to ballet class, and drop her son, Lee, at soccer practice, and return to the dance studio. Her husband, Del, would pick up their son on his way home from work.

Richard Stoli's living room drapes barely rippled, as he pushed a few inches aside to observe the neighbor woman leave her gold Lexus parked at the curb. Stoli hated her Lexus, the fact that she owned one and he did not. The fact that her husband owned a black Mercedes luxury sedan, and he did not.

His lips parted in a ferocious smile at the gorgeous Hispanic woman's face wreathed with rage. She scanned the houses up and down the street. Stoli watched her long firm muscled legs stride along the walk. Her fake leopard spotted high heeled shoes snapped a staccato cadence to her front door. She fumbled with her keys, opened the door, then rushed inside to the display pad to turn off the alarm.

Stoli didn't have an alarm. He couldn't afford one. He couldn't afford to pay for soccer shoes and a uniform for his son to play in a youth league, like the nigger boy across the street. He couldn't afford to buy a leotard and pay for his daughter to take dance lessons, like the little Mexican girl across the street.

At least his own house wasn't on the same side of the street right next to theirs. That would have been intolerable. That the Mexican family had even moved into the neighborhood was intolerable. That and the fact they had bought one of the more expensive homes with a market value of $600 thousand. Stoli's home had been assessed at $205 thousand, even with the upswing in California real estate. But he had done nothing to improve it.

He kept thinking maybe he should sell his house and move his family back to Texas where he could find a real job. Texas had a true leader in the Governor.

Stoli had been layed off as an aerospace assembly worker after thirteen years at Boeing and had been unemployed for one year until he found a part time job at the local big box store driving a forklift. His pension and benefits were gone. If it weren't for his wife, Ruthie, working as a grocery store checkout clerk, they wouldn't be able to pay the mortgage and would have to go to ER for medical treatments.

In his search for another job, no one cared about his knowledge of machined and fabricated parts and how to assemble and install wire harnesses, or so he thought. His inability to accept the reality of being laid off was transparent during the three interviews he was granted. He could not repress his anger and fear of not regaining what he once had, what he considered his earned sense of entitlement as a white skilled laborer.

Stoli frequented white supremacist websites. The expressions of hate and vitriol fed his imagination and shaped and formed who he was becoming. He worshipped the gospel of hate radio and could not get over the mid-term Presidential election. He didn't know what the word demographics meant and didn't give a shit.

He dominated the family television, watching wrestling and mixed martial arts. Ruthie and the kids closeted themselves to escape his shouts and curses, a steady stream of profanity, as he sucked cigars and drank cases of beer. His sour body odor and tobacco smoke permeated the living room.

Mikaela accessed her husband's number. Her hand trembled as she pushed back her Leontine luxurious brunette hair and slapped the iPhone against her left ear. Her gold hoop earring jingled in resistance at being displaced.

"Del, where the hell are you? Answer your goddamn phone! Jesus, don't send me to your voice mail! Pick up! Pick up!" She terminated the connection and called again.

"Micky, I'm with a customer. I'll call you back in five."

"Don't hang up on me! This is an emergency. Some mother fucker on our street spray painted our garage door with the word wetback."

"What the hell? We've lived there for seven years. There' s never been any problem."

"Well, we've got a problem now. What do you want me to do? Oh, by the way, don't pull into the driveway when you come home. There are nails and screws scattered all over it."

"Take a photo of the door and send it me. I'll be home in an hour."

"What about Lee's soccer practice and Shana's dance lesson?"

"You go ahead and take them. I'll paint over the word as soon as I get home. I don't want them to see it."

"I was thinking I should call the police and the Orange County Register."

"If you call the police, the media will show up. We don't want a circus. Let me handle it. Just take care of the kids. I have to get back to my customer."

"I can't believe it. This is Orange County."

"That's the point. It is Orange County. I'll see you later. Any gawkers?"

"There's no one on the street. No one. Everybody in the neighborhood can't be like that."

"It only takes one. Later."

"Shit." Mikaela ended the call and walked back outside across the strip of front lawn where she could get an angle framing the garage door. Her iPhone captured the ugly word. She emailed the digital photo to Del, then returned to the house.

Mikaela was a tall stunning beautiful Latina woman who looked to Stoli like she could be in a television series or the movies. That she lived in the neighborhood caused him to resent his own frumpy wife with her thick legs and midriff bulge that had replaced her flat abdomen hardened by hours of high school girls water polo practice. He had fantasies about the Mexican woman. Stoli's old faded brown Nissan had a rusting dented rear door and fender and broken plastic taillight held together with duct tape. Stoli would never admit it, but he envied the handsome features and tall athletic build of her husband, Del, and the cars he and his wife owned.

"No wetback should look like that," he reasoned. "He looks like a white man. He has the face of a white man. Even his nose and chin look better than mine. He shaves his head and looks great. I'm half bald and I look like shit."

Stoli always rooted for the white guy whenever there was an Hispanic fighter on the wrestling channel and Mixed Martial Arts, his two favorite television programs, over-watched to the point of saturation. He didn't care if they were Mexican, Cuban, Puerto Rican, or some shit hole South American country. He screamed and ranted at the combatants. He wasn't satisfied unless the white guy turned the brown face into a bloody pulp. He marveled that the brown guy's blood streaming down his face looked black instead of red, but the white guy's blood looked red.

When two white guys fought, he rooted for the one who was not as good looking to beat the living shit out of the other guy who was a drama queen. Stoli hated the drama queens with their long flowing blonde locks like some transvestite with enormous pectoral tit muscles. Stoli believed the drama queens were gay and deserved to have the shit beat out of them. Whenever they made a throw and held their opponent down for the count, Stoli boiled up out of his frayed easy chair and filled the air with inspired profanity. He laced almost every sentence and phrase he uttered with a "fuck" or "shit" or "goddam cock sucker" since he had been laid off. Having to settle for a temp job driving a warehouse forklift did little to soothe his disposition.

Del would forever associate his wife's phone call with the odor of processed rubber in the tire distribution warehouse. He gazed through his second floor balcony office viewing window at the long steel racks of thousands of palletized tires of every size and tread. He managed sales, inventory, and distribution to automotive dealers and tire companies throughout Southern California with products made in Africa, Southeast Asia, and South America.

Diesel trucks lined the receiving docks along one side of the massive five acre warehouse and an army of giant container eighteen wheelers departed from the docks on the other side to navigate the endless convoys monopolizing the freeways passing to and from Ontario and the Inland Empire, the center of commerce east of Los Angeles and the Port of San Pedro.

The warehouse ran three full shifts of receiving and shipping clerks and forklift drivers seven days a week. Even though much of the operation used automated conveyor, inventory barcode and packing systems, Del often worked fourteen to sixteen hour days to stay on top of and monitor the demand for his products.

The business was his bank and the manifestation of his success as a regional manager reporting to the parent company in Michigan. The photo of his defaced garage door that his wife emailed him shattered his illusion and fueled his rage. He walked up and down two aisles of the warehouse to temper his anger before he dared to go out and get behind the wheel of his car.

The erratic vertiginous swarm of traffic slowed his progress along familiar surface streets and freeways that he now perceived as passageways through an alien landscape. His hands clutched the wheel with a desperate grip to maintain his focus. The word 'Home" on the orange and white signage of the warehouse quelled his disconnectedness. Home was his family, his property, his community, his self. He had never doubted its sanctity until now. The threat of intrusion had barely existed on the periphery of his thoughts. His occasional brush with racist slurs as a boy had not had a significant impact. Schooled by his mother and father, he had sloughed off their remarks, but he couldn't avoid seeing and hearing about the ongoing plight of struggling Hispanics in the news media.

From the time he was born, poverty had never touched him and on military bases he had commingled with children of Asian, white, Hispanic, and Black ethnicity. The word nigger painted on his garage door shattered the continuity he had enjoyed in high school and college academics and athletics and his unbiased acceptance into the business world on the strength of his scholarship.

On an intellectual level, he perceived that he lived in a world of social boundaries and could avoid complicating his life by not dating a white girl. A romantic association with a white girl would make him seem to be seeking acceptance in white upper-class society. He and Mikaela had achieved that goal together, being bright and beautiful and Hispanic.

They lived in a predominantly white and upper-middle class mixed Hispanic and Asian neighborhood and worked in white managed companies. Their children attended white schools taught by white and a few Hispanic and Asian teachers. Their friends were from different cultural and family backgrounds and did not engage in distinctions because of skin color and ethnicity.

Del did not want his children to see the racial slur on their garage door and create an axiomatic doubt about their equality and validity.

He parked his car at the center of the crowded lot and silently cursed himself for passing up an empty space near the entrance to avoid meeting the gaze of a scruffy bearded white contractor wearing paint-stained coveralls and loading raw lumber into the back of his red Dodge Ram.

Not fully understanding his avoidance impulse, Del crossed over to the next aisle and strode quickly past other cars and trucks to the garden entrance. Barely noticing the trays of green seedlings and flats of bright colored flowers on mobile aluminum racks, he swept through the garden supply section and, in his search for the paint aisle, side-stepped customers pushing their orange carts along the wide front access walkway.

The labels on the shelves of stacked spray paint cans blurred as though denying him a clear identification of what he sought. He rubbed his eyes and blinked to restore his focus and purpose and located two cans that confounded him. He was unsure whether to select a flat white or a semi-gloss white. The choice derailed him. He grabbed a can of each and rushed back along the aisle to the front checkout counters.

With a squeal of brakes, his sharp turn onto *Calle de Paloma* in the Yerbe Verde tract laid a sheen of tire tread. He slowed abruptly at seeing the small crowd of neighbors clustered at the foot of his driveway taking photos of the garage door with their iPhones.

"No," he moaned. "Oh, God, no!" He recoiled at the thought of the insulting image being sent out over the Internet. He stopped at the curb, kicked open the door, grabbed the plastic bag containing the paint cans, and approached the one middle-aged man and seven younger women exclaiming their dismay and disapproval in sensational tones that such an act had happened in their neighborhood.

"Did any of you see who did this?" Del's voice thundered.

The group turned toward him and Del saw photos being taken and one camera capturing him on video. "Do not take photos of me," he ordered. "As a matter of fact, unless you can tell me who did this, I want all of you to leave. Just go home. I don't need my privacy invaded any more than it already is. Please go now, all of you. I have to clean up this mess."

"You must be very angry and upset," said one of the women.

"Yes, I'm angry and I'm upset. Please do me the courtesy of leaving."

"You going to call the police?" asked the man.

"I don't know what I'm going to do. But right now, I'm just going to clean it up."

"This is an outrage to all of us," said an Asian mother. "This is against the law."

"He knows," said the man. "We need to let him take care of it, clean it up. We need to all go back home now." He spread his arms wide to encourage and herd the women away.

"The news media should come and see this," said another woman. "This should be on the evening news."

"No media," shouted Del. "Don't go calling any media."

"If it was my house," said a fourth woman, "I'd have the police and the news people right here on the spot. I'd want an investigation and I would prosecute."

"It's not your house," said the man. "This is more of a shock to him than to any of us. Let him take care of it in his own way." As the group moved off down the street, the man half-twisted back to call to Del, "If there's anything we can do to help, let us know."

Del vehemently shook his head, then, kicking and shuffling at the screws and nails scattered across the surface of the driveway, he went to the door confronting him with the despised word that made his skin crawl.

The uneven shape of the letters bled in erratic streaks and bumps, indicating that whoever had put them there had been in a hurry and not made any effort to be precise. As he slowly obliterated them with white spray paint, Del thought the ragged edges a sign that the perpetrator did not want to risk being recognized and caught in the act. Maintaining anonymity was his leverage and the key to his cowardice.

He conjectured that no one outside the block would know or even care about the Romero family living there, unless someone from a neighboring tract had decided to express his opinion.

Although they didn't interact with Del and Mikaela socially, the next door neighbors on either side waved and said 'Hi' and acknowledged them on a first name basis since they had bought the newly constructed house and moved in seven years ago.

With one or two exceptions, people were friendly in a noncommittal way, which was standard suburban behavior. People tended to lead private lives and occasionally had family and friends from outside come to birthdays and dinner and pool parties and to celebrate national holidays. Del and Mikaela had both Black and white friends park expensive cars at their curb and along the street. No one had ever objected. Del considered the vandalism on his garage door as a bizarre social anomaly, more than a prank, the acting out of a sick white supremacist fantasy.

Liquid white paint leaked from the spray nozzle, pooled in his finger nail quick and dribbled in rivulets down his forefinger. Upon finishing the laborious task of covering the black letters, he stepped back and noticed their slight imprint still visible through the skein of white. He switched cans and blasted the pattern with yet another layer until the word was obliterated to his satisfaction.

He went into the house and washed his hands at the kitchen sink, then entered the garage.

From a crack at the edge of his living room drapes, Stoli watched Del carrying a broom and dustpan come out of the garage and sweep the sharp metal into small piles on the driveway. He wheeled a trash barrel from around the side of the garage and deposited the debris.

Concealed behind his curtain, Stoli had observed the small gathering of neighbors taking photos of his handiwork on their iPhones. He had seen Del drive the rubberneckers away and paint over the letters. He breathed a sigh of relief that no police arrived to investigate and knock on doors. He did not want to talk to police officers. He could continue his campaign undisturbed to force the Mexican family to move out of the neighborhood.

Ruth slid the barcode of the boxed white rice across the horizontal scanner of her checkout counter, scanned the middle-aged customer's coupons, then tapped a few computer keys to bring up the discounted total on the flat screen beside her.

"One hundred seven dollars and thirteen cents." She watched the woman swipe her debit card and saw the digital payment register on her computer. A moment later, she pulled and looped a two foot long receipt and several coupons from the printer and handed them to the woman. "Have a nice day."

"Thank you. You too." The woman moved to her cart, as the Hispanic teenage girl positioned a final plastic bag filled with vegetables next to a carton of range free eggs and a loaf of wheat bread on the upper section. "Thank you, dear." The woman pushed her cart toward the exit.

"It's time for my break, Ruthie," the girl smiled.

Ruthie silently marveled at her smooth immaculate brown skin and rosy compexion. “Sure, go ahead. No one waiting. End of my shift. I’m going to close out.” She turned off her number five station light and placed a ‘closed’ sign, ‘please go to next checkout’ on the rubber conveyor, and waved the supervisor over to observe her balance her cash drawer.

“Good to go, Ruthie,” the overweight blonde woman beamed an approving smile, as she locked down the computer and cash drawer. “Have a great evening.”

“Thanks, Kristin, you too.” Ruth moved along the central food aisle in an unhurried walk to the employee area next to the stock room. Her feet ached despite her ergonomic shoes. After a day of standing at the checkout, the extra thick soles made little difference. Her legs and hips also throbbed.

She had been a clerk for ten years and worried how much longer she could keep it up. But when her husband lost his job, she knew she had no choice. As a forklift driver, he made only a third of his former income at Boeing and they had seven to eight years of child support ahead of them.

As Ruthie pulled into her driveway and stepped out of her car, the next door neighbor woman came over to greet her. “Ruthie, you just missed it.” She raised the iPhone she clutched in her right hand.

“Hi, Gladys, missed what?”

“Look at this.” She held up the digital photo of the racial slur on the Romero’s garage door.

“What’s that?”

“The Romeros across the street.”

Ruth craned her head around to look at the house across the street, then back at the photo. “There’s nothing there.”

“The owner painted over it. Someone painted wetback on the garage door.”

“I guess I didn’t miss anything.”

"A group of us got pictures. We're putting it on the Internet."

"Did the police come?"

"No one called them."

"Someone should have called them."

"The owner told us not to."

"That's strange."

"We think he doesn't want any publicity. He told us that. He didn't want the news media coming here."

"I can hardly blame him."

"He can't stop us from sharing it with our friends on Facebook though."

"Why do you want to do that?"

"This happened in our neighborhood. This is news."

"No it's not. It's just some kind of prank. Teenagers or something."

"He was really upset."

"Who?"

"The owner."

"Wouldn't you be?"

Gladys shrugged. "Don't have to worry about that. His wife got here before he did, then drove away. I could tell she was mad."

"Gladys, you should get out and find something to do besides spying on your neighbors."

"I beg your pardon, Ruthie. I don't spy on my neighbors. A lot of us went over to look at it. You would have too, if you'd been here. Someone said it was a tagger."

"The owner must have been embarrassed. I wouldn't have bothered him."

"It did bring something to our attention."

"What was that?"

"They're the only Mexican family in *Yerbe Verde*."

"So, what's that supposed to mean?"

"Nothing for me personally. I don't have any problem with Mexican people as long as there aren't more of them than me."

"Gladys, we've been friends and neighbors for a long time, and we're friends, so our opinions are just that, opinions. You have yours and I have mine. But I'm telling you as a friend, you're coming off sounding like a bigot and a racist."

"Well, whoever put that word on the garage door is the bigot and racist, not me. I say hello to them. I wave when I see them. I don't ignore them."

"That's good of you, Gladys."

"Since you're throwing stones, what about you, Ruthie? I haven't seen you rubbing shoulders with 'em."

"I welcomed them to the neighborhood. Stoli and me are a lot older than they are. They have little kids. We have teenagers. They're highly educated and have good jobs, professional jobs. Stoli and me, we don't have anything in common with 'em."

"That's for sure. They're brown and you're white and you have an excuse. So don't shake your finger at me, Ruthie. We're longtime friends, so we can be honest with each other. You're just as prejudiced as I am."

"It really doesn't matter what we think. We just have to accept each other. They have a right to live here. We have a right to live here. That's what it comes down to. Whoever put that name on their garage door doesn't have the right."

"Well, it's done. It's over and none the worse for wear."

"It might be done, but it's not over, not what they're feeling."

"It's got nothing to do with us."

"Is that why you're going to send it to everyone you know on Facebook?"

"It's just something that happened. That's all. It'll pass and no one will remember it."

"People do remember it and the only passing is it gets passed around. That's why I won't let my kids have Facebook accounts. I talk to people at work whose kids do. You read about those suicides because of what some kids put on Facebook. They don't have any common good sense. They just put stuff on there that's sensational so they can hurt someone else and feel important. I've got two kids. I know how their minds work. If you send your photo out, you're just gonna hurt that family. Think about it, Gladys."

"I don't know where you come off acting like you're better than the rest of us."

"It's called human decency, Gladys. You know, do unto others."

"Well, Ruthie, you know as well as I do that in today's world it's do others before they do you."

"What does your husband have to say about it?"

"Sam's not home from work yet. You should ask your husband though."

"Was he out in the street with the rest of you?"

"No, but he was watchin'. He came out to the front yard, then went back in the house. He doesn't like havin' them Mexicans livin' over there. I heard him say so to Sam."

"Don't pay any attention to him. Stoli's havin' a rough go of it, his job and all."

"You're just makin' excuses for him."

"Okay, so I am. He's in a bad way, but he's still my husband."

"You're too good for him, Ruthie."

"I'll be the judge of that. Have to go in and get dinner ready. Nice talkin' with you."

"Nice talkin' with you too." Gladys turned away and walked across her front lawn. "Have a nice evening."

"Yep." With a quick glance across the street at the Romero house, Ruth walked to her front door. Surprised to find it locked, she knocked and rang the bell. "Open up, Stoli. It's me. I'm home."

As Stoli opened the door, she stepped past him inside. "What's the door doing locked."

"Didn't know it was. Thought you locked it when you left this morning."

"Don't remember that I did."

"Force of habit."

"Kids home?"

"In their rooms, doin' homework."

"Not likely. You gonna help me with dinner?"

"I'm in the middle of a match," he referred to the professional wrestlers on television body slamming each other against the ropes and onto the floor of the ring.

"Have a good day off?" Ruth dropped her purse on an armchair as she moved toward the kitchen.

"Any day off is a good day." Clutching a can of beer, he returned to the couch.

"Read in the paper that Boeing is hiring again," she called back while pulling a skillet and a saucepan from the cupboard. "They have a big new contract. Have to replace old airplanes being retired."

"I'll call human resources tomorrow," he shouted over the noise of the wrestling match spectators.

She filled a large pot with water and set it on the stove to boil, then unwrapped a two pound package of hamburger from the meat keeper and set it aside while she chopped half an onion and sautéed the pieces in olive oil in an over-sized skillet. She poured a jar of Italian seasoned tomato sauce into the saucepan and waited for the water to bubble before siphoning in a package of stiff spaghetti pasta, then turning the gas flame to low under the sauce.

With the meat sizzling and the water boiling behind her, she stepped to the kitchen door. "I saw Gladys in the driveway. She said something happened to the neighbor's house across the street today."

"I saw some people over there, but I didn't pay much attention."

"Gladys said someone spray painted the garage door with the word wetback."

Stoli pushed his pudgy body up off the couch and went to the living room window. He held back the drapes and looked out. "There's nothing on his garage door. Are you sure Gladys wasn't drinking? She takes meds too, you know."

"She showed me a photo on her iPhone."

"Well, good for Gladys and her iPhone. That garage door is clean as the day it was installed."

"Obviously the owner painted over the word."

"I'd paint over it too and forget about it. It must have been a prank."

"You don't forget about it when you're Hispanic living in a largely white neighborhood."

"No one cares if they're Black or brown or yellow as long as they keep up their place." He dropped the drape and returned to the couch.

"I can't help thinking what they must be going through," said Ruthie.

"Don't be such a bleeding heart. It's not your problem."

"All this Internet and Twitter and Facebook stuff – it causes problems. It's a good thing we don't allow our kids to use it."

"They have cell phones. If a kid has a cell phone, they're doin' it."

"Maybe we should take their phones away."

"Not a good idea. Kids today, you do that and they'll kill you in your sleep and post it on the Internet."

"Our kids aren't like that."

"Ruthie, don't be naïve. Our kids are like all the other kids. The Internet only makes it worse because they share things faster. That's where they get their ideas. That's what they believe in, not what you and me got to say about anything. My friend at work told me. He has two daughters who dress like whores. He showed me their picture on his iPhone."

"On his iPhone?"

"Yeah, he wants to show what he has to complain about. He has all kinds of photos of things he doesn't like and he complains about. When we have lunch, it's like show and tell."

"Does he have photos of anything he does like?"

"Now that you mention it, no. If he does, he never showed me. He's a whiner and complainer, one of these guys who whines and complains all the time, about everything."

"Sound familiar?"

Stoli's head jerked up from watching the television screen. "What's that supposed to mean?"

"Does it sound familiar?"

"No, it doesn't."

Ruthie smirked.

"What's that look? What's that look on your face?"

"I guess it's my Facebook."

"There are things I have a right to complain about."

"It's all right to complain, but it's better to do something about it or try to do something."

"I do things about it. I'm a highly skilled aircraft assembler and now I'm workin' at a piss ant ware house for peanuts."

"It's a job. Better than no job."

"I'll be callin' Boeing tomorrow."

"You'll get your old job back. I know you will."

"I don't need you to be a rah rah cheerleader."

Ruthie grinned. "You need some cheering up, Stoli. You're a sad sack. Rah Rah!"

"Go make dinner. What're we havin'?"

"Spaghetti."

"My fuckin' favorite."

"That's what I like to hear, my fuckin' favorite."

Chapter 14
Image

Mikaela dreamed of seeing her name on signage in women's fashions in leading department stores, on dress labels and suits and sports clothes and swim suits. But now she could not erase from her mind the image on her garage door. The word superseded and obliterated her vision like an invading mental worm.

Sure, some narrow-minded racist cretin had put it there, someone in the neighborhood, someone who wanted them gone, some white supremacist who wanted them to slide back down the social ladder because their presence threatened the Aryan illusion he held of himself just as the foul word on the garage door contaminated their lives.

Prejudice was not unfamiliar to her, less so when she had been an unaware young girl growing up in a Los Angeles suburb than reading and hearing about it in the media. She witnessed its impact on her two older brothers who had been awarded sports scholarships to prominent universities supported by their academic records demanded by their father who was a civil rights lawyer.

During her own college years, white boys were more interested in her natural beauty and aggressively tried to gain access to her body rather than acknowledge her superior intellect. She graduated with honors among the top ten of her class.

Although she worked in banking, she understood she could capitalize on her beauty because fashion attached itself to her. She had an artistic creative eye for style, for the lines and curves and colors of material.

Just as she valued her own beauty, she had met her male counterpart in Diliberto Romero, who she thought could have become a movie star rather than a tire salesman. She even suggested that he try that career route, take acting classes, model men's clothes. He protested he didn't have the ego for it and didn't handle rejection well. He wasn't thick-skinned enough. His gentle self-effacement was among the qualities she admired in him and caused her to fall in love with him.

She never thought of him as a fighter. She thought he would agree with her that they sell their house and move out of the neighborhood as quickly as possible. This wasn't their dream house anyway. They had discussed plans to buy up in a few more years. Interest rates were low. Housing prices were rising. It was a seller's market. These were positive encouraging signs that corresponded with their own jobs and economic success. "Let's make the move," she argued. "Why wait?"

"Because some bastard is trying to force us out with an insult on our garage door."

They waited until their son and daughter were asleep before having the conversation. She had picked them both up from school, which was a break in the routine. Lee wondered why his dad wasn't taking him to soccer practice and was told that his dad had to work late.

Lee scrunched down in the back seat. He liked that his dad picked him up and took him to soccer practice. His dad had done that since the beginning of the season, and now this. He didn't resent that his mom was driving him to soccer after dropping his sister, Shana, off at the dance studio for her ballet lesson. But he and his dad talked about the day. His dad talked to him about sports and listened intently to what Lee had to say about his schoolwork and teachers and friends. His mom didn't seem to be as interested. She would listen all right, but today, she wasn't even listening. She tuned him out. She gripped the steering wheel like she was trying to choke a snake and she just kept looking straight ahead at the traffic, which was okay. But she hadn't even smiled at him when she picked him up at the school parking lot. She had handed him his gym bag and he had to change into his soccer shorts and gear while they were driving, which he didn't mind doing when his dad was driving, but his mom? He told her he'd change when he got to the practice field. He didn't think she even heard him. She didn't pay any attention. She just said, "We don't want you to be late."

"They start with warm-ups anyway," he said.

"I'm sorry we had to drop Shana off first," she said.

"It's okay, Mom. It's no big deal. I can play if I warm-up or not."

"Well, I don't want you to have a muscle cramp or something."

"I don't get muscle cramps, Mom. I'm a kid. Don't worry about it."

"I always worry about you and Shana."

"We're okay, Mom. We're okay."

"Has anyone on our street ever stopped you or said anything to you, like when you're riding your skateboard or your bike?"

"Other kids talk all the time. You mean grown-ups?"

"Yes, grown-ups."

"They say hi. They're nice. I like my soccer coach. I have friends on the soccer team. Why are you asking me?"

"I'm trying to deal with a neighborhood situation."

"What kind of situation?"

"Actually, it doesn't really involve you. I was just curious."

"Is something wrong?"

"Yes, but it doesn't involve you. Do you and Shana like where we live?"

"Yeah, we like it a lot," said Lee.

"I know you're both doing well at school and your teachers like you."

"I have awesome teachers."

"It helps to have awesome teachers."

"Did something happen?"

"Actually, your dad and I are doing well and he and I will be discussing the possibility of moving."

"Moving! Why?"

"Our house has appreciated in value and the market is right for us to sell it and move up."

"Move up to where? The mountains?"

"Not that kind of up, to a better home, more expensive and in a better neighborhood."

"You're not gonna make Shana and me change schools. What about our friends?"

"We'd wait 'til the end of the semester, and you'll make new friends. Moving is a good thing. It gives you a new perspective about people and places and broadens your horizons. Your dad grew up in a military family and lived in many different countries around the world. His experiences were beneficial."

"I know. He told us about them and Gramma and Grandpa showed us pictures and told us stories about them. But I like it here. I have friends. I don't want to move."

"I haven't even talked with your dad about it yet. It was something we planned for the future, down the road a few years, just before you start high school."

"That's a long time away."

"Not so long. Look how the years whip by."

"I wish I could stop time and keep things the way they are."

"Change is good, dumplin'. It's also necessary and nothing can stop it."

He looked over at her. "You haven't called me dumplin' since I was five years old."

"Well, you're older. I didn't think you wanted me to keep calling you dumplin'."

"It's a little kid's name. I'm almost as tall as you."

"Except in my heels. You have a few inches to go."

"I want to be as tall as dad some day."

She smiled. "I expect you will."

From that point in the conversation, she just focused on the traffic so she wouldn't plow into some other car and so she wouldn't cry.

"Dad," Lee looked up from his plate of salmon, broccoli, and brown rice across the table at his father. "Mom said we might move."

Del set his fork on his plate so it would not clatter. He slowly chewed his mouthful of fish and rice while staring intently at Mikaela.

"I told him we would be discussing it," said Mikaela. "We talked about it as part of our future plans."

Del swallowed hard, then gulped from his tall glass of water. Normally, he and Mikaela would have wine with the evening meal, a pinot noir with salmon. Tonight, wine was absent from the table. His son's unexpected comment made him want to break out the Scotch. He would have that drink later when the kids were in bed and he and Mikaela would compare notes of the day.

"Can I still go to dance class?" asked Shana.

"Of course," said Del. "Nothing has changed. We haven't decided anything definite about moving." His warning glare chased Mikaela's avoiding glance.

"I don't start high school for three more years," said Lee.

"What about high school?"

"Mom said that's when you planned to move, but now you were changing your mind."

"Nobody's mind is changed."

"I was explaining to Lee about the current market conditions," said Mikaela.

"He doesn't need to know about the current market conditions. He just needs to be a boy."

"Change can be positive," said Mikaela. "I reminded him of your childhood living in different countries."

"I don't want you to leverage this conversation with Lee and Shana at the table. We can talk about it later."

"I didn't say anything important."

"Good. So, Shana, how was your dance class?"

"We're starting to learn a new routine to get ready for the dance recital in May."

"Your mother and I look forward to seeing it, and, of course, your brother."

"Not me," said Lee. "Those dances are boring."

"I come to see your soccer games," said Shana.

"Are you bored?"

"No."

"That's because soccer isn't boring."

"We're all supportive of Shana's dancing," said Lee. "We all stand by each other in whatever we do. That's what being a family is all about."

"I'm not saying I won't go and see her," said Lee. "She's good. I could never move around like that. I just don't like all that tippy toe music."

"So, what's your favorite kind of music?" asked Mikaela.

"I like Justin Bieber and Matty B. All my friends have them on their MP3's."

"I like Kelly Clarkson and Taylor Swift," said Shana. "But we can't dance ballet to them."

"Modern dancing or jazz maybe," said Mikaela. "You'll be adding that class next semester."

"Yeah, if our teacher lets us. She picks all the music."

"You can always offer a suggestion," said Mikaela.

"Miss Wenger is strict, but she's nice too."

Later that night after their children were asleep, Del tossed back a triple scotch straight and continued the conversation.

"We're not going to let some asshole force us to move."

"The damage has been done. We have to leave. We owe it to our children to leave. Whoever did this is crazy, a sociopath. Who knows what he might do next."

"We owe it to our children to stay," said Del.

"We owe it to our children to move. That's just your pride talking."

"You're goddamn right. I want to catch the son-of-a-bitch."

"And then what?"

"Have him arrested."

"If you want someone arrested, you call the police," said Mikaela. "That's their job, not yours."

"Not yet. The other thing I don't want is to get us smeared all over the news. We don't need to draw attention to ourselves. Think about our jobs."

"I am. I'm thinking about further discrimination because it's out there in the workplace and it's real," said Mikaela. "If you want to keep this clean, we should just move."

"No, I'm not going to let some narrow-minded racist prick do this to us. We have every right to live here. We've earned it."

"Whoever did it broke the law. Let the law handle it."

"If it happens again, I will, and then we'll move, but it will be on our terms, not his, whoever he is. We won't give him the satisfaction."

"What about Lee and Shana? Whoever put that word on the door is a sicko. He might do something to harm our children. I don't want to risk that and you shouldn't either."

"This guy's a coward. He's not going to hurt little kids. He knows that'll get him a life sentence."

"Only if he's caught."

"Lee and Shana are always with us or with other kids. We never let them go anywhere alone. It's not safe in this neighborhood or any neighborhood."

"Well, what are you going to do?" Mikaela threw up her hands. "You can't stay home all day and up all night."

"Video surveillance."

"Video surveillance? Are you kidding? We're not a bank or a company."

"It's inexpensive wireless technology, relatively inexpensive. The cameras are small, about the size of your fist. They can be tucked up into small corners and I'll have motion sensor lights installed."

"If lights come on, don't you suppose that will scare the guy away?"

"That's fine. If he can't even get to the house, he can't pull this shit again."

"This isn't just about the shit, Del. It's the attitude, the perception. It's being pointed out to the rest of the neighbors that not only are we Hispanic, we are not accepted."

"No one has the right to do that to us, no one. I'm going to fight this, Micky, and I'm going to win."

"If it doesn't work, we're moving. We're just flat out moving. You agree?"

"I won't agree to anything until I see what happens."

"When are you going to put up your surveillance cameras?"

"Tomorrow evening. I'll pick them up on the way home from work."

The next morning, Mikaela's agonized cry echoed through the house. "Del, they're out there."

"Who?"

"Out in front. Television vans are lining up."

"What the hell!" Del dropped his razor on the bathroom counter, grabbed a hand towel and wiped away remnant lather from his jaw as he followed Mikaela to the living room window. As curious neighbors gathered on the street, one of the three news cameramen was videotaping the front of the house.

"What the hell are they filming?" Del started for the door.

"Del, put on a shirt, even a T-shirt. Don't go out there like that. You're half naked."

"Shit, are the kids up?"

"I was just going to wake them, when I looked out the window."

"Don't let them see this 'til I find out what's happening. It has to have something to do with yesterday." He raced down the hall to the master bedroom, snatched a plain blue T-shirt and pulled it on over his head as he returned to the living room. "Stand by the door. Don't come out there unless I call you and definitely don't let the kids wander out there." He opened the door, stepped onto the porch and slammed it shut behind him. He looked in the direction the television camera was pointed.

The word had again been spray painted on the garage door.

He saw the camera lens pan toward him. He stepped aside hoping to avoid being caught standing near the garage door and the despised word as a label.

Tracked by the handheld camera, an attractive young Hispanic reporter rushed toward him. Thrusting her microphone at his face, she called out, "Sir, Sir, would you please tell us your name."

He tried to wave her away and return to the front door.

"Do you have any idea who did this? Someone in the neighborhood?"

"No comment. I don't have anything to say."

"Is it the first time this has happened?"

Two other reporters and their camera and sound crews moved forward across the lawn from their vans. Now that he saw what was happening, Del wanted desperately to escape back into the house.

"Please sir, you must have something to say about this!"

"Sir, you do realize you're the victim of a hate crime! It's against the law!"

At that moment, red and blue lights flashing, three black and white police units rolled into the area and parked next to the news vans. Doors flew open and six officers stepped out of the vehicles. Two went directly to the upside and downside of the sidewalk to warn away and contain the gathering of gawking neighbors clicking photos with their cell phones. The other four young officers approached Del, who decided he now had no choice but to remain and be questioned, but at least he would be responding to legal authority, not harassment by the journalists.

Two officers ordered the three female reporters and their crews to stand back and give them room to talk with Del. The officers and Del remained on camera and the sound engineers amplified the microphones attempting to catch the conversation.

"Good morning, sir. I'm officer Hernandez and this is Officer Harkinson. Would you tell us your name."

"Del Romero."

"Thank you, Mr. Romero. Are you the owner of this house?"

"Yes, my family and I have lived in this neighborhood for seven years." Del figured he was at least fifteen years older than the two lean athletic men, one Hispanic, one white, in crisp dark blue uniforms. Wide black belts hung with holstered handguns, tasers and cuffs reinforced their image of authority. All four had clean-shaved heads. The radios clipped to their shirts crackled with intermittent statements from a dispatcher.

"When did you discover your garage door had been vandalized?"

"This morning. My wife saw the neighbors and news vans out front and told me. I just came out a few minutes before you arrived."

"Have you given any comments to the media?"

"No, I'd prefer not to have this blow up into something bigger than it is. A word can be erased."

"That's true, Mr. Romero, but our concern here is the intent of the perpetrator, who could be one of your neighbors. Our crime scene investigators are on the way to take a paint sample and photos and gather any evidence that can assist in identifying the individual or group that might have done this. They have broken the law and will be subject to arrest."

Del noticed three other officers cordoning off the driveway and front yard and instructing the journalists, their crews, and curious neighbors to stand behind the yellow crime scene tape.

"My wife and I have to take our children to school and go to work. Are we allowed to leave?"

"We have to ask you both some questions, but, yes, you'll be able to take your children to school and go to work. Is your wife inside?"

"Yes, she's getting dressed and about to get the kids up to have breakfast."

"We have no reason to enter the house, but we do need to speak with both of you. You can ask her to come outside, or, with your permission, we can talk with you inside."

"Give me a moment to see if she's dressed and what's happening with the kids."

"Of course, Mr. Romero. We'll wait right here." Officer Hernandez spoke into his phone. "The owner has stated we have permission to enter the house to speak with him and his wife. The crime scene is taped. As soon as CSI arrives, they can begin."

Del nearly collided with Mikaela hovering just inside the front door.

"What is it?" she clutched his arm.

"The police want to talk to both of us."

"In here?"

"I told them it would be all right to come in. Those cameras are running out there. I don't want both of us to be on the evening news."

"What about Lee and Shana."

"Have them get dressed and come down to breakfast. We can't shield them from this. They're exposed. We'll have to explain it."

"Do you believe me now when I say we have to move? We have to put Lee and Shana first."

"The subject is not off the table."

"Thank you for that."

"Not what I wanted, but this is out of control."

"Will there be a lawsuit?"

"Only if the police can find out who did it."

"Someone must be sure of himself, to do it twice."

"There will be an investigation."

"I still want us to move."

"We'll talk about it. Get the kids. I'm going to let the officers in. They can start with me."

Back in New York, eating lunch at the local deli, Luna Romero related to Bernadette what had happened to her son and his family in California.

"He called to warn me he was going to be on the national news and it's not a pretty picture. It started off in the local media, but then it went viral."

"I haven't watched or read the news in the past few days," said Bernadette.

"You would think things like this don't happen in California," said Ella.

"What happened to your son? Is he all right?"

"He wasn't attacked or shot at or anything like that, but look," Luna took her cell phone out of her purse. "I don't keep things like this on my cell, only family pictures, but look at this." She handed the phone to Bernadette.

Her eyes narrowed at the photo of the word 'wetback' in black spray-paint at a left to right upward diagonal across the white garage door. She handed back the phone. “Was your son able to do anything about this?”

“He said the police asked him a lot of questions and the news people were all over him. He got a call from the District Attorney's office and other hate crime victims associations. There are hate crime sites all over the Internet, and not just the white supremacists. There's anti-race, religion, gender, politics, you name it and someone has a website against it.”

“What did your son do?”

“He wanted to stay and claim his right to live there, but as soon as he said that on the news, he received anonymous death threats against his wife and children. So he moved.”

“Did the police find out anything?”

“No evidence. Del said they talked to most everyone in the neighborhood. There are other ethnic types. Del and his wife and children are the only Hispanic family.”

“I don't know what to say, Luna. I'm so sorry. You're a good friend. It bothers me when things like this happen.”

“Well, thank you, Bernie, but we learn to cope with it and roll with the punches.”

“There's more going on here than punches.”

“Yeah, it's getting worse. It's almost like the Civil Rights Act isn't a law. To a lot of people, it isn't a law, at least not to them. They think if they ignore it, it will go away. The stink of discrimination is still with us. My son was profiled and pulled over once because he drives a Mercedes. The cops searched the car for drugs. Of course, they didn't find any, but they made him get out of the car and roughed him around a little, hoping he'd fight back. That would give them a reason to arrest him. But he's a big strong guy and just did what they ordered. In some states, if you don't have or can't get a photo ID card, they won't let you vote. They don't want to let Blacks and Hispanics vote. It never ends.”

Bernadette shook her head.

Chapter 15
Vibrations

Stoli waited patiently in the short line of assembly workers at the tool crib. He shifted his tool belt into a comfortable position to accommodate his protruding belly. At the cage, he signed the stock receipt for a drill and a rivet gun and walked out into the massive one hundred yard long hangar at the Boeing aircraft assembly plant.

The bay doors stood open. Swamp coolers descending from the high ceiling and industrial fans the size of diesel truck tires perched on tall metal poles blasted air at assembly workers arrayed on scaffolds alongside the fuselage of a Boeing 737. The movement of oil tainted air did little to minimize the summer heat. He adjusted his yellow hard hat over the red bandana that encapsulated the top of his head to keep beads of sweat from dripping into his eyes.

He stopped to chat briefly with the assembly supervisor studying engineering drawings spread open on a long table top. Stoli nodded his understanding of the supervisor's direction from the section to which he pointed on the drawing, then ascended the steel steps to the opening that would later become the door, and entered the fuselage cabin devoid of seats. The metallic chatter of hand drills and rivet guns ricocheted from the titanium steel sheet metal skins being systematically attached to the ribs of the frame.

He crouched to grab a handful of rivets from a metal tub, then positioned his battery powered rivet gun to install a sequential vertical line like a succession of bullets. He clutched the handle more tightly at each insertion, then relaxed his grip at the moment the rivet was seated. The slight vibration of the tool and the sense of control it provided soothed him.

Getting his old job back at the aircraft plant gave him a huge sense of relief. With the progression of time, his children had become intractable teenagers, and his wife the primary breadwinner. That she made four times his meager Walmart wage for the past two years and with benefits gnawed at him. His stress had escalated at the lost control of his established patterns. At least Ruthie had the good sense not to remind him who was keeping the family afloat. But now that stress was gone.

Keeping the family financially secure had always been his job, including the benefits. He was a highly skilled, well paid aircraft assembler. Even with his years of tenure, his union had not been able to save him from the layoff. The funding of contracts was beyond their control. And that's what griped him, that his life was governed by politicians and financial bureaucrats. That was not how things should be. He should be able to call his own shots, not kiss ass to their laws that made them billionaires and him unemployed. Fuck 'em! Fuck 'em all!

After two hours of riveting, he felt the need to smoke a cigar and have a cup of coffee. His energy level was dropping. He needed a jolt of caffeine.

Smoking was not allowed on the production line or even inside the hangar. He had to walk outside to a designated area covered by a canvas tent awning and marked off by yellow painted lines. He claimed a folding chair at one of the small round plastic tables and covered the surface with his open thermos and insulated lunch carrier. Steam rose from the half-filled metal cup.

He lit up his cigar and exhaled clouds of gray smoke that would discourage anyone from joining him, even another smoker. He didn't like to visit and talk with his fellow workers. They made him feel uncomfortable and uneasy. He had to work too hard to come up with a topic of conversation, which quickly faded after a reference to the recent score of a football or a baseball game. Most of his co-workers didn't watch professional wrestling. They said it was just choreographed and fake. Stoli thought the baseball players and footballers were just a bunch of *prima dona* pussies by comparison. They were paid far too much money just for playing a game and they were treated like royalty, like stars. They're jocks. That's all, jocks.

He hated jocks, because of what they did to him years ago in high school. Raised on a heavy starch, fatty meat, and sugar diet (cookies, cakes, ice cream, pies), he had always been overweight along with his parents and brother and two sisters, called fatties by their classmates.

Considering Stoli's 250 pound bulk at six feet, the football coach, Orin "Bull" Brannigan, had tried to recruit him to be a lineman during his freshman year. He had told Stoli the training would toughen him up. He would shed excess weight and convert his fat to hard muscle. Girls would "admire" him.

Stoli liked the image of himself envisioned by the coach, who needed bulk meat in the line. Brannigan spoke in a tough manner, reminding Stoli of a hawk-nose drill sergeant he had seen in a movie. He ordered Stoli to get a short buzz cut like the rest of the team. Bull wanted his boys to look and talk like him. Stoli's new haircut made his face look like a pumpkin. Bull complimented him on the haircut and said his thick neck and fat jowls would protect him in head to head contact.

Training began during August with soaring temperatures of 95 to over 100 degrees. Stoli showed up wearing the standard summer workout uniform of red gym shorts, white T-shirt, shoulder pads, helmet, and cleats. Sweat poured off his body. He could barely move his arms and legs. The hard body jocks laughed at his stumbling jog excuse for a wind sprint. He didn't have any wind. He could barely breathe in the heat.

The coach told Stoli it would take him a couple of weeks to get into condition and that workouts were always hardest at the beginning. Stoli had never worked out in his entire young life. He had been a couch potato, eating chips and candy and reading comic books and watching hours of mindless television.

The physiological shock to his body left him feeling comatose. He could barely walk home from school. His mother was alarmed at the redness of his face, an apoplectic flush. Although he had drunk a gallon of Gatorade at practice, he went to his room and downed a liter of regular Coke, which did nothing to assuage his thirst (the sugar only increased it) and replenished the calories he had shed that afternoon.

His ass and thigh muscles ached and throbbed. Except for raising his head to gulp from the trademark red plastic bottle, he lay unmoving on his bed. He hadn't showered at the school, just stumbled and staggered home, but not without overhearing a few parting shots that he didn't want others on the team to see the size of his "tiny dick."

He didn't think it was so tiny. He had measured an erection while masturbating and was pleased to discover its tumescent eight inches. But in its relaxed state, it withdrew into folds of flesh like a turtle's head into its shell.

Stoli didn't know if he could survive a second day of training. He did show up and told the coach he wasn't feeling well, but he would try his best. Bull said that was all anyone could ask.

Fifteen minutes into the practice, Stoli collapsed on the field.

The paramedics arrived and Stoli woke up in the nearest hospital. His distraught mother and father came to see him in ER, where the attending physician kept him overnight until he stabilized.

He told his parents that Stoli was not in any physical condition to go through football training. His blood pressure, glucose and cholesterol levels were far too high. He pointed to the intravenous feed and catheter attached to Stoli's right arm.

"We're restoring his electrolytes. They were dangerously low. Given the symptoms, at his young age, he's at risk of having a heart attack. He needs to be on a gradual weight loss diet and modified exercise program for at least one year. I'm referring you to a dietitian."

In one sense, Stoli had been relieved to hear that advice, especially coming from a doctor who didn't look to be more than a few years older than himself. Stoli wondered how he could be a doctor and look that young and healthy and be so smart.

In another context, Stoli's anxiety reasserted itself.

He would be glad to never again have to work out with the shouting, sweating, grunting, body bashing team members. Bull Brannigan expressed his disappointment, but said he understood Stoli's health and safety issues. He told Stoli he had potential. But on the other hand, Stoli had been subjected to insults and derision by the jocks for quitting before he even got started. The ridicule seared his soul.

He knew he could not endure four years of high school without doing something about the condition of his body. He had to prove he was a man.

He tried out for the wrestling team. With weight training and foot work, he learned to balance and move his body. He learned to use the force of his bulk to take down and pin opponents in his heavyweight class.

After one year, his weight dropped to 210 pounds. When he looked at himself in the mirror, he saw the growing definition of muscle in his upper arms and shoulders and thighs. What he admired most was the disappearance of fat that had once been his sagging belly and the appearance of a waistline that allowed him to replace his wide body jeans with a medium slender cut. His jaw surfaced from the loose fat that had concealed it. He had become a man.

Now, he wondered where that image and sense of himself had gone, his pride and confidence and caring of his body, all just fading away. Now, the world of professional wrestling displaced who he had once been as a young man. He identified himself with the glistening muscle bound contenders, steroids coursing through their blood, stomping like apes and roaring meaningless threats of pain and mayhem at each other. The illusion sustained him and distorted his view of himself and of the real world.

Stoli hadn't counted on the attention his despised word would draw and the vitriolic response in the media. He hadn't realized so many people disagreed with his point of view. He thought people were sick of the invasion of Hispanics in white neighborhoods. The unexpected house to house investigation taking place raised the possibility that the two empty cans of black spray paint nestled deep in his trash barrel beside the garage might be discovered. He would remove them that night, take a drive into the foothills, and bury them.

At 3:30pm, he returned his drill gun kit to the tool room and electronically signed out for the day by scanning his barcoded employee badge at the laser time clock station. He waved to the uniformed guard seated in the security kiosk as he passed through the heavy black wrought iron gate. He waited at the tram stop for a lift to the center of the Boeing employee parking lot.

Driving along the industrial zone street bordering the aircraft plant, he thought through what he would do next. Because he started early in the morning, he arrived home two hours before Ruthie. That gave him time to grab the paint cans and get rid of them without her there to question what he was doing.

For the past year, she had become too nosy about everything he did, as though she lumped him in with the kids to be checked on and harassed, especially after the time she caught him surfing porn websites. They had stopped having sex shortly after he got laid off. He had been drinking heavily ever since.

"It's not me with the problem, Stoli." Her words rang in his head. "I'm here for you. You just aren't here for yourself. You're the one stayin' away from me."

As he pulled into the driveway, he pressed the control button on the remote to raise the garage door. He stepped out of the truck and went directly to a box of black trash bags. He billowed open the pressed synthetic plastic as he walked back out the door and around to a row of large trash barrels at the side of the garage. He flipped up the lid of the nearest container and peered inside. A gaseous cloud of rot and decay forced him to step away and gulp a lungful of fresh air.

He returned to the garage for a rake so he would not have to lean into the malodorous maw of refuse. He manipulated the rake through the lumpy bags until he found the one that concealed the paint cans. He pulled them out and quickly stuffed them deep into the lawn bag and knotted it closed.

Driving away down the street, he saw his daughter balancing her school books and talking on her cell phone as she came along the sidewalk. She ignored his wave.

The Yerbe Verde residential tract nestled against a range of chaparral covered rolling hills that formed an elongated canyon populated with spreading live oak trees, cypress, and stands of birch and maple.

Concentrating on the narrow road ahead, he missed seeing a gray Toyota Camry that followed several car lengths behind since he had entered the canyon. He turned off onto a deserted forest service trail head parking area. The car following continued down the road for a short distance and stopped. The driver executed a U-turn and drove back to the trail head.

Carrying the black trash bag and a shovel, Stoli left his truck and hiked quickly up the dirt trail. He didn't see the car pull in beside his truck and didn't notice the dark-haired woman following him until he stepped off to the side of the trail and began digging a hole. The stabbing strokes of the shovel blade muffled her steps as she came up behind him. He sensed her standing there and turned with a startled grunt.

Bernadette watched him shake and tremble. Sweat ran in rivulets through his day old beard and down his neck, soaking his shirt. His eyes rolled back into his head. His skin quivered and shriveled, falling away in red flakes until his muscles and tendons and veins and arteries were exposed. His cellular vibrations steadily increased and his physical presence began to fade, then accelerated to a high pitched hum. He became a vapor. Then he was gone.

That night, Ruthie called the police and reported that her husband was missing. Her daughter had briefly seen him drive out of the tract that afternoon. The officer on the phone asked if Stoli might be visiting a friend, maybe staying over night. Ruthie flared at the insinuation. She would have to come in and file a missing person report.

Two days later, a park ranger discovered Stoli's deserted pickup truck illegally parked after 9:00pm when the trails were closed. He issued a citation. When the truck had not been moved three days later, he contacted the police to have it towed and impounded. Then he walked up the trail to see what might have become of the hiker. Maybe he had been injured or fallen over a steep ledge. He found the shovel and the two spray paint cans in the black lawn trash bag and brought them back with him to the station.

The police reported to Ruthie that her husband's truck had been found, but there was no sign of what might have happened to him.

Ground searchers and a police helicopter combed the area where Stoli had disappeared. The ranger handed over the shovel and lawn bag with the paint cans. A police inspector made the connection between the black paint cans and the defacing of the Romero family's garage door. They came to a dead end regarding a suspect who could be involved in Stoli's disappearance.

One week later, Ruthie discovered her husband, dead, sitting on the living room couch. His vacant eyes were wide open watching a wrestling match. Her screams brought her children running and then her daughter's screams rent the air.

Chapter 16
Aftermath

The teenage girl lay twisted in a pool of her own blood staining her light pink and blue dress with dark splotches. The dress had flapped up like a bird's wings taking flight to escape the children's screams and the rattle of automatic gunfire. Long dark hair entangled her thin right arm thrown back over her head. Her eyes were closed, her delicate face a rictus of fear and pain.

The acrid fumes of nitrogen from scattered spent cartridges hung in the turgid air.

Three medics checked for vital signs among the ten other children prostrate under their desks. The rasp of a metal zipper underscored the intermittent blast of comments on police radio phones as the coroner closed the body bag containing the classroom teacher, Mrs. Macomber, who was wheeled out on a gurney.

George and Lily Guthrie's daughter was not among those who had been escorted out of the classrooms to the gymnasium and united with their parents to undergo a cursory examination for physical trauma. An emergency staff of seven psychologists seated at tables off to the side conferred with those least able to cope with the emotional shock.

"When can we see our daughter?" George Guthrie held his sobbing, trembling wife and tried to get the attention of a helmeted officer wearing a flack jacket.

"I know this is difficult, sir, but we have to wait until the medics are done."

"She didn't come out with the other students. Does that mean?" He left his question unfinished.

"We don't have all the information yet."

"Her name is Stephanie Guthrie. Have they identified the children who were…?" Again he could not bring himself to make the concluding statement.

Outside, a police helicopter thundered overhead executing sweeps back and forth with video cameras monitoring the carnage, fire engines, paramedic vans and trucks, a fleet of twenty ambulances. Yellow crime scene tape defined the area barricaded with thirty black and white police units controlling access and egress to and from the school property. Restrained by uniformed officers, clamoring media journalists leaned in shouting for information.

George and Lily walked through the teachers and family melee in the gymnasium and stepped outside at the same moment twelve gurneys bearing body bags were being wheeled in a train by paramedics from the heavily guarded classroom.

"Stephanie!" Lily's high pitched scream echoed from the walls of the open courtyard. "Stephanie!" She broke from her husband's grasp and ran toward the departing gurneys.

Two police officers intercepted her flailing rush and deflected her pummeling fists by holding down her arms until George arrived to take her.

"I want my daughter! I want my daughter! They can't take her away! They can't take her! We have the right to see her!" Wet black mascara streaked the sides of Lily's angular face. She sank to her knees and twisted and writhed and groveled in mourning that would become her way of life.

George tried to inhale. His throat choked on the words he tried to speak to her and to the officers. His heart and lungs seized. He couldn't breathe. He thought he was having a heart attack. He sensed he was crying. No tears rimmed his eyes.

Clutching his wife, they stumbled across the quad and out to the parking lot where another officer prevented them from following the gurneys being lifted into ambulances. The rear doors closed concealing the body bags.

"We just want to know which one is our daughter," George rasped. "Who is going to tell us? When will we know?"

"I know how difficult this is, sir," said the young officer. "It's best that you wait inside. Once the coroner confirms her identification, someone will come and see you."

"When will that be? How long will we have to wait?"

"I'm sorry I don't have an answer, but they will let you know as soon as possible."

"Let us know? Let us know?" Lily choked. "Will we get to see her?"

"They'll tell you, ma'am."

"They can't keep us from seeing our daughter," said George. "She is our daughter."

"No one will keep you from seeing her, I'm sure."

"We'd better go inside, Lil. We'd better go inside." George supported her as they stumbled back to the gymnasium.

She grabbed a tissue from her handbag, but it wasn't enough to staunch the flood of tears and mucous. She pressed her nose and eyes into his shoulder.

Joanne Harper noticed them stagger through the crowd across the gym floor to the bleachers. She had seen them go out into the quad. They had returned shaking and huddled in despair, which meant the worst. She rose from her table and went over to them.

"I'm Doctor Harper. I'm so very sorry. I'd like to do what I can to help you."

Lily's grieving face stared up at her charitable expression. Joanne was a slightly older woman, late middle-age. Her graying hair reminded Lily of her own mother. "Can you help us see our little girl? Her name is Stephanie Guthrie."

"We just want to see her," said George.

"Are you certain she's among the victims?"

"She isn't here with us."

"Of course. I'm sorry. An arrangement will be made for you to identify her."

"When?" George's horrified suffering expression unsettled the psychologist's professional demeanor. Although several years younger than her own husband, he projected a similar keen blue-eyed intensity crackling with emotion. "You're a doctor?"

"A psychologist. There are seven of us. We're here to talk with the parents."

"What is there to talk about? There's nothing you can say or do that will bring her back."

"The loss of your child is difficult. I share your grief."

"What the hell good is that? She's not your daughter. It's not your grief."

"I'm someone who empathizes with you. I'm someone you can talk to and help you get through this."

"Get through this?" Lily's voice tightened into a wheeze.

"There is no getting through this," said George. "Did the police kill the guy who did this?"

"He was shot and killed. He was shot multiple times."

"I wish to hell I had my hand on the God damn gun."

"Do you have other children?"

George shook his head. "Stephanie is our only child."

"Do you have relatives who have children?"

"We do, but you know, this is taking us nowhere."

"It's important to say things, to get things out."

"We just want to know what's happening to Stephanie. We'll take care of how we feel in private. This is never going to go away. We know that. What is it we're supposed to do now? What do we do next?"

While driving to the coroner's office, George struggled against a wave of disorientation, a sensation of emotional compression, an illusionary shield to block any further tragedy and to prepare them for what they must next do. Lily was unable to go beyond the lobby of the coroner's office. She said with a tense whisper, "I want to remember Stephanie alive. I don't want to see what happened to her. I don't want that to be my last memory of her."

George nodded and helped her to a chair. Other parents were arriving and being escorted in, one couple at a time. The screams and wails of two other women penetrated Lily's progressive darkness.

As George entered the lab, he blinked rapidly at the impersonal metallic shine of examining tables and metal gurneys in the florescent glare . He saw that four other children had been removed from their body bags, covered with sheets, and were waiting for the arrival of their parents.

Wearing a lab cap, green scrubs and blue latex gloves, the coroner motioned George to follow him. "Mr. Guthrie, please come this way, sir," the gentle voice encouraged him. "You might want to put this on." He handed George a cotton face mask similar to the one that dangled under his own unshaven chin. A brief reflective flash in the coroner's glasses from the blinding overhead examining light gave George the sense he was with some other worldly creature. But the cherubic compassionate face offset the scrub's dehumanizing effect.

The shrunken naked body of his daughter nearly brought him to his knees. He clutched a corner of the table. A purple scar marked the wound where the hollow point bullet had entered and shredded surrounding tissue as it passed through her spleen and left kidney and exited taking a piece of her vertebrae. He stared in disbelief at the blue pallor of death that painted her skin. Stinging bile surged up into his throat at the asphyxiating odor of formaldehyde.

The coroner asked, "Is she your daughter, Stephanie Guthrie?"

George nodded. He could not speak. He choked and looked around wildly. The coroner grabbed a metal bed pan and thrust it at George's chest as he tore away the face mask and vomited.

The coroner waited until George finished his violent upheaval and observed him for signs of fainting. He held an ammonia capsule ready.

"Sorry. Sorry," George muttered through the discolored drool dripping from his lips and the tip of his nose. "So sorry."

"It's all right, Mr. Guthrie. It's all right. Come over to the sink. You can wash yourself off." He turned on the warm water and pulled several paper towels from the wall dispenser. After George rinsed and patted his face dry, the coroner handed him a small Styrofoam cup of cold water from a nearby cooler. George nodded his appreciation.

He followed him back to the examining table and watched him cover Stephanie's face. "Thank you, sir. A representative from the police department will be contacting you to discuss further arrangements."

George nodded. His tall broad shouldered frame shuddered with uncontained grief. The coroner took his arm and gently escorted him back to the lobby.

The despair in his wife's eyes encroached on his own, his attempt to mentally erase what he had just seen, his blue child. Even if Lily asked him to describe Stephanie, he would refuse. She imagined he could have actually said goodbye to her, that she would still possess some impulse of life, perhaps even a spiritual presence that would recognize and hear him. Clinging to such a fantasy was all Lily had left. The random killing of her daughter snuffed out reality.

She leaned against her husband as he helped her through the glass doors and out into the parking lot to their car. When they arrived at their condominium, Lily used the bathroom, scanned the medicine cabinet for a bottle of Motrin, and swallowed down four with a glass of water. Staggering and supporting herself against the walls, she went to Stephanie's bedroom. She selected her daughter's favorite plush stuffed bear from a collection on a high shelf, pushed off her shoes, and crawled into the girl's twin bed without removing her clothes.

George stared at a bottle of Jack Daniels kept in a kitchen cupboard for special occasions. He desperately wanted a drink, a strong drink or two or three, drinks to shut down his mind, to send him into oblivion. He struggled with the concept of a special occasion. A special occasion was supposed to be a happy one. The irony of the death of his daughter as being a special occasion of the opposing kind did not escape him. But he knew there would be no more of the happy kind.

He pulled the rust colored bottle from its shelf, removed the stopper cap, tipped the opening to his lips and swallowed, five gulps coursing down through his esophagus in successive stinging waves. A great gasp escaped him when he lowered the bottle. His chest and torso bucked with several gut heaving coughs. He grabbed the edge of the kitchen sink until the spasms subsided. His tearing blurred eyes came to rest on a snapshot of his daughter wearing her purple and white cheerleader uniform. He removed the photo pinned to the refrigerator door with a small souvenir magnet and sat down heavily at the table. He pushed the bottle to the center of the table and cradled her image cupped in both hands.

He studied her image for the physical features of her Mom and Dad she had inherited. She had been their legacy. Now, all that remained were photographs and memories. *She has her Mom's nose,* he observed silently to himself. *Small, narrow with a slight upturn at the tip that gives her that sweet mischievous expression. She has my eyes though, that gray green from her Irish ancestry, and my big ears. No wonder she wanted such long hair, to cover up her ears. Doesn't matter. They are beautiful ears, beautiful dark hair, character eyebrows like mine, high cheek bones, perfect skin, that tight knit athletic body. No wonder so many boys wanted to date her. Too young for that though. But the next year in high school, I wouldn't have any say in the matter. Never go to parties, never take the biology and chemistry subjects that you love, never wear a prom dress, never go to college and medical school like you talked about. You would have made a great doctor. A surgeon. You have the hands for it, the finger dexterity from all your years of playing the piano. Your Mom and I will miss hearing you play the piano. We'll miss seeing you jumping and dancing with your cheer leading team at the school games. We'll miss having meals with you at our table together and hearing about school, your friends, your day. We'll even miss watching you send text messages. We'll just plain miss you, Steph. We love you. We will always love you.*

His chin dropped to his chest and be began to snore. His head lowered to the table and he slept on his daughter's image.

George and Lilly sat on folding chairs along the sideline with other bereft weeping parents. The location was the very spot where their daughter and her cheer team had leapt and danced and bounced and pranced leading the enthusiastic crowd of students and adults seated in the bleachers rising behind them, now silent. Barely a murmur was heard as the solemn memorial service began.

At the raised podium, against a backdrop of photos of the victims projected on a muslin scrim, a chosen speaker, a close friend, a sibling, or a parent conveyed the unique qualities and achievements for which the eleven students and their teacher would be remembered.

The photos did not depict the grisly images of murder, but the attestation to the wholesome positive lives they had led, images of their beauty and exuberant smiles.

A non-denominational clergyman delivered the invocation.

A gathering of news media vans, journalists, their sound and camera crews, and a host of newspaper reporters clustered outside the fence and the parking lot entrance blocked by police officers and barriers denying them access.

The church services and Facebook and Twitter outpourings of religious believers and faith organizations praying for Stephanie on their behalf put George in a silent rage. Prayer did nothing for him and his wife. All it did was exacerbate the reality of their child's death in a Godless world. He didn't believe in God anyway. There was no proof of his existence. There never had been and never would be. Faith just gave people a comfort level to cope with life's problems and provide some behavioral standards that were mostly ignored. That's why society depended on law enforcement. But even that had not kept their child from being murdered. George wished all the faith mongers would just go away and leave them alone.

Lily had been heavily medicated for stress and depression. George hit the bottle several times a day and late into the night. He knew that in a few weeks after the furor over the mass killing had died down, he would have to return to work and act like a normal human being again with his colleagues. He and Lily were both undergoing psychological counseling with Joanne Harper.

A normal human being – he wondered what that actually was. Had the man who killed the teacher and children been normal once upon a time, or never. Had the latent impulse for his act been incubating many years before, maybe in his childhood. He knew nothing about the killer. Nobody did except for the police, who had not yet spoken to the media or to the parents of the dead children. The parents wanted some kind of revenge, some redemption, but there was none to be had.

The killings had escalated the debate for gun control between the Gun Rights Association GRA lobby and gun control activists. The GRA lobby declared themselves blameless.

George's perception was the gun lobby was using the second amendment and political fear mongering as an excuse to manufacture and market automatic weapons and profit from the killings and murders, so more people would want to buy guns believing they would be able to protect themselves. But George knew that no one was safe. No one.

Chapter 17

Trail

Ignatius Stroud watched the television news of the memorial service with emotional detachment. He crushed his cigarette in the overfilled clamshell ashtray on his cluttered kitchen counter. He reasoned that the mass killing of eleven middle school classroom children and their teacher had nothing to do with him, even though he had indirectly sold the AK-47 to the man who used it. The gun laws in his North Carolina town were loosely enforced, if at all, which created a market that attracted GRA members. His on-line retail website, Guns R' US, with an online video testimonial by Jimmy Richter, a prominent state gun lobbyist with ties to the Washington D.C. lobby, had established Ignatius as a major reliable source for gun buyers.

The demand for automatic weapons exceeded his capacity to supply them. He had to use straw buyers to get around one-gun-a-month restrictions and had arrangements with out-of-state non-licensees to legally sell their weapons to straw buyers residing in North Carolina who would channel them back to the original buyers. The laundering of firearms had become a lucrative business for Ignatius. One of those transactions became the AK-47 purchased by the killer. Otherwise, Iggy, as his friends and customers called him, kept careful records in compliance with the Federal Firearms Law. On the surface, he ran a clean business. He had never been audited by the Feds.

A year ago, he discovered a way to boost his profits through black market gun-trafficking and circumvent the need for background checks and reporting sales. Because the arrangement involved a high legal risk, since most of the weapons were sold to non-licensed owners who lived in other neighboring states, he did this infrequently to avoid establishing a pattern. If he got into trouble, he could rely on his brother, Jubal Stroud, a New York attorney, to get him out of it. He figured once the gun was no longer in his possession, he wasn't responsible for what the buyer did with it, and the sale could not be traced back to him.

His Washington connection knew about the deals and, twice, was involved in facilitating the transaction for deep pockets GRA supporters. Jimmy Richter didn't agree with most of the Federal Firearms Laws anyway and lobbied heavily against Congress and the Administration to not interfere with the sale of high powered automatic weapons with removable magazines.

The gnawed bones of slow-cooked baby back pork ribs lay in a crisscrossed mound on a stained white plate where a fat black fly had taken residence, inert after its hours long gorge of congealed barbeque stains. The rising aroma of last night's dinner still hung in the kitchen air.

Iggy lifted the plate to the trash barrel and watched the bones tumble into the plastic liner. The fly made a sluggish escape to the window above the sink and clung to the dust coated glass.

Iggy gulped his cup of cold coffee and held a slice of toast dipped in three runny egg yolks so as to avoid dribbling on his chin. He slotted the streaked plate and food-spotted utensils into the washer emitting a rancid smell from a three day accumulation of dirty dishes. He poured green soap granules into the dispenser and closed the door, pressed the start button, and walked away into the adjoining living room as the sound of gurgling water increased in the machine behind him.

He rubbed the dark stubble of a two day growth of beard and debated whether or not to shave before going to his store. He sported a short cut square goatee. At the age of forty-six, even with a beer belly bump pushing over the top of his belt buckle, he felt he could pass for a younger man. His unblemished boyish features and accommodating brown-eyed gaze suggested to customers he had integrity and their personal interests at heart, and served him well when hitting on women.

He touched the remote to turn off the television, then strode down the long hall to his bedroom. He pulled on a pair of jeans and a red polo shirt displaying his store name and logo over the right side of his chest. He jammed his white-stocking feet into black cowboy boots, stood up from his king bed, and tugged at the sheets and blankets to smooth out the wrinkles. He envisioned his girlfriend in those sheets that night.

He gargled mouthwash to reduce the taste of breakfast and cigarettes, then brushed his teeth and gargled some more. If he brushed and gargled twice a day, he believed he would not have to go to the dentist and had not done so for five years.

A finger full of gel briefly restored the upright position of his short spiked black hair snugged flat by his favorite NASCAR baseball cap. He grabbed his keys off the dresser, and went out to the weed-infested front yard.

He barely noticed the odor of decay and cacophony of trilling crickets rising from a vast nearby swamp. The dank oppressive humidity increased as the sun rose and cooked the fertilizer spread on thousands of acres of green unharvested tobacco fields. A mile away above the treetops, thick white steam from a paper mill evaporator billowed into the morning sky.

Pulling out of the driveway, the Ford's over-sized wheels spun and kicked up loose gravel. His gabled ranch style house in a rural area placed him in the middle of indigenous wildlife in the surrounding pine and kudzu choked forest. He had once taken a six point buck with a shotgun right from his back porch.

Reba MacIntyre's lilting voice filled the truck cab from a Raleigh country & western radio station. He maneuvered the winding curves along the narrow two lane road past the local fish house where his girlfriend, Ramona Dunrobin, worked as a waitress in the family owned restaurant. At noon, it would be packed with locals. The Dunrobins owned and operated catfish, bass, perch and shrimp farms on the river that flowed a half mile from the store.

He saw Ramona's purple Toyota Corolla next to her father's pickup at the outer edge of the gravel parking lot that fronted the small prefab building. Lights were on inside. He detected movement through the windows. The family members were at early food preparations for the day.

He would talk to Rae at noon when he was having lunch with Jimmy Richter to discuss the birthday present for his son.

He bought a cup of coffee at a drive through, then continued three blocks to a newly renovated strip mall. Except for a few scattered pickups and cars of other store owners and fast food patrons, the parking lot was empty. To accommodate customers, he pulled into a space away from his store front. He unlocked the black wrought iron bars that blocked access to the door and windows and shoved them rattling along their overhead track to the edge of the wall.

Upon entering, he walked quickly to an electronic keypad hidden behind the counter and disarmed the security system, then went back to lock the door from the inside. The store would not be open for two more hours. He checked the multi-screen views on a desktop computer of the exterior surveillance cameras covering the moderate size parking lot, front entrance, and the back garage door for receiving and shipping weapons and ammunition.

Six closed circuit cameras scanned the store interior. Embedded security alarm circuits rimmed locked reinforced glass display cases containing over two hundred rifle and handgun models, a full range of ammunition, and a variety of camouflage hunters clothing on outlying racks and shelves.

The smell of gun metal oil permeated the store.

In the backroom warehouse on a worktable, he disassembled and cleaned a Model 70 rifle that Jimmy Richter bought for his son as a gift on his 14th birthday. They would come in later that afternoon when the boy was out of school.

Iggy pulled up a screen on the sales computer at the counter and checked his inventory data base. A sealed crate of Mossberg rifles and shotguns was scheduled to arrive that morning.

Pheasant and deer seasons were only two months away. He would advertise a promotional sale of the popular Mossberg's and other manufacturers' models.

A mud-spattered black truck lurched to a stop taking up three parking spaces in front of the store. A stocky, gray-bearded man wearing ankle top hiking boots, baggy jeans, a red T-shirt with the black letters GRA emblazoned across the chest, and a camouflage cap dismounted from his elevated cab. He scanned the gun store display window to see if anyone was inside and detected movement. He shoved the truck door closed and walked to the store entrance as Iggy noticed him and came out from behind the counter to let him in.

"Hey, Jimmy, thought I wouldn't see you 'til lunch."

"Sorry, can't make it. Got a call from D.C.. Have to fly up for an emergency damage control meeting because of the school killing. Fuckin' media's givin' us a bad rap. Have to rev up our campaign strategy. I came by instead of callin'. I'm out of ammo at home. Need a dozen boxes of 270 soft points and another half of 20 gauge."

"What about your boy? I have his model 70 in the back."

"He'll come by after school. Could you give him a lift home?"

"Sure, glad to."

"Take him through cleaning and safety?"

"Part of the package," said Iggy. "So, what's happening?"

"Media interviews of the parents whose children were killed are getting prime time play joined by bleeding heart liberal senators to expand the god damn gun laws."

Iggy unlocked the counter case, lifted out the boxed cartridges and set them on the glass top. He swiped Jimmy's credit card and arranged the purchase in a plastic bag. "You in Washington for a while?"

"Don't know yet. Have to do what it takes."

"Think you'll make the monster rally?"

"Don't count on it. Rae goin' with you?"

"Wouldn't miss it. She's in to crashin' and bangin'."

"Like in the sack."

They burst out laughing. "Sort of like," said Iggy.

"Any thought of hookin' up?"

"Nah, she don't want it and neither do I. She says why spoil a good thing. We're havin' a good time. Gettin' married 'ill spoil all that. Her parents aren't happy about us. You know, church people. Rae's older Sister moved to Nashville to get away from them. Took a secretarial job until she gets her real estate license."

"I read you. Goin' up to D.C. gives me a little diversion. Nothin' serious. Just a little fun on the side."

"Sounds like you got a good deal goin' there."

"That's what it's all about, Ig, gettin' a good deal. Have to go home and clean up. Have a flight in three hours." Jimmy snatched up the plastic bags and headed for the door.

"Thanks for stoppin' by, Jimmy. I'll take care of Denny."

"He thinks of you like an uncle."

"Nice to know. Uncle Iggy. Has a ring to it."

"Great day, great day!"

"Yeah, you too. Good flight."

"Thanks." Jimmy climbed up into the truck cab, started the engine, and gave Iggy a thumbs up as he drove away.

Iggy relocked the door, since the store wasn't due to open for another hour.

The thought that Jimmy had been called to the GRA lobby in Washington because of the shooting jarred his complacence. He didn't know who ended up with the particular assault rifle used to kill the school children. It obviously exchanged hands and ownership after it passed through his store and crossed three state lines. He didn't think the F.B. I. could trace the sale back to him, but transactions made under the radar always left him feeling nervous. The serial number of the weapon had been published in the media. It matched the number in his inventory records. The mass killing using a weapon he had touched put him on edge.

The gravel parking lot in front of The Fish House was jammed with pickup trucks and cars that spilled out along the sides of the narrow road. Iggy parked his truck at a canted angle on the shoulder overgrown with kudzu and weeds at the edge of the encroaching pine woods.

He dropped his half-smoked cigarette in the metal depository just outside the front entrance, then held the door open for an elderly man and his wife leaving the restaurant. He stepped inside and stood next to a bulletin board covered with a pastiche of personal business cards and small ad clippings for plumbing, electrical, construction, handyman, hauling, horse and dog boarding, janitorial, dress-making, and other services. He moved to make room for several patrons lining up to pay at the cash register.

Rae waved at him to come over and take the vacated table she was clearing with a clatter of utensils and food and crumb encrusted dishes.

He breathed in the aroma of steam rising from the buffet selection of breaded deep-fried fish, French fries, sweet corn, foil wrapped yams and potatoes, coleslaw, and garlic cheese bread.

Mill workers leaned on their elbows over their food amid bottles of ketchup, barbeque, and hot sauce cluttered at the edges of the hard plastic tabletops.

As he scrapped his aluminum café chair into position, Iggy grinned appreciation of his leggy, big breasted Rae, approaching him with her order pad and pen. She tossed her shoulder length brunette hair. Her red lips swooped upward toward high cheekbones in a rakish smile.

"You want the usual or something different?"

"You got any specials?"

"Everything we serve is special. You know that, honey." Feral gray-green eyes flashed with amusement.

"It's only special when it's served by you."

"Complimenting the waitress will get you extra large portions. Be sure to leave an extra large tip to go along with it."

"You take any time off this afternoon? You're the portion I want."

"Love to, sweetheart, but we're really busy. I'll make up for it tonight."

"Sun can't go down fast enough to suit me."

"All in good time, love. All in good time. So what'll it be?"

Iggy looked across the crowded room at the buffet line. "I'll order off the menu today."

"You need to see a menu?"

"After fifteen years of comin' here, I know what's on it."

"Got it memorized."

"Got it memorized. I'll have the dozen deep fried jumbo shrimp with fries and coleslaw."

She jotted down his order. "Any catfish on the side?"

"Nope, shrimp'll fill me up. It's rich."

"High in cholesterol."

"We don't think or talk about that. Besides, you want people comin' in here askin' for shrimp."

"Yeah. What about to drink?"

"Sweet tea, plenty of ice and extra lemons."

She finished her note with a flourish. "Short wait what with all the customers."

"Not in a hurry. Gives me more time to watch you work."

"Gotcha."

"Gotcha."

Denny hated the .22 rifle his father had forced on him. “It’s my most precious gift to you. Father to son,” Jimmy Richter had said. “Now, here, these go along with it.”

His father had placed a box of .22 caliber shells in front of him while he was playing a video game and ordered him to get his gun ready. Denny’s first impulse was to resist, to say no, he didn’t want to go, but he feared the angry diatribe his father would heap upon him.

“This time, you’re not going to miss. I’ve seen you hit targets at the range.” Denny cocked his head away from his father’s threatening hot breath in his ear.

Sighting down on the unsuspecting rabbit, Denny hoped it would sense its impending death and run away but it continued to nibble on the abundant sweet clover. Denny didn’t dare let the gun barrel falter or waver. He had trouble sighting and missed most of what he shot at. His father’s critical eye watched over his shoulder. Denny didn’t like to kill small animals. He knew his reluctance to kill the rabbit was irrelevant to his father. He had never asked Denny how he felt about anything.

Denny didn’t know why his father told him to stop by the Guns ‘R Us store. He’d been there a number of times to please his dad and always pretended an interest in the discussion of firearms with Iggy Stroud.

Denny took a roundabout way from school to the gun store. His reluctant steps stopped at the entrance, but he did not go in until Iggy happened to notice him standing outside and came to open the door.

“Hi, Mr. Stroud.”

“Hi, Denny, how you doin’?”

“My dad said to come by your store on my way home.”

“Did he tell you why?”

“No, he said you had something for me, a surprise.”

"Actually, it's a birthday present from your dad."

"Oh, he didn't tell me."

Iggy's broad grin discomfited the boy. "Well, that's what makes it a surprise." He gestured with his arm. "Come on. I have it in back." He gestured again. "Come on, boy. You're gonna like this one. It's an upgrade from your .22."

Looking at the guns displayed in the glass case, Denny shifted his book pack and walked around the counter. Iggy placed an encouraging hand on his shoulder. Denny objected to his touch, but didn't wince.

Iggy opened the gun case, removed the Winchester Model 70 it contained, and placed it gently next to a small can of gun oil, cloth patches, and a bore on the outdoor patio table. He pressed down on the bolt stop and pulled the bolt to the rear to remove it and checked the magazine to be sure it was empty of rounds.

"As you can see," he explained to Denny, "even though I know this gun is empty, I check and double check it before I start cleaning. See here? This is the safety. You put it in the intermediate position.

"Always check to see if anything is blocking inside the barrel like powder fouling. Some dust or dirt or particle could be in there and later cause a jam. The way we're goin' to do that is take out the barrel and the action. I don't have to tell you to keep the muzzle pointed away from you and the house, but I'm tellin' you anyway. Now here, watch me." He removed the two action screws and lifted the bottom metal from the stock. He looked down the inside of the barrel, then handed it to Denny. "Here, now you look."

Denny closed one eye and saw clear light without any protrusions at the opposite end.

"See anything?"

"No, sir."

"Good." He took back the barrel and action. "Now, you watch me clean, then you do the same. This here," he picked up a long slender rod, "is a cleaning rod. You put a patch on the end like this and soak it in nitro solvent. I use a copper solvent 'cause the shell casings are copper. Then you poke it down inside the barrel and breech end and firmly pump it back and forth to dislodge any residue. You do that enough times 'til you're sure you got the barrel clean. Next, you put some gun oil on a cloth and rub it lightly over all the parts. You don't have to take the firing pin apart. Just leave it as it is. You don't want to grease everything up. You just want to leave a light film. Everything clear so far?"

Denny nodded and breathed in the metallic odor of the gun oil.

"Good, now you reassemble the rifle. Don't put live ammo in the gun to test it. Don't ever do that. I'll watch. Do it the same way step by step the way I showed you. Then I'll bring out another gun for you to clean. This is all close to the same way you clean your .22. Your dad asked me to show you. He plans to have you graduate to a higher caliber. He wanted me to show it to you before he brings it home."

"Yes, sir."

"You can call me sir, if you like, but Iggy will do fine. This ain't the Army."

"Okay," Denny nodded.

Denny detected the change the day after he saw his best friend, Randy Schieble, holding hands and walking across the high school campus with a pretty blonde girl unknown to Denny. He and Randy had been good buddies all through elementary and middle school. He started toward them and waved and called out, "Hey, Randy," and was stung at how they snubbed him and quickly went off in another direction. His emotional insecurity plagued him enough as a ninth grader dealing with the first day of the fall semester.

Even when Randy wasn't with the girl, he ignored Denny, wouldn't even talk to him when Denny offered to buy him a soda after school. Denny turned his back on him and told him to "bug off. Stay away from me, asshole."

The sting of his friend's words seared Denny's brain. Even if Randy had a girlfriend, Denny did not understand how he could trash their friendship.

When he finally saw the photo and message on Facebook, he knew Randy was behind it, or Randy and his girlfriend. It was a digital photo Randy had taken of him masturbating in Randy's bedroom.

The abrupt ending of their friendship confounded Denny. Growing up as neighbors and classmates, they had both been athletic avid tree climbers, built tree forts, rode bikes, were active members of Cub and Boy Scouts. They had camped, fished and swum in lakes. They were obsessive video game players and shared favorite action and horror movies. Both were able to execute handstands, ride skateboards on high curved ramps in the park, and played youth soccer and baseball sponsored by the recreation department.

Randy's sharp features underscored a persistent authoritarian expression that could dissolve into mirthful giggles. He took pride in his dark spiked hair and rarely missed an opportunity to view his image in a reflective window. He liked to be in charge when it came to making decisions about "what to do."

Since turning thirteen, they had discovered YouTube videos of sex acts on pornographic websites. They would take breaks from their summer school studies to watch the videos and masturbate together.

In the beginning, they avoided touching each other. Then one afternoon, in a flush of erotic passion, Randy had suddenly thrown his free arm around Denny and they fell over, lying on Randy's bed. Randy's hand groped Denny's tumescent penis. Within moments, they were masturbating each other ejaculating sperm over their legs and abdomen.

But Randy didn't stop there. Copying the action on the video he licked Denny's now drooping penis to bring it up again and gasped at Denny, "Do me."

The erratic intensity and frequency of their sexual activity continued for one year until now when Denny finally saw the photo on his own computer. His slender wiry body was splayed out naked on Randy's bed. His right fist clutched his erect penis. His eyes were clenched shut from his exertion. His reddish Justin Beaver style haircut was askew and his thin jaw had dropped open at the pleasurable moment of ejaculation.

As he read the caption, he choked on the scream rising in his throat.

Chapter 18
Indifference

Jimmy was sitting at his desk in Washington when his wife called.

"Jim, this is Roberta," her ragged sobs choked into his ear. "Denny shot himself with that new rifle you bought him."

"What the fuck? What do you mean he shot himself?"

"He blew his head off, Jim." She waited at the vast silence. "Jim, are you there?"

"Yes, I'm here. I can't believe it, not after all the training he's had."

"He was twelve years old."

"He knows how to handle a rifle, loaded or unloaded. This was an accident, right? Tell me this was an accident."

"The police are here now. I don't know what it was."

"What the hell is he doing with a loaded gun in the house? He knows better."

"He doesn't know anything, Jim. He's dead."

"There was nothing wrong with him. He's a normal kid. He wouldn't take his own life."

"There were things he was having problems with."

"Things? What kind of things?"

"You know, all that bullying that goes on."

"Bullying?"

"On the Internet."

"The Internet?"

"Don't act stupid, Jim. Yes, the Internet."

"But Denny has friends. He's a popular kid."

"There were things he didn't tell us."

"Why not?"

“Because of you. Everything had to be your way. He didn’t think like you. He’s dead, Jimmy. Our son is dead,” she screamed.

“Bullshit! I don’t believe this. He didn’t really shoot himself. It had to be an accident. Is he at the hospital?”

“He’s at the morgue, you fucking moron!”

“I can’t believe this. We were pals, Berta. We were pals.”

“Only in your fucking mind. You better get home. I can’t handle this. I can’t do it myself.”

“What do you mean, only in my mind?”

“He told me when you were gone on one of your trips.”

“Why didn’t you say something?”

“He made me swear I wouldn’t tell you. He was afraid of you.”

“Afraid,” Jimmy gasped. “I love him. I think the world of him.”

“He didn’t know that. He didn’t feel that.”

“Who was bullying him, some kids at school?”

“Yes, some kids at school. I can’t talk about this on the phone. I’m hanging up.”

“Wait! About what? What could they bully him about? He’s just a normal kid like them. A great kid.”

“Denny was gay, Jim. Every kid in school saw his picture and an ugly, ugly caption.”

“What kind of caption?”

“Stop asking questions. I’m going to vomit.”

“God damn it, Berta, tell me what it said.”

After a long pause, she choked out, “Faggot Denny Richter sucks dick.”

“Holy shit,” he whispered. “Holy shit. I’ll be home on the earliest flight.”

“Denny is at the coroner if you want to see him.”

“Yes, I want to see him. Why would I not?”

“His face is gone.”

"Oh, fuck," Jimmy exploded in tears. Coughing, he choked out, "I have to hang up." He heard the click at his wife's end of the line.

"What happened, Jim?" His colleague, Marston Livingston, noticed him crying.

"My son, he shot himself. He killed himself."

"What? Listen, I am so sorry to hear that."

Jimmy waved him away. "I have to get home."

"Don't let this turn you, Jimmy." Marston grabbed his shoulder and looked him in the eye. "It was an accident. They happen all the time. Don't let this turn you."

"What the fuck are you talkin' about? He's my son."

Marston stepped back. "How did it happen?" He listened impassively to Jimmy's news. The mass killings, drive-bys, gang and domestic murders were what Marston called collateral damage of a gun society. His role was to promote greater production and distribution of weapons of violence, a complete reversal from who he had been in his other life before his transformation.

In his other life, he had been the Reverend Lawrence Livingston. He had informed his wife that he was going out for an evening stroll. He explained that he needed to assemble his thoughts for the summit the next morning and there was a church a few blocks from the hotel where he wanted to stop in and pray. A conversation with the Lord would help to clarify the muddy theological waters that lay ahead.

She cautioned that walking alone in the city at that time of night was not particularly safe. He just laughed and said, "God is always with me. God is my bodyguard."

"Well, if you're gone more than thirty minutes, I'm calling the police."

"You worry too much." He gently reached down and touched her lightly freckled cheek. He loved her freckles. They were a

feature that had caught his attention twenty years ago during a conference in Columbia, South Carolina. She had that sun fresh southern look with gray-blue eyes that bespoke a deep emotional sincerity and faith in God. Her blonde-tinted brown hair draped back over her shoulders then was now worn in a shorter mature style, but her natural beauty was unchanged. He marveled at how youthful she appeared, even after bearing and raising four children.

Married life had been difficult during their early years. Beth had worked two jobs as an accountant while he was building his ministry. He had visions of one day heading a world-wide network. Ten years ago, that dream had come to fruition thanks to a generous financial gift from a wealthy venture capitalist who was among Larry's ardent admirers and was dying of cancer.

Although Larry denied he possessed "star power," his wife and other followers convinced him that he had a special charisma that attracted people to him. From the pulpit, the stadium stage, and on television, he projected a calm but forceful intensity when he delivered a sermon. He had the lean Nordic face, challenging blue eyes, and muscled body of an Olympic athlete that many women in his audience perceived as a natural and acceptable sexuality for a religious leader.

There were those among them who called him Larry, rather than the formal Reverend Livingston, and pretended intimacy. By his nature, he promoted such a casual personal reference, but he had tactfully discouraged numerous suggestions of availability and advances by smitten young and middle aged females. He took the precaution of always leaving his private office door open when women came to seek his advice on personal matters. Visitors were aware that his secretary could see what transpired and, for the most part, hear what was said. Reverend Livingston had no use for scandal and lawsuits.

As he stepped off the elevator and walked briskly across the expansive hotel lobby, he was followed closely by a well-dressed businessman wearing a dark suit and solid color tie. He carried a laptop side bag slung over one shoulder and conversed earnestly into a headset attached to his left ear.

The businessman was only a few steps behind Reverend Livingston when the green liveried doorman grasped the polished brass handle. Lawrence diverted his glance from the elaborate hotel monogram on the glass door to nod his appreciation as he passed through onto the canopied entrance. While turning at the sidewalk and setting out in the direction of the church five blocks away, he briefly overheard the man request assistance of the doorman in getting him a cab. He had no reason to pause or glance back and notice that the man declined the cab when it pulled up, but continued to follow him at an unobtrusive distance.

The church signage of St. Stephens engraved in granite and on a wall plaque at the front entrance did not deter him. Lawrence was not a Catholic. He was famous for encouraging and promoting the acceptance and value of all religions, since they all had the purpose of trying to explain and understand man's existence in a spiritually meaningful way. There were many of his own constituents and other ordained religious leaders who profoundly disagreed with him. They believed in the exclusivity of their faith and relationship with their named God.

What was at issue and was the underlying reason that Lawrence had organized the summit conference of religious leaders of all faiths from around the world was the abuse of religion for personal, political, and economic gain. His opening remarks the next morning would be that God in any manifestation was not on anybody's side. During these times of Islamic and Christian fundamentalist radicalism, he placed himself and his career at great risk. He knew that a summit conference would do little to change diverse cultures and societies and the greed and intolerance that pervaded the world overnight, but someone had to start somewhere. He felt it was his calling to do so.

The conference had drawn the attention of the media and the prospect of a terrorist act as another of the mindless programmed incidents of violence that only perpetuated religious conflict and animosity and accomplished nothing. Lawrence believed that man was a sufficiently high-reasoning being and that he would find the ways and means to prevent the exploitation and ultimate destruction of the planet. New technologies could provide the resources the world needed to sustain life and alleviate the continual competition for land and food and water and sources of energy. Promoting the mutual acceptability of different belief systems was ten times more difficult.

The church's imposing hand-carved oak door opened with a slight effort at his touch. It remained unlocked for late worshippers until midnight. He noticed a few older people seated or kneeling and praying inside the cathedral. In deference to the Catholic ritual, he dipped his fingers into the font near the entrance and appropriately crossed himself, then walked up the central aisle to the altar and knelt.

He did not immediately set his mind into the meditative act of prayer, but studied the architectural structure and milieu of the church interior. The vaulted ceiling under the dome spread like an octopus to the buttressed heavy gray stone that enclosed the nave and transepts designed to block out the world beyond the walls. Detailed stained glass scenes of saints allowed filtered light to penetrate the holy sanctuary and inevitably drew one's gaze to the sculpted rendering of Christ on the cross extending high above and to the rear of the gold filigreed altar. The two gothic spirals of the church towers seized an onlooker with the impression that these were elevator passages for one's soul to ascend heavenward.

As Lawrence closed his eyes and bowed his head in over his hands folded against his chest, he heard and sensed the presence of the one individual moving in and kneeling beside him. He did not open his eyes, but focused his mental energy on an appeal to the Lord in guiding him during the problematic days ahead.

Understanding the essential privilege of privacy in communal prayer, Lawrence nevertheless sensed that something was drastically wrong. He opened his eyes and stood and the man who had followed him into the church rose with him shoulder to shoulder. He quickly glanced at his face, but the man continued to stare straight ahead at the figure of the suspended Christ. Lawrence wondered if his sudden clutch of fear was unwarranted, except for the bizarre message of the man's prayer. The close proximity of the man raised a second premonition.

The man then turned his head and looked past Lawrence at a bald figure only he could see. Translucent milky blue eyes, pale skin, and his shaved head rendered Pearl an other-worldly appearance. At six feet five inches tall with a body like iron, he projected a lethal aura that did not invite casual conversation.

Lawrence looked over his shoulder and saw that the few people who had been seated in the pews were now gone. He was alone with this man whom he now sensed meant to do him harm.

The sudden pin prick of a sharp needle penetrated the side of Lawrence's neck. He lurched away with a cry and snatched at the invasive instrument, but it had been immediately withdrawn.

The chapel slowly began to spin. His eyes blurred and he clutched at the air as he collapsed on the steps. Arms and legs spread wide, Lawrence's dimming gaze watched the blue and gold stain-glass rendering of Mary Magdalene that dominated the transept wall under-lit by flickering candles blur and fade to darkness.

The fading vestigial memory of what had happened when he had been human existed somewhere in the depths of his mind, but was disconnected from his current life.

When Jimmy arrived home, he discovered his wife had removed every rifle and handgun in the house.

"What did you do with them?"

"Is that all you can think about? You're more concerned what I did with your guns than your son committed suicide? The police have the birthday present he used to kill himself. I got rid of the other guns so you'll never know where to find them."

"What are you thinking? Guns are my life. Guns are part of your life, part of our life as a family. You're a shooter."

"I'm a mother first. I let that important fact slip by me. I should have stood up to you before. Now, it's too late."

"Too late for what?"

"Our son and daughters are our life, not your god damn guns. There's no use for them. There never was any use for them."

"We'll have to talk about this later."

"Your son committed suicide."

"You don't have to tell me that again."

"It doesn't seem to have registered. Our lives will never be the same."

He stared at his wife. "I'm sorry, Berta. I can't think straight right now."

"After you go to the coroner and see Denny, you should understand what I'm saying."

He knew what she was talking about. He had known ever since he took the job as a lobbyist that required him to be in the Washington office for two weeks out of every month. He had noticed the change in his wife ever since the day Marston Livingston had flown down from D.C. to recruit him ten years ago. Denny was only three years old then and Jimmy was a county supervisor who also did volunteer work for the GRA. His contributions on behalf of the GRA were noticed by the Washington office, which was expanding its staff and lobbying efforts to exert a stronger influence in promoting their conservative political agenda.

Roberta Cummins had met Jimmy while working in the county department of roads and highways. She processed work orders he issued and maintained the library archives of new projects and maintenance files.

Although his office was in another wing of the county building, they saw each other almost daily when she brought oversize engineering drawings to planning meetings. Her soft smooth features and sunny smile caught his attention. Light brown hair trailing down her back gave the impression she was younger than her twenty-six years. She moved with the souciant grace of a teenager in a firm athletic body. He worried that she might consider him too old, but she accepted his invitation to a first date. One month later, she moved out of the apartment she shared with a girlfriend and into Jimmy's luxurious home on the north side of town. He insisted on a large wedding. Roberta wasn't comfortable with the huge crowd of Jimmy's boisterous friends and well-wishers, in addition to a long string of relatives, but she didn't object to the arrangements. She went along with whatever he wanted and rarely asserted herself, a quality that Jimmy insisted on in their relationship.

His controlling nature dominated their family life. His abusive shouts at their son during youth soccer and baseball games contaminated the viewing experience of other parents seated around them. Five times, referees stopped the games until her husband, hurling invectives, left the spectator stands.

Roberta recalled Randy's parents chaperoning Denny and Randy and their two daughters, Hillary and Samantha, on Halloween. Glued to the television, Jimmy refused to even answer the door when trick-or-treaters rang the bell. After seven years of marriage and giving birth to her son and a daughter, Roberta realized that her husband did not care for children. He refused to interact with them as infants, wouldn't change their diapers, bottle feed them, and later, relegated to her the "chore" of reading them bedtime stories and tucking them in.

The image of his son's shattered face caused Jimmy to step back from the examining table with his right hand groping blindly for a place to sit. The coroner grasped him by the upper arms and supported him to a bench.

When Iggy received the call from Jimmy telling him that his son had shot and killed himself, Iggy had a difficult time hearing Jimmy's voice on the cell phone. The cacophonous noise of crashing crunching metal overlaid by the manic roar of the crowd and piped in hard-driving country and western music drowned out half of what Jimmy was saying. So Iggy didn't fully understand what had happened.

He and Rae had consumed a six pack of beer and were starting on a second, but the anxiety in Jimmy's digital voice pinged in his brain. He touched Rae's arm and motioned with his head that they had to leave.

"What?" she shouted at him.

He held up his cell phone and tapped the screen, then canted his head again and gently tugged her arm. She shrugged and nodded and followed him stumbling over the knees and feet of other spectators in the aisle.

When they are clear of the noise and the crowd, he called Jimmy back and listened to his frantic message. He told Rae, "Jimmy's boy, Denny, shot himself with that new rifle I gave him today."

"Shot himself? Not on purpose."

"It could've been an accident, but Jimmy said his wife told him that might not be the case."

"He committed suicide?"

"Maybe."

"That's unthinkable."

"I only hope it was an accident. But he knows how to handle guns, safely. Jimmy brought him up on all that."

They didn't speak as Iggy maneuvered the truck out of the stadium parking lot.

"I read there are a lot of teenage suicides," said Rae. "They have a lot of problems."

"Don't know about that." He was silent and subdued for a few minutes. "Denny was like a nephew. Thought of me like an uncle, 'cording to Jimmy."

"You going over to his house?"

"Not tonight. Says Berta has really lost it. Don't want to have to deal with that."

Iggy was alone in the store when the attractive brunette wearing a business suit entered through the front door and approached the counter. He had not seen her arrive. There was no car parked in front of the gun store. Visitors and customer foot traffic had been slow that day. He had just returned from lunch at the Fish House. Three beers with his oyster sandwich and fries had given him a slight afternoon buzz.

"Yes, hello, ma'am. Can I help you?"

When she didn't respond, he looked at her more closely. Her dark eyes held him riveted.

"Ma'am, is there something wrong? Are you okay?"

Bernadette watched him shake and tremble. Beads of perspiration erupted from the pores of his skin. Sweat ran in rivulets through his day old beard and down his neck, soaking his shirt. His eyes rolled back into his head. He felt a burning surging sensation that originated in his stomach and intestines and spread down through his legs and upwards consuming his pounding heart and exploding lungs and sending an electric charge to his brain. His skin quivered and shriveled, falling away in red flakes until his muscles and tendons and veins and arteries were exposed. His vibrations steadily increased and his physical presence began to fade, then accelerated to a high pitched hum. Then he was gone.

News on the police scanning network was relayed to Leon and Berzinsky. When they questioned Rae Dunrobin, she told them Iggy's disappearance occurred a day after his phone conversation with Jimmy Richter. One week later, his corpse suddenly appeared in the store, seated behind the counter. There was no sign of blood or cause of death. Following the initial investigation, the local police had no explanation. The similarity of the bloodless murders left Leon and Berzinsky without a trail to follow.

Chapter 19
Fraud

The deafening explosion consumed him in a concussive wave, lifting and tossing the HUMVEE like so much jetsam. Tearing pain cut across his left side and he heard nothing as his head throbbed into whirling darkness. He had no memory of being pulled from the twisted metal wreckage and no sensation of the oxygen mask being placed over his face and the prick of the IV needle entering a vein in his right arm. He suddenly existed in a soundless world he could not see.

Days later, he detected the movement of undefined images against dim sporadic lights. He heard muffled sounds and low voices. He tried to lift his arms, but they did not respond. He had no sense of time, no sense of day and night, no sense of sleep and hunger, no sense of direction, no sense of purpose, no sense of life.

He tried to think of something concrete, something he remembered. He tried to think. He wanted desperately to think, to make his brain work. The impulse of desperation, of anxiety was all he had.

He began to come out of his mental darkness when he heard his name spoken by a military doctor. "Derek Harper."

He didn't look for his wife and parents in the greeting pavilion crowded with returnees. He watched the gradual merging of civilian clad men, women, and children commingling with uniformed soldiers, heard shouts of greeting, cries of glee, women sobbing, saw glistening tears running down distorted faces, hands clutching tissues, small children shouting "Daddy" being lifted high and hugged with intensity by their smiling grinning fathers calling their names. What he saw and heard was all meaningless to him. The people and what they were doing did not register. He stood quiet and unmoving in the midst of the swirling noise. A familiar figure separated from the pressing humanity and stood in front of him. He could not recall her name.

Her blue-gray eyes bathed him with love and anxiety. Her lightly red-tinted lips split into a wide smile from an uplifted expectant childlike face at the center of an explosion of dark curls that reminded him of a forest animal.

Her arms reached up and encircled him around his neck and her body crushed into his. Her lips pressed hard against his grim dry mouth. His arms remained at his sides. At his lack of response, she tilted her head slightly and he heard her low-pitched voice speak his name.

"Derek, it's me, Denise, your wife. I'm so glad to see you. I'm so glad you're home."

He stared beyond her over her head at the crowd and saw his mother and father separate from the bodies and move into position at either side of Denise. Joanne Harper slipped her left arm under and inside her daughter-in-law's embrace and planted her head against her son's and choked her emotionally charged greeting into his ear, "Welcome home, Derek, we love you." Her nose twitched at the touch of freshly barbered bristles at the side of his head. She remembered he had large ears like bookends containing a young innocent face. She saw her husband's scarred hand come to rest on top of Denise's intertwined fingers. His face hovered in on the other side of Denise's head. "So glad you're home, son. We love you. So glad you're home."

Derek felt like he was trapped, smothered and confined in a small space. He jerked away and stepped back using his hands and arms to ward them off rather than embrace them. He saw their expressions change chameleon-like from joy to shock and concern. He didn't understand why. He felt no emotion, only that they had physically closed in on him. He did not want anyone to be close.

"Just allow him space," said Joanne. "He obviously underwent extreme trauma. He needs time to reorient himself. I'll arrange to get him into VA assessment counseling as soon as possible. For now, we have to relate to him only in a functional way. As much as we want to show him affection, show him how much we love him, we can't. We have to give him time. We have to give us time. I'm so sorry, Denise, this will be hardest on you. Just be patient with him. His relationship with you and your original love for each other are the most critical factors that will help him."

"Come on, son," said his father, "Let's go home."

Without expressing any affect, Derek stared at the man wearing an open-necked shirt, dark blue sportcoat, gray slacks, and brown loafers. He recognized features similar to his own, the rugged face, once engaging friendly blue eyes, and more hair on his head than Derek had.

"Myron," said Joanne, "let Denise." She motioned the young woman forward.

Denise hooked an arm through Derek's. "Time to go home, dear. I'm going to make a great dinner for you."

Joanne and her husband, Myron, had planned earlier to drop Denise and their son off at their apartment to be alone together that first night.

After a moment's hesitation, Derek nodded, his first sign that he acknowledged them, and walked through the crowd with Denise clutching his arm and his parents following close behind.

During the ride home in the car. Myron's half-hearted single attempt at jovial enthusiasm met with a sullen silence by his son in the back seat, as though Derek didn't hear or understand what he was saying, and did not wish to acknowledge his father's intent.

Upon arriving at the apartment complex, Myron parked at the front curb. By silent agreement, neither he nor his wife got out of the car. Her face a mask of smiling anxiety, Denise waved goodbye to her in-laws, then guided her husband through the entryway into the courtyard spotted with a few wrought iron metal tables and chairs around a small swimming pool in need of cleaning.

"Welcome home, Sweetie. This way." She nudged him in the direction of the second door at the patio ground level. She released his arm to fumble for keys in her purse, unlocked and pushed open the door, then motioned for him to come inside.

The inexpensive furnishings and two large prints of an autumn scene of long dry field grass and mallard ducks landing in a pond and the second, a forest grove with a doe and her fawn stepping out of the shadows into a slanting splash of sunlight stirred a memory of another life before the darkness had enveloped his mind.

For the first time, he associated the young woman with the room and the prints and recalled her saying at the greeting center, "Derek, it's me, Denise, your wife." He sensed that she was being kind to him, but he didn't know why.

"Want to watch a football game while I make dinner?" She ushered him across the small room to the couch, picked up the remote from the coffee table and aimed it at the flat wall screen. "I don't know who's playing, but we can see if there's a Steeler's game. They're yours and your dad's favorite. She found the ESPN channel and tuned in at the center of an ongoing play with the announcer's voice overriding the background noise of the crowd.

She noticed that he was visibly upset at seeing the brutal physical contact of the players. "I think a comedy might be better." She clicked the remote to change the channel. "You always liked this one. They're still on the air. I'll watch a little with you before I get started on dinner. We're having lasagna. You always loved lasagna. I just have to pop it in the oven. Sweetie, would you like a beer?"

For the first time since his arrival, he looked at her as though he recognized her and nodded.

"One cold beer coming right up. How about some chips and pretzels with it?"

He nodded again. She felt encouraged, even though she thought it unnerving that he didn't speak to her or to his parents during the car ride home from the military base at Dover. He had just stared out the window as though he were entering or reentering a strange new world.

As she went to the refrigerator, she unbuttoned the top three buttons of her silk blouse to expose the soft cleavage of her breasts. Handing him the cold bottle of Coors, she leaned in toward him, hovering close to his face. He took three rapid gulps, then suddenly chugged the rest.

"Wow, you must be thirsty. I'll get you another."

He shook his head.

She sat beside him on the couch. "I love you, Derek. I'm so glad you're home. I missed you so much." Aching to push her body close to him, she reached over to place her arms around his neck and moved her other hand down to touch his groin. He back handed her with a slap that raised a welt on her cheek. She cried out.

"My God, Derek. I'm sorry. I'm so sorry. I didn't know you aren't ready. I'm sorry. I can understand what you must be going through. It's okay, Sweetie. We don't have to hurry."

The young man who had come home was not the man she had married. He was unalterably changed, as though he had gone away as the person she had known and returned as a stranger.

Unable to cope with his erratic mood swings, Denise finally told Derek's parents that she had to move out until he could undergo therapy and regain some sense of normalcy. He was evicted from his apartment for failure to pay the rent. His mother insisted that he move in with her and her husband until his situation improved. Living with him would give her the opportunity to work toward his recovery from traumatic brain injury.

Jefferson and Candace Jergen operated out of a small office in a low rent commercial district of Fort Lauderdale, Florida. Using only a post office box as their business address allowed them to maintain a low profile, a key element in their strategy to make it difficult for anyone to trace them. They marketed their services through a self-designed patchwork website that established their nonprofit 501c tax exempt status and lured donors to their professed cause on-line in support of military veterans returning from Afghanistan and other Middle East wars.

Of their net non-profit, less than one percent trickled down to benefit veterans, just enough not to raise any issue with the IRS.

Jefferson mined a revolving panoply of veterans and their captioned photographs from invitations to submit their stories to the website for a modest compensation.

Having both served short jail sentences for check forgeries, Jefferson and Candace discovered the Internet provided a failsafe opportunity to work their scam within the parameters of the law. They had only to appeal to the patriotic altruistic impulse of Americans weary of the war in Afghanistan and disgusted with the Federal Government's shabby treatment of returning veterans.

One of them was the son of Joanne Harper, a counseling psychologist with Luna Romero's inner city support group.

Jefferson's prize possession was a raised pilot house luxury yacht for deep sea fishing and cruising among the Florida Keys. The earnings from the nonprofit supported the two million dollar vessel and provided the financial resources to purchase a ten million dollar mansion at the beach with their own private inlet and dock. Candace arranged for catered house parties and Jefferson hosted trophy fishing trips to the Keys and to Grand Bahama for their friends.

Joanne Harper never would have known about the Jergens, except that she began researching financial support options when her son returned from Afghanistan and was placed on a three year waiting list with the Veterans Administration for the assessment of his disability and what the VA would be willing to pay him. He was among the thousands of wounded and physically and mentally disabled. Joanne read that despite the 1.7 trillion U.S. dollars in war spending, no funding had been provided to deal with the unprecedented aftermath projected to bring the cost of the Middle East wars to 6 trillion dollars.

She discovered Derek's photo and story caption along with hundreds of others sold to the Jergens by a clerk at the VA. When she asked her son about the photograph, he didn't know how it got there. He had never seen the website before.

When she Googled the name, no performance data was available. She contacted the IRS and learned the nonprofit ranked among the lowest in providing service and benefits and did the minimum to maintain its nonprofit status. Stung by the posted net worth of twenty million dollars, she went searching for who the Jergens were and could not trace them until she came across their police arrest records.

For most of the time, Derek stayed in the room of his childhood. Through the closed door, JoAnne could hear either silence, as he listened to music on his IPod, or him playing video games. He would come downstairs to the kitchen for meals, but then return to his room with his food on a tray. Joanne and her husband did not push him. She explained to Myron that their son would interact with them only when he was ready.

After three weeks, he would leave the house after lunch and be gone for the rest of the afternoon. She knew he spent the fifty dollars a week she left on his dresser, but not on what, and she didn't pry. The fact that he was outside reorienting himself to civilian life in some way encouraged her. She did no more than ask how his day was and received the same answer, "Okay," but no details.

She had to caution her husband to curb his impatience with the imperceptibly slow progress being made with their son living with them and the stultifying bureaucracy at the local VA hospital.

"That's what Joanne told me," said Luna Romero munching on her corn beef and rye at the deli where she and Bernadette met for lunch four or five times a week. "Her son came back from Afghanistan a mess, traumatic brain injury she called it. He's living at home with her and her husband now, but she's concerned he might be getting into drugs. She doesn't have any proof, but there are signs. She's a psychologist. She knows."

"Has she found out anything more about that nonprofit veterans organization you mentioned to me the other day?"

"She can't find where they actually are, only on the Internet."

"No phone number that can be traced?"

"Not even a phone number. How's your sandwich?"

"Pesto chicken isn't my favorite, but thought I'd try it, because of the artichokes. I like the turkey Reuben better. What's the name of that website?"

With Simonetta's intervention, Bernadette found them. The pink two story mansion behind a high stone wall and a black wrought iron entry gate nested among a grove of Florida palms, banana trees, magnolias thrusting white blossoms into dappled sunlight, and cascades of bright red, purple, and yellow tropical foliage.

As they lounged on their pool deck sipping rum daiquiris, they never expected to see the woman, a stranger, striding purposefully toward them along the flagstone path from the front of the house. She was wearing a business suit.

"Who's that?" said Jefferson. "How did she get in here?" He stood up from his cushioned lounge chair. "Excuse me," he called out to her. "You have no business here. Did the maid let you in?"

When Bernadette was within a few yards of the pool, she spoke. "I let myself in."

"What the hell?"

She continued walking to them until she was two steps away.

Candace removed her sunglasses and shaded her eyes to look up at her. "Whoever you are, you're trespassing."

Bernadette watched them begin to shake.

"What is this? What's happening?" Jefferson cried out. He grabbed his left arm to still the trembling that only increased.

Beads of perspiration erupted from the pores of their skin that began to melt as though it were made of butter. Their eyes rolled back into their heads. Their skin quivered and shriveled, falling away in fleshy flakes until their muscles and tendons and veins and arteries were exposed. The vibrations steadily increased and their physical bodies began to fade into ash, then accelerated to a high pitched hum. Then they were gone.

One week later, the house maid discovered their unmarked corpses seated at the dining room table.

II

The Black Spiral

Chapter 20
Fugitives

Sometimes, Bram Vernon felt like a rodent traversing the subterranean sewers of Manhattan. He tried to erase his identity through the use of ten aliases that removed him further and further from whom he had been. During the past year, he had grown a ragged gray beard and wore the shabby clothes of a street vagrant when he left the seedy hotel room he rented for only one month at a time before moving on to another.

Although he had a substantial amount of money deposited in five different banks under five different names, his intent was to be invisible to those at the First World Corporation who were searching for him.

A recent newscast about the death of the Wall Street billionaire, Gale Walsh, caught his attention because of a lack of evidence as to how the bizarre murder occurred. The news anchor, John Morley, reprised his theory of Satanic murders he had originated with the grisly bloodless killing of the prominent religious leader, Reverend Lawrence Livingston at the altar of St. Stephens Cathedral one year ago. Bram knew how close Morley was to the truth, but could never come forward and reveal himself to corroborate the suspicion with the facts he held in secret.

The murder of Gale Walsh changed Bram's position. If he did not risk sharing what he knew, the dark energy momentum and events would only escalate. But he could not go to the media or send a message over the Internet. He would be looked upon as another nut case. Except for the crazies, people did not believe in Satanic cults, let alone what was being unleashed by his former employer, the First World Corporation.

Even if anyone believed him, the spiritual invasion had advanced too far to stop it from spreading like a cosmic cancer into every facet of life. It existed on a parallel plane and was consuming and taking over its competitor, the original physiological genetic phenomenon of biological evolution. Individuals and groups, whole societies could only react to its influences.

They could not escape it and there was no defense, no counter-acting mechanism that he had been researching until the First World management discovered his secret activity and forced him to go underground. For the moment, he had eliminated his identity and they could not find him. But they confiscated his research and buried all his data with the exception of what he carried with him on a 5 terabyte mini backup drive from which he had made five copies and stored in separate safe deposit boxes.

He conjectured what might happen if he contacted the FBI profiler who had investigated the Reverend Livingston case. Bram worried that the FBI would think he was in collusion with the killer, not acting as an informer. They might not believe what he had to tell them anyway, just another nut case. But the nature and circumstances surrounding Walsh's murder raised a serious doubt and Bram had an hypothesis of the evolution and existence of an intelligent dark energy world.

As a genetic microbiologist, he discovered an evolutionary branch that was hidden at a cellular level and mutated into an unknown sphere. He traced its gradual migration from theory to fact, the formlessness and flexibility of dark energy shapes that over the centuries had evolved into human-like alien forms.

Bram discovered the juncture of an unexplained branch of the evolutionary family tree in the black spiral DNA helix while he was employed as a researcher at the Unicell Division of the First World Corporation. He had been hired to conduct research on inventing new synthetic pharmaceutical drugs subjected to FDA trials. These were nutritional substances and genetic hormones that could be introduced into the human food chain through an expression vector recombinant DNA in target cells. The cells would be replicated and subsequently hybridized and transformed within the host food sources like a genetic tapeworm.

The First World Corporation owned and operated seed factory fields and processing plants in three regions of the United States and in India, South America, and South Africa.

His research used microbial cells, eukaryotic model systems, molecular biology and biochemical techniques. He discovered the black spiral helix during the physical mapping of a DNA sample taken from a substance to be widely introduced into seeds and plant forms, fertilizers and water tables, distributed through ocean currents and assimilated into the food chain of marine life forms, and consumed by species of fowl and mammals from grains and grasses.

Ultimately, the harvested and processed food sources would then be consumed by humans and assimilated into their genetic DNA and passed along to their progeny, their children and grandchildren who would perpetuate the DNA characteristics through the next centuries of biological plant and animal life forms.

Bram had cut the DNA fragments and separated them by electrophoresis. He had then applied an external electric field to the electric surface charge of the particles suspended in a solution. The DNA migration pattern created a genetic fingerprint from which he could identify overlapping DNA stretches in clones and sequence the clones to reveal the DNA sequence of the organism. The black spiral did not have any relationship to nor could he trace it to any previously known biological forms.

At that point, he began exploring what he suspected might be a was a missing branch of the evolutionary tree that could lead to a shadow world.

Beginning with the existence of human and chimpanzee ancestors four to seven million years ago, his studies related to genetic adaptation to extreme climate changes.

He used the analytical tools and methods of potassium argon dating, argon-argon dating, carbon 14 radiocarbon, and uranium series that measured the amount of radioactive decay of chemical elements.

Optical Thermo-luminescence and electron spin resonance measured electron absorbance inside sedimentary rocks and skeletal bones. Paleomagnetism analyzed the direction of magnetic particles in the identified sediment layers.

Through his application of biochronology, he compared the changes of animal species in different geographical regions over time and conducted molecular clock analysis of genetic differences between living organisms and rates of genetic mutation related to how long ago living species shared a common ancestor.

He studied the bipedal features and characteristics of the Ardipithecus group that existed four million years ago, the Australopithecus group, Paranthropus group, and Homo group.

On a parallel evolutionary track, the black spiral DNA developed a parasitic existence in the early human forms when stone making tools appeared 2.6 million years ago and the migration of Homo Erectus out of Africa to the Middle-East, European, and Asian regions of the world.

Bram believed the mythology of Satan was only a literary device to simplify and explain the existence of the evil element in man. Bram determined that In Biblical times, the fictional moral tale of Lucifer, God's son and his fall from grace had been created at around six thousand years ago.

The Biblical story portrayed the character of Satan as a beautiful cherub created by God as the most powerful of His angels. As described in the myth, before the creation of man, (established in biological time at seven million years ago), Satan competed with his Creator for the worship ascribed to Him. Satan recruited one-third of the angels to rebel with him against God. The ensuing battle with the archangel, Michael, ended with Satan being cast down to earth. Continuing the myth, being a shape changer and not done with the conflict, Satan transformed himself into the famous snake that convinced Eve to eat the apple from the tree of knowledge of good and evil in the Garden of Eden.

The black spiral helix could not be carbon dated or its origin determined by other analytical technologies, because it could not be traced to a biological source until Bram's mapping showed that it had come into existence seven million years ago and was carried forward as an undetected embedded mutant DNA structure throughout man's evolution, which predated the Biblical rendering of the mythological Satan and Garden of Eden story by six million nine-hundred and ninety-four thousand years.

He concluded the possible existence of beings created in a parallel universe from dark energy.

Not wanting to leave a digital trail, Bram sent a sealed letter with no return address to Leon Safullo at his FBI office in New York City. In it, he said, "I've been following the news about the death of Gale Walsh. There's a relationship between how he was murdered and how Reverend Livingston was murdered one year ago. I can help you. If you are interested, I will be the homeless vagrant standing near the front entrance of your building at 10:00am on August 1st. In so doing this as a whistleblower, I will need the protection of your agency."

Bram assumed that the plainclothes civilians loitering around the front doors of the FBI building were agents. Two wearing business suits closed in on either side of him, as he approached.

"Mr. Vernon, please come with us," said Berzinsky.

They escorted him into the building and directly into an elevator.

"I'm Agent Berzinsky and this is Agent Safullo. We appreciate you contacting us. We didn't see anyone watching you and we will ensure that you are safe and protected. We have some questions."

Bram nodded.

Following a three hour video recorded interrogation, under armed guard, they escorted him back down the elevator to an underground parking facility. They did not tell him where they were taking him. An hour later, they introduced him to Maximilian Schultz.

Chapter 21
Discovery of Simonetta

"Look at this."

Hieronymous Blum transferred the image of Bernadette Garcetti from her holographic image at his floating workstation to the viewing area of Hiram Bean's command center. She was walking along a busy street in downtown Manhattan.

"Watch closely. Do you notice the blonde woman walking close behind her?"

"Yes."

"Familiar?"

"Yes, she's Simonetta."

"She's an aura. Watch what happens."

Simonetta's spirit aura moved closer, emulating Bernadette's walking cadence until her image merged with Bernadette and disappeared.

"She's using that woman as a disguise," said Bean.

"I've been tracking the movements of the woman. Her name is Bernadette Garcetti. She was present at the murder and disappearance of four victims who were under our influence and control."

"Simonetta's misusing her powers of possession. She's gone rogue on us. She's in violation."

"There's more." Blum moved his right forefinger across a holographic virtual touch screen that brought up the image of Bram Vernon. "I discovered where Bram Vernon is hiding."

"Are you sure that's actually where he is? He creates these impressions, but when Mars Livingston goes to find him, he's never there."

"He creates numerous false digital trails to throw us off track, but I think I've nailed him."

They watched the giant floor to ceiling holographic essence where the ethereal shapes of human spirits evolved, twisting and turning from the roiling void of darkness.

In his human persona, Hiram Bean posed as a billionaire real estate executive who experienced a life change when he survived the crash of his private jet in shark infested California coastal waters. His head struck the instrument panel upon impact and he lapsed into an artificial self-induced coma that lasted seven days. The Coast Guard rescued him within thirty minutes of the time his plane went down or he would have purportedly died in the sinking wreckage. Of course, Hiram Bean did not die.

A few years earlier, he arranged a news story about his wife prevailing against breast cancer; and their autistic youngest son, one of four children, showing signs of recovery.

In addition, Unicell, a medical research and development division of his diversified holdings, made the discovery of an unusual black spiral DNA structure that Hiram held in the utmost secrecy. The black spiral DNA was man's link to the dark energy of the universe. He believed that no one outside of the evolutionary scientist, Bram Vernon, who uncovered its source and himself knew of the structure. There had been no announcements and no papers published. All evidence was kept locked in a secret vault.

Notwithstanding the trauma to his head, as part of his media spin and deception, Hiram told the media he interpreted these auspicious events as a sign that God was personally sending him a message, to use his wealth and influence to become the Lord's political organizer on earth in preparation for the second coming of His son, Jesus Christ. So he devoted his massive wealth, the First World Corporation, and his personal life to the service of his Lord God. He said he believed in a literal interpretation of the Bible and its mythic prophesies.

Hiram followed a rigorous diet of complete nutritional balance, which was widely published. He was a compulsive exercise fanatic devoted to a routine facilitated by a professional trainer who was a devout Christian. He believed he possessed the charisma and physical appearance of a leader, tall, a full but lean face with prominent features and a patient benign expression.

For Hiram, spirit was a process that began with pure thought or logic, went on into other beings and pictorial presentation or nature, and returned from nature to complete self-consciousness or the spirit proper. He did not believe that what he thought and did was evil.

As he programmed his agents sent out into the human world, he instructed them, "To be evil, one must be conscious of the norms one rebels against and will ultimately obey. I do not recognize the norms. Self-consciousness is the true reality. God as a picture must die in order that God as a thought might live, one with every man's deepest self-conscious. The religious consciousness has never fully identified itself with God, the object of its devotion, but pictured itself as coming together with that object at some indefinite future date in an existence it calls heaven. I provide the means for that future consummation and it is nothing like you and other men and women might imagine. It is the realm of darkness, the ultimate reality.

Cultures and societies can maintain their organization and activities for varying lengths of time by capturing energy and expending it according to needs in the maintenance of its ordered state. I know that life, in any form, adjusts its structure and behavior in such a way as to remain adaptive to environmental conditions and that the persistence of life on earth in the face of death's certainty depends on the ability of organisms to reproduce themselves. But they can repair and adjust for only so long before they inevitably pass into death.

"What endures on earth over the millennia is not the individual, but the race, and its endurance depends on the act of reproduction as the bridge that spans mortal generations. We are perfect. We do not exist in their reality but we have the power to create and to destroy life. This fact further reinforces the insignificance of mortality. The concept of the change of form is founded in quantum physics. It is within quantum theory that we discover and harvest souls."

In Hiram's world, the phenomenon of light energy was given off and absorbed in tiny definite units called quanta or photons. Light appeared to be in a steady stream or continuous flow, but was a series of many small actions. Radiant energy was transmitted in waves in ranges of certain frequencies or spectrums. When the atoms of a substance were disturbed in a mental or in a biological form, the death of a plant, animal or a human, all the atoms of that substance began to vibrate and the energy radiated outward and escaped just as a vapor dissipated into the medium of air from boiling water. The atoms of substances became dark energy.

"So what can we do about Simonetta?" asked Blum. Despite the wrinkles that layered his face and neck, he emulated the sleek black retinue of his superior, including the shaved head.

"What is happening out there?" asked Hiram. "What is she doing?"

"She's created a virtual simulation," said Bloom. " A SIM. After she murders her victims, she deposits their spirits into the virtual worlds she controls and returns their physical bodies. There is no escape for them. They are imprisoned and we can't get to them."

"What about her?"

"She can disappear into any one of her worlds, and we can't pursue her. She has a multitude of Gateways that she can erase like electronic burrows, pulling the openings closed behind her, rendering her incapable of being followed. We have no way to follow her and find her."

"Find a way. I'll contact Mars Livingston. He has to terminate her and Bram Vernon."

Mars Livingston left his office promptly at six that evening and strolled leisurely along the busy outlying streets of the Capitol to his three story townhouse on George Street.

Hiram Bean's holographic image sat waiting for him in Marston's living room.

"Sir," Marston bowed his head, then, locked into Bean's telekinetic gaze. "To what do I owe the privilege of your appearance?"

"I have a mission for you. It's unfortunate when we have to terminate one of our own, but we've discovered a renegade."

"Do you have a lead?"

"She hasn't been in existence very long, only one year since she was created."

"A she?"

"One of our early female prototypes. They can be subject to issues and malfunctions, but that is why we send them out into the world, to be tested."

"What is her identification?"

"Simonetta Vespucci. Her image is represented in a famous painting, *Birth of Venus*, by the Renaissance artist Sandro Botticelli. But there is yet another problem that is more important that I want you to handle first. His name is Bram Vernon. He's a human, a genetic scientist we employed in the Unicell Division of the First World Corporation. He destroyed our black spiral DNA research files that I believed were secure. Then he disappeared, taking with him all of the existing research and genetic design data and material of the black spiral triple helix.

Until now, the black spiral helix has been impervious to mutation. There's no trace in our system that a gene transfer could be introduced to attack it, not by microinjection or a delivery vector. Bram Vernon has changed that possibility. He was our lead scientist at the Unicell Laboratory developing biological viral DNA delivery systems and chemical non-viral delivery systems. Black Spiral DNA is unknown to human genetic research. Even if it is discovered, their genetic scientists will not be able to unlock the genetic code. To our misfortune, Bram Vernon has that code. Since he discovered black spiral, he is the only one who can unlock the code. He was working on that project when he disappeared on us. He is the only one. No other entity is able to do that, human or spirit. Our opposition with humans is not biochemical. It's intangible, their values and belief systems. We don't have a trace of his existence. He's done something to block us. We were about to introduce black spiral into the human food chain. If we detect a resistant strain in the spiritual world, that will give us an indicator of where to find him. But we can't wait for that to occur. I want you to undertake a physical investigation to track him down and terminate him."

Mars nodded.

"I have channeled to you what we know about him since his departure from Unicell. The information will provide you a trail to follow. As we learn more, you will receive it through my spiritual transmission."

Mars watched Hiram's image collapse and dissolve into indecipherable molecules and fade to infinite nothingness.

Chapter 22

Mars Livingston - Assassin

Mars liked the feeling of cool air caressing his porous skin, which was always slightly warm to the touch, one of his artificially programmed human thought processes, and sensations that were embedded in his black spiral DNA chip.

Prior to Mars' implantation into human society, Hiram deprogrammed and deconstructed his soul, identifying Reverend Lawrence Livingston's conscience, engulfing it in a magnetic radiating imaging field and overwriting his previous spiritual features which disintegrated into molecular trash consumed by the massive dark energy universe that replaced it with the immoral psychogenic code of a sociopath.

He had been subjected to a training regimen to awaken and experience the features and impulses of his simulated human life that would be most useful to him in his covert role as an instigator of chaos and as an assassin. His core conscience had been reprogrammed and left him with no attachment to anyone.

"We must win at any and all cost," said Hiram. "For us, collateral damage does not exist. Our goal is to destroy all things that humankind considers of positive value and its brand of morality. Whoever or whatever is taken along the way is irrelevant."

While driving through North Carolina to see Jimmy Richter, attend his son's funeral, and investigate the death of Ignatius Stroud, Mars passed through the small town where he had started his previous career as a preacher. Seeing the main street, his church, and the people recalled a positive impulse that his reprogrammed mind crushed.

From time to time, prompted by a place, a person, an object, or a memory that had not been completely erased in his spiritual reprogramming, vestiges of his prior existence surreptitiously crept into his thoughts to be promptly snuffed out by a watchdog, a spiritual virus detector. He did not know or recognize that his last name, Livingston, was his code name given him by the spiritual programmer, Hieronymous Blum.

Mars could absorb Simonetta's spore through his skin. She left a lingering molecular vapor in the air wherever she had been concealed in the persona of Bernadette Garcetti. He detected it now at Ignatius Stroud's Guns 'R Us store.

He met Jimmy Richter and the local sheriff, Leland Pentegraft, in the parking lot in front of the store. As a favor to his drinking buddy, the sheriff had agreed to allow them access through the posted yellow crime scene tape. Jimmy and the sheriff pulled into the parking lot a few minutes after Mars. They stepped out of their cars and briefly shook hands.

"Nice to meet you, Sheriff. Mars Livingston. Thanks for helping me out. Jimmy and I work together."

"So Jimmy tells me." Leland's tall thin lanky frame aligned itself with an involuntary quiver. "Nice job bein' a lobbyist with the GRA." Leland ejected a viscous gob of Redman Chewing Tobacco into a Styrofoam cup carried in his left hand. A remnant of the dark red juice adhered to his thick handlebar mustache.

"That's right. Puts me at the center of the political fight."

Leland removed his reflective lens sunglasses, exposing milky blue-gray eyes. He tipped back his tan western hat. "We're all sorry to hear about his boy."

"As I am, Sheriff. It saddens me to hear that young people, children, are killed or being killed."

"It's a sorry thing when it happens. But it's usually for odd reasons, crazies outside of our control. My point is we don't want to have our guns taken away 'cause of the crazies. Guns are part of our way of life. So don't cave for them gun haters."

"Believe me, the GRA is not caving."

The sheriff removed a key from the ring attached to his ammunition belt and unlocked the metal barrier and the front door. As they entered, he asked, "anything specific you're looking for, somethin' you want to see?"

"I just need to spend some time in the store. The GRA doesn't take it lightly when one of our retailers is hit like this. It's bad for our industry and bad for the economy."

"I don't know if Jimmy told you, but the Feds were down here from New York snoopin' around," said Leland.

"The FBI?"

"Yeah, from what they said, this isn't the first murder of this kind."

"Of this kind?"

"No blood. Not one damn drop. Damnest thing you ever seen. Iggy disappeared and then one day we found him back behind the counter, stone dead and no sign of a wound, and not even a heart attack after the coroner finished with 'im."

"Did they say anything about the case, share anything?"

"Not with me. They barely tolerated my hangin' around, even though I was the first law enforcement on the scene. They asked me questions I couldn't answer. I mean what happened to Iggy is too weird for words. Know what I mean?"

Mars nodded. "Are there any suspects identified? Anyone local?"

"We've got people who practice voodoo around here, but nothin' like this. They can't make people disappear 'less they kill 'em and sink 'em in the swamp. I don't like to say it, 'cause I don't believe in shit like this, and I'm a good Christian, a God-fearing man, but what happened here seems like it was supernatural."

"Not likely. There's an explanation for everything. I'm sure scientific forensics can find the answer."

"That's askin' for a lot with somethin' strange like this, especially when there ain't no evidence of foul play. The coroner said there was nothin' in 'im or on 'im that could've killed 'im."

Mars moved away from the sheriff to detour from the discussion and further imprint Simonetta's presence much as a bloodhound identified and recalled a scent through his olfactory memory.

He scanned the display of rifles, shotguns, handguns, ammunition, and hunting and camping gear. Without looking back at the sheriff, he asked, "Who reported Stroud's body appearing back in the store?"

"His girl, Rae Dunrobin. She was the one first called in he was missing. A week before his body turned up again."

Mars turned to face Leland and Jimmy. "When was the FBI here?"

"A few days ago, for the second time."

"How did they find out about Stroud?"

"Me. I called 'em," said Leland. "Thought he was kidnapped or somethin'. Then when his body showed up a week later and no blood or nothin', no cause of death, I called 'em again. They got on a plane and were down here the same day, a private jet no less." Leland raised his hat and scratched at a bald spot with the hatband, then settled the crown over what remained of his receding brown hairline.

"Do you remember their names?"

"Sure, you might even know 'em. Agent Leon Safullo, an older guy, and Agent Ed Berzinsky, a middle-age body builder type. Kind you wouldn't want to git into a scrape with."

"Did they take prints?"

"My lab already done that. Took some photos though. Had some questions about Iggy. I told 'em the best one to talk to was his girlfriend. So they went off and done that. You know 'em?"

"Lot of agents in the Bureau. Sometimes they pull a GRA officer into an investigation. I never worked on a case with them, but sure, I know them." Mars had discovered early on in his reincarnation that he had no difficulty lying, felt no repercussions, no remorse. Lying and distortion of the truth were normal behaviors, business as usual, in his work as a lobbyist and throughout his Senatorial and Legislative contacts in the Federal Government.

"You packin'?" asked Leland.

"I beg your pardon?"

"You carryin' a gun?"

"I keep it in the car."

"Both them agents carried a Glock. You too?"

Mars nodded.

"Can do some damage when you need it."

"Fortunately, I've never had to use it."

"Shot four men in my job," said Leland. "Just four. Could've been a lot more. Didn't kill any of 'em. Just wounded. I was merciful, even though they pulled on me."

"Obviously, you use discretion in making an arrest."

"Call it what you want. It's a gut feeling. Never fails me. I kin read people. Know how far they'll go."

"That's a good ability to have." Mars continued to peruse the guns. "Where can I find Rae Donrobin?"

"The Fish House just off I-95 north where it intersects with Palmetto Highway down the road from the paper mill. Can't miss the mill. Smell it 'fore you see it. Blows big clouds of steam into the air. Can't miss it. Rae works there with her mom and dad. Family place."

"I'll stop by and talk with her."

"She's in a bad way, grievin', if you know what I mean. She and Iggy were real close for years. Never got married. Plannin' on it. Too late. Strange how this happened. Real strange. You find out anything, mebbee you'll let me know. Those agents was tight-lipped. Even though this is my jurisdiction, they wouldn't tell me nothin'. Heard the FBI is like that, kinda territorial. You ever had to deal with 'em like that? Ignored me like I was a snot-nose kid. My badge is the same size as theirs."

"They're gun people, just like us," said Mars. "We get along."

"All in the family is what I say."

Mars nodded. "All in the family."

"You comin' to the boy's funeral?"

"That's my real reason for being here. Jimmy's a close friend and I represent the GRA."

"My missus and Jimmy's friends local here are givin' a barbeque reception after the church service. You're welcome to join us."

"Was Stroud buried?"

"Still at the coroner. Funeral's next Sunday."

"Well, I need to check in to a motel and pay a call to Rae Dunrobin along the way." Mars extended his right hand. "Thank you, Sheriff, for your assistance. My superiors at the GRA are anxious to hear any news or insights I might have to take back with me."

"Pleasure's mine, Mr. Livingston. Pleasure's mine." Leland spit into his cup as the three of them walked outside.

Mars and Jimmy waited in the parking lot for Leland to lock the door.

The Fish House was crowded with local customers as usual at the dinner hour forcing Mars to wait outside with several others until tables were vacated and cleared. He opened the door and looked around the dining area. Rae Dunrobin bustled back and forth from taking orders to the kitchen and returning with a tray filled with steaming platters of fish and shrimp and fries and tall plastic cups of sweet and unsweet iced tea. A line of men and women at the salad bar loaded small plates with lettuce, tomato wedges, pickles, corn, garbanzo beans, and black olives heavily doused with dressing, then shuffled back to their tables.

Having identified Rae, Mars realized he would not be able to engage her in conversation while she was working. He walked back to his rented car parked on the narrow shoulder with many others in a long line. He would return later when the restaurant closed at ten, according to the sign in the window.

Rae saw the man leave his car and approach the door as she said goodnight to the last three customers, workers from the mill. The sound of their pickup engines droned away down the dark road into the night. As Mars reached for the door handle, Rae pointed at the sign indicating the hours and mouthed her words through the glass window, "We're closed."

Mars flicked open his wallet to flash his GRA card as though it were a badge. "FBI," he shouted. "I'm here about Ignatius Stroud."

Rae stared at him for several seconds, then opened the door a crack. She could hear her mother and father cleaning up in the kitchen behind her. "What do you want? I already talked to the FBI."

"I'm here about his killer. I'm trying to find her."

"His killer's a woman?"

"Yes, I have a question you might be able to help me with."

Rae opened the door a little wider, but did not let him in. "Did those other agents send you here?"

"Yes, but I'm also a friend of Jimmy Richter. Sheriff Pentegraft told me I could find you here."

"I have to close up, but go ahead. Ask your question."

"First, I'd like to express condolences on behalf of the GRA. I work with them, which is how I know Jimmy Richter."

"I can't keep standing here. Ask your question."

"Did you and Ignatius know or ever meet a woman by the name of Bernadette Garcetti? She's about five ten, short cut dark hair, attractive face."

"I don't know anybody by that name. If Iggy did, maybe through his business, he never told me. He did business with a lot of people, not just here, but all over, other states, other cities. Did she kill him?"

"That's what I'm investigating. She's a prime suspect."

"How could she be able to do that? She's a woman. Sheriff Pentegraft told me Iggy was kidnapped, then brought back dead."

"There's more to what happened to him that we don't know. That's why we're talking to people who were close to Iggy."

"I wish I could help you, but there's nothing more I can tell you."

"I appreciate your taking a few minutes. We will find his killer. I'm sorry for your loss, Miss Dunrobin."

"Did Jimmy tell you my name?"

"Yes, and you're in the bureau of records."

"What's your name?"

"Agent Livingston, Marston Livingston."

"Well, I hope you find her. Goodnight, Mister Livingston."

"Good night, Miss Dunrobin." Mars turned away and walked back to his car. He heard the door close and the dead bolt lock click shut behind him.

Forging through the night, his headlights picked out the image of two small children walking hand in hand along the shoulder. Startled, they turned and looked at his approaching car. He slowed and stopped. The four year old boy appeared to be his son and the two year old girl his daughter as he remembered them. As he stepped out of his car and walked toward them, they dissolved into the swamp mist drifting across the road.

Chapter 23

Abduction

With a polite, "Thank you." Ashley Huggins sipped at the hot coffee the female police officer handed her. The officer seated herself across the table next to the undercover detective and told Ashley their discussion was being recorded on video.

"Obviously you aren't working alone, and you don't act like a pro."

"I'm not. I really am not. I was kidnapped in a mall parking lot. He is forcing me to do this. I was shopping for clothes to get ready for college. I'm enrolled at Cornell as a freshman this coming fall."

"Who is your pimp?"

"He calls himself Blade. That's all any of us know about him. When he did talk to us, he always brought out his knife and held it like he would stab us at any moment. He kept us in different motels every few days. He kept moving us around, sometimes to different towns and cities. We wouldn't stay in any one place for long."

"What kind of car did he drive?"

"He had an old van of some kind. I think it was a Dodge caravan. The side doors slid open and shut."

"What color?"

"White I think, or gray. It was covered with dirt and dust. I didn't pay attention. It had a lot of dents."

"How many were you? How many girls?"

"Four, including me."

"What can you tell us about the other girls? Do you know their names?"

"He gave us names. We didn't know each other's real ones."

"What were the names, starting with yours."

"Because of my red hair, he named me Red. He didn't introduce the other girls. I found out their names when we were on the street or I heard him speak to one of them. He told them my name was Red."

"Did you ever tell him your real name?"

"When we were in the van, he took my purse and cell phone with all my ID. He could tell who I was. He told me if I tried to get away or contact anybody, he would kill my family. He must have seen their photos in my wallet. I started crying and asked him to please let me go. He told me to shut up or he would hurt me."

"How and when did he take you?"

"I arrived at the store opening hour and parked in an isolated space for employees with no other cars beside me. I knew that in about two hours, the other spaces would be filled but I liked to leave myself room to maneuver when I was backing out to leave.

"I was thinking about my planned freshman curriculum in human ecology at Cornell. I had been studying the course catalogs of the Human Biology, Health, and Society undergraduate program. I would be studying physiological and biochemical human health issues from a broad and multidisciplinary perspective. What particularly interested me was I could select what I wanted to investigate through the wide array of courses related to human health and well-being. I was especially interested in the resistance to disease and factors in the normal growth of children. The biological processes of normal and abnormal behavior, and social, political, economic and cultural factors related to healthcare would be topics of my post-graduate research. But they were five years away."

The police officer and undercover officer glanced at each other. Ashley's intellect and vocabulary surprised them.

"When I returned to my car, this battered white van was wedged in so tightly next to mine, I wondered if I could even move my car. I tossed my backpack into the trunk and was walking around to the driver's side when somebody rushed me from behind. Before I could turn, a black sack enclosed my head and face. I screamed and choked and struggled. Then I felt the prick of a knife against my ribs.

A man's voice warned, "Don't fight. Don't scream. Don't say anything. You do and I'll kill you."

"I stopped trying to resist as he tightened the draw string at the base of the sack around my neck. I stood rigid and trembling, afraid he was going to strangle me. His free hand roughly grabbed my arm and I followed the pressure of his hand and body guiding me. I stumbled around the rear of the van to an open door on the passenger side."

"Step up," he ordered. "Get in." He followed me inside and pushed me down onto a back seat. He did not remove the black sack he had forced over my head and face. I heard the rasp of duct tape and felt my wrists being bound in my lap with snug wraps of the tape.

"His voice was very strange," she told the detective, "like he was trying to force it to sound deeper. It sounded almost like a woman's voice."

"In what way? Was it high, mid-range?"

"When he was mad, it would go up, like he was straining. You could see his neck muscles and his face turn red. And he was always waving his knife around when he talked like that was the only way he knew how to gesture, like it was part of his hand. Sometimes he tossed the knife back and forth from one hand to the other."

"Can you describe him? What did he look like? Our sketch artist will try to create a resemblance."

"I never saw his face until he took me to the motel."

"Can you describe him?"

"I'll try." Ashley gulped back tears. "What about my mom and dad and my brother and sister? Blade knows you arrested me and he knows I'm here talking to you. He said he would kill them."

"A police unit is on its way to your house."

"Thank you."

"Start with his face, any visual characteristics that stand out?"

"He has a dark brown mustache and a scrawny goatee. His hair looked like it doesn't have any place to settle so it sticks out in different directions kind of receding from his forehead like a clown. He's skinny. His clothes kind of hang on him. He smokes cigarettes and drinks a lot of beer in the van, especially when we were on the street at night. His face looks young, like a gaunt teenager. He has a long straight nose and a pointy jaw. The goatee makes it more pointy."

"Do you remember the color of his eyes?"

"Chocolate milk. They reminded me of chocolate milk."

"Did he have any tattoos, scars, any other marks?"

"He had daggers on both arms."

"Anything else?"

"The one time I saw him naked, he had swastikas on his chest."

"When did you see him naked?"

"The time he raped me. It was the same day he kidnapped me. He took me to some dirty motel. I don't know where. He took the sack off my head so I could see where I was going. The motel didn't even have a name. He took me to a room on the first floor."

"He stripped off my clothes, pushed me down onto the bed and raped me. He held the knife blade raised in the air like he was riding into battle. I thought I heard him say 'My name is Blade.'

"I didn't dare say anything. I wanted to scream. I had never had sex with anyone before, not even my boyfriend. I didn't know what to think. I was a normal girl raised in a normal family and now here I was being raped by a maniac. Afterwards, he told me to take a shower. I kept trying to think how I could escape. But when I got out of the shower, he had stuffed my clothes into a laundry bag and left me with nothing to wear, not even a pair of panties.

"I crawled under the stained sheet and thin covers and cried myself to sleep.

"He woke me that night. Made a lot of noise coming into the room. He told me to get up and put on some clothes he had brought. I'm tall, so a couple of things were snug. He arranged the silk blouse so most of my breasts were exposed. He gave me back my shoes. I'd been wearing dance slippers. The skirt was a maroon denim wrap around with a side zipper. He gave me a brush and told me to brush my hair. He told me I had good hair, that John's liked it long. He gave me back my purse. My wallet was gone. There was some makeup and hooker things, some sex jelly and clean wipes. He told me if I tried to run or get away, that he was faster. Then he told me again he would kill me and my family if I tried to run. I promised I wouldn't. He also told me that from now on, my name was Red, because of my hair. Then he took me out to the van. There were three other girls inside."

She recalled in her own mind what happened next.

"Blade parked the van on a side street. We were near a main thoroughfare. "He ordered us to get to work."

"As the other girls stepped out of the van, I held back. 'I don't know what to do,' I told him."

"Stay with Jasmine," he said. "She'll show you what to do."

"I think she was Chinese," Ashely told the detective, "but I couldn't tell for sure. She did have a beautiful face and long black hair, longer than mine. Hers was all the way down to her waist. She was wearing a red colored Asian dress with gold flecks in it and she wore tan heals with suede anklet wraparounds. The other two girls had stiletto heels. The one called Ruby was a Black teenager. At least she looked like a teenager. She had streaks of blonde in her hair and a lot of costume jewelry around her neck and bracelets on her arms. She rattled them a lot. She was attractive. The other girl, her name was Blue. She had very sad blue eyes. I think she was probably a runaway Blade had taken off the street. She looked like a teenager dressed in sexy clothes like a rock singer. She had long blonde hair too, but it was thin, wispy I would call it. She and Ruby went off in a different direction."

"I'm smart and I notice things. The street was like at a carnival with blue and red and gold neon signs and rows of bars and seedy hotels and fast food takeout restaurants on corners. The overhead city street lights were silver-gray instead of white. They diluted the color of everything like a zone of fog. I saw about fifty prostitutes parading back and forth or posed near the entrances of bars. Others smoked cigarettes at the corners in the flash of moving car headlights.

"I was walking with Jasmine when a medium tall man wearing basketball shorts followed us for a short distance. He had a numbered purple jersey and athletic running shoes. He nudged in between us and grabbed our arms.

Jasmine jerked away, but kept walking. "Don't touch," she warned him.

"Sorry. Sorry. So, hey, girls, how you doin' tonight?"

"We're doin' fine," said Jasmine. "You lookin' for a good time?"

"I like your friend here," he bumped his unshaven jaw against my head. "How you doin', Red. You look great. I have a soft spot in my heart for redheads."

"She's fresh," said Jasmine. "What're you lookin' for?"

"I'm parked down a side street, a block away. A private spot. No lights. We can talk about it there. You can come along if you like. But I want her. Can I call you Red?"

"Yes," I said.

"Tell us want you want," said Jasmine, "and I'll give you the price."

"Get right down to business, don't you? Red here is more the quiet gentle type, my type."

"You buyin' or you just talkin'," Jasmine growled like she was a fighter.

"I'm buyin'. I'm an easy goin' guy. You don't have to worry about rough stuff with me."

"I ain't worried," said Jasmine. "You get rough and it'll come back atcha."

"I'm on the up and up. Name's Roger."

"Well, nice to meet you, Roger. It's nice to meet him, isn't it, Red?

"Yes. It's nice to meet you." My heart was racing.

"What you buyin'?" repeated Jasmine.

"Red here has a good body. I want to feel her titties."

"That's one hundred."

"I want to finger her cunt."

"That's up to three hundred."

"Expensive cunt."

"Anything else?"

"I want her to top me off with a blow job."

"Now you're up to a thousand. You got the cash?"

"I've got it."

"Pay me before you and red get in the car," said Jasmine.

"How 'bout I pay for the feel and the finger fuck, then see if we go for the rest."

"You take us for suckers? You don't pay up front, you don't get no rest."

"If I like the blow job, there's an extra five hundred in it. You ever give a blow job?" he asked me.

"I shook my head."

"You sound like a virgin. You a virgin?"

"Yes."

"Awesome, not many of you around anymore. I can help you out with the blow job."

"Can I just masturbate you?" I asked, as we approached the car.

"Nah, I can do that myself for free. I want to feel your warm tongue licking around my cock. Big difference. You get the picture?"

"His hand rubbing my breasts made my skin crawl with the sensation of lice moving over my body. His crotch smelled like farts and sour piss. I didn't swallow his cum and spat it onto the floor of the car. He slapped me and said he would not pay the extra five hundred.

"As I backed out of the car seat, I hit the direct dial that connected to Blade I had a none payer. The man yelled at me to get the fuck out of his car. I stalled. The driver side door was jerked open and Blade pressed his knife into the man's neck without breaking the skin. He ordered the man to hand over his wallet. Blade removed one thousand dollars in twenties, took five credit cards and tossed the wallet into the street as he ran off into the night. I had run off as soon as Blade arrived. I crouched in a doorway, buttoned my open blouse and cleaned my mouth and hands with the sanitizer and wipes in my purse.

"An hour later, I was standing back out at the curb when a businessman offered me three thousand dollars to go with him to a motel. I called Blade on my cell phone and relayed the information. Blade left his van and walked over to the black Lexus. I'm sure he was thinking big money. Still on the cell, he ordered me to go with the John to a certain motel. He told me to get the cash in advance while I was right there in the car. I got into the car and told the John he would have to pay me first. As soon as he handed me the money, he showed me his badge and identified himself as cop. He placed me under arrest and took back the money. A nearby police unit on the radio pulled up behind the Lexus. Two officers got out and handcuffed me. They read me my rights and put me in the police unit. They talked some code words on the radio, then drove to the police station."

Upon her return home, Ashley underwent a medical and psychiatric evaluation to determine if she needed therapy before and during her first few months at college. As she told the doctors, "I'm okay. I can handle this. I don't want to think about it. I just want to get on with my life."

Prior to her departure for Cornell, the local police discontinued their surveillance of her street and her parents ended the private security services of a bodyguard.

***

Maggot had no idea why his mother had given him such a name. He didn't even remember having a mother. She spent more time away from the apartment than in it. And when she was home, she stayed in bed, passed out from drugs and alcohol. From the day she deserted him at age five, he had disowned the name and dedicated his efforts to living it down. In place of it, the voice in his head had created a new name that established and reinforced his desired image of himself.

The name had come to him in a dream from the voice of Heironymous Blum who often spoke to him, advising him and telling him what to think and do among the many dreams and random thoughts that flitted through his mind day and night, thoughts he would attempt to hold, but faded away like smoke and shifting striations of a dark substance that fueled his frustration and anger. The voice encouraged him to fixate on the anger, which stayed with him for longer periods and, through repetition, he was able to call up at will. Anger was the only emotion on which he could consistently rely. The presence behind the soothing voice had arranged his life that way.

The boy had not even known what a maggot was until his first year in the foster care home. When he told the man and woman who ran the home what his name was, he didn't miss their quick glance at one another, and wondered why they said they would call him Maggoy. But from that time on, he answered to the name without question.

One day in their play area, he had joined the six other children, all three to four years older than he, looking at a dead rabbit eviscerated by a neighbor's cat. Bulbous white worms swarmed over the exposed pinkish-red organs.

"What are those?" he asked.

"Maggots," a frail girl standing next to him said.

He did not repeat the word. Coughing on the vomit in his throat at the rising odor of animal decay, he quickly moved off to the far side of the jungle gym to distance himself from the scene of death.

Whenever anyone asked, he would always give his name as Maggoy until the day he left the foster home, the day he became Blade Maggoy.

He feared and avoided the gangs, especially the African American gangs who had established turf in the larger cities and relied on widespread prostitution business using hundreds of girls to financially support the gang lifestyle with less risk than drug trafficking. The money gave them power and respect. Blade had to operate on the periphery to find his market niche, which turned out to be a strategy of mobility and staying small.

When Blade finally escaped from the school for the emotionally disturbed, Bloom arranged for the next phase of his training wandering homeless on the streets of New York. Bloom directed another of his dark spirit creations, Tyler Reddick, to introduce himself to Blade and become his mentor.

Standing outside a ghetto mission, Blade grew nervous about the middle-aged man watching him. He wasn't dressed like other homeless men lurking about the entrance waiting for the next meal or a cot to become available. His graying hair was trim and his clothes and shoes were clean. His lean clean shaven jaw and strong rugged features reminded Blade of a professional sports athlete, especially since he was wearing a blue and white nylon sports jacket. Blade tensed, prepared to run as the man approached him, if he turned out to be an undercover officer in search of runaways. But his deep blue eyes twinkled in a friendly way that matched his smile and hearing his name spoken surprised Blade.

"Hello, Blade, I've been waiting to meet you." He extended his right hand. "I'm Tyler Reddick."

Blade backed away one step and did not take his hand.

"It's okay. I'm not a cop or someone from social services."

"How do you know me?"

"We have a mutual acquaintance. He told me you would be here and he sent me to help you."

"What kind of help?"

"I want you to come and work for me. It's part of a plan for your life. You weren't meant to wander around the streets homeless like this."

"What kind of work?"

"It's something you can do very well. You were meant to do. You were born to do."

"I don't know what you're talkin' about."

"You'll understand once we start working together. But first, I'm offering you a place to live. I have a nice apartment toward mid-town. You'll live there with me. You'll be safe. I'll provide everything you need. You'll never be hungry. You'll have new clothes. You can take a shower and brush your teeth every day, if you want, or even if you don't want. But it feels good to be clean. Sound all right to you?"

Blade stood aside for an alcoholic vagrant with greasy hair and wearing layers of filthy clothes stumbling blindly to get inside the mission.

"I guess it's okay."

"It will be a whole new life for you, Blade."

They started walking away down the street.

"How did you know my name?"

"Oh, our mutual acquaintance told me."

"Who is that?"

"His name is Bloom, Hieronymous Bloom."

"Weird, I can't even pronounce it."

"Doesn't matter. He's looking out for you. That's why he sent me to get you."

"Will I meet him?"

"No, he has other ways of getting in touch with us."

Blade lived in the same flat with Tyler and slept on a futon on the floor. Tyler fed him well and let him smoke cigarettes and drink beer. Blade never expressed any gratitude for what Tyler was providing him. He had no feelings about it one way or the other, except that he preferred his new situation to scrounging in dumpsters.

He did notice a difference between Tyler and the men at the school. They were big and rough and didn't hesitate to use wrestling choke holds on him when he had raging episodes. They would hold him still while a nurse injected him with medication.

Tyler was tall and slender and spoke with the clipped vowels of a Boston accent that sounded slightly British, although Blade didn't know the difference. Relocated from the foster home, during the thirteen years he had spent in the special needs school for emotionally disturbed children, he had heard a mix of harsh New England, Puerto Rican and Black ghetto voices. Tyler didn't sound like a New Yorker and he never laid a hand on him. He showed Blade where things were in the apartment and told him he could cook or microwave his own meals if he would like. Blade could watch any program he wanted on television and select video games from Tyler's library. Blade preferred the games that were the most violent.

For the first month, Tyler left Blade alone in the apartment. He would return a few hours after midnight and sleep late into the morning. He never told Blade where he was going or what he was doing until one night, he said, "I'm taking you with me. I want to show you something."

His first meeting with Tyler's ten girls was unexpected. It took place near downtown Manhattan on side streets populated with bars near the theater district. Tyson explained the area was "fertile" as he put it. "Patrons who come to this part of town have money, lots of money, and they spend it. My girls can get three times the average rates than in the bad areas."

"What is it you want me to do?" asked Blade.

"I want them to know that you work for me and you're a real badass and if any one of them shortchanges me, you and I will come to see them. When I introduce you, I want you to show them your knife. That should be all they need is to see the knife."

"I can do that."

"What happens if they short change you? What do I do then?"

"We'll both go visit the girls where they live, and you'll do a little light carving on them. On their bodies, not their faces. They need their faces and I need their faces to do business, but we will threaten to change their faces. So I want them to see you out here at night along with me. I want them to know you are my enforcer. I don't want to have to come out here every night. So sometimes I'll send you out here alone."

"What do you do?"

"I'm their manager. They give me their money and I pay their rent and medical bills and give them a food allowance."

"Do you get all their money?"

"Most of it. When I send you out here alone, you will make the collections. They all will know that. When they see you, they'll come over and pass along the money. It's that simple. It's just business. We're going to make a good living together, you and I."

Once a week, Tyler would bring one of his girls home for Blade to have sex. His desire for sex became addictive and he asked Tyler to bring girls home more often. Tyler obliged.

After ten years in the merchant marine working on freighters as an engine mechanic, Tyler had saved over three hundred thousand dollars deposited in the credit union. In foreign ports of call, he had noticed the heavy traffic of prostitutes working in brothels and the armies of street walkers soliciting sailors and seamen and single tourists and businessmen. He became aware of the multi-billion dollar pornography industry on the Internet and saw his opportunity to become wealthy in a second career.

Early on, he decided the Internet as a marketing medium was not for him. Girls and women could deal directly with their Johns and bypass the middle man, the manager, the pimp. He would manage and work his girls on the street.

Eventually, Tyler entrusted Blade with making bank deposits and gave him password access to two of his many accounts under different names. He told Blade that eventually he could build his own business and have his own accounts. This happened sooner than either of them expected.

The night Tyler was arrested for dealing drugs in a sting operation and he didn't come back to the apartment, Blade went out to talk to the girls. They told him what had happened and that Tyler would go to jail for a long time. Seven of them told Blade they were crossing over to another handler. Blade convinced three of the girls to stay with him by promising them more of a cut in their money and he would take them traveling. He said he would drive them to Florida on a vacation. He took Tyler's van and continued to do business on his own.

When he drove his van into a city, he would scour the central and outlying areas for gang graffiti as sectors to avoid. The most lucrative locations were bar and nightclub districts, but his girls often ran into competition. Blade would pull his girls out rather than risk their direct confrontation and injury, especially to their faces.

He had never anticipated that one of his girls would be arrested by an undercover cop. That this had happened to his newest property unnerved him. She wasn't seasoned and sufficiently under his control for him to trust her. He knew she would identify him. And for that, she would pay.

***

The discovery of Ashley Huggins' slain body was the main topic of the morning news. She had been reported missing to the campus police by her roommate when she didn't return from her night class, a biology lab. The location of her body in the brush along a dimly lit wooded path connecting the dorm to the main campus suggested the killer, dressed as a student, had been stalking her, perhaps for days, learning her patterns.

Mr. and Mrs. Huggins could not control their insurmountable grief. Luna Romero and other members from their church came to their house to try to console them with prayer and spiritual comfort, to no effect.

***

"Seven times! She was stabbed seven times!" So shaken with sobs, she could barely stand, Luna Romero reached out for Bernadette's support. Bernadette guided her to a cushioned bench in the women's room down the hall from her office.

Tears streamed down Luna's florid face. "Ashley and her family were members of our church. They were friends. I've known them for years. She just started as a freshman at Cornell. She had her whole world, her whole life ahead of her. And now this. It's too much. It's just too damn much." She accepted the handful of tissues Bernadette held out to her and dabbed at her eyes and wiped her runny nose.

"What is the world coming to, Bernie, I ask you? What is the world coming too? She was a beautiful young woman. Her parents said she'd been abducted and forced to become a prostitute. How could that happen? The police pulled her out of it and everybody thought she would be safe. Not so. Not so. He got to her first. They're looking for her killer. He's out there. He got away. I feel so helpless. This could happen to my own daughter, to anyone's daughter. There's nothing I can do. Nothing I can do."

Bernadette slowly looked at herself in the mirror.

***

In an outlying Cleveland suburb, Blade pulled the van into the parking lot of a Howard Johnson's motel. He checked himself and his three girls into a single room as a family of four under a fictitious name. He told them to watch television until he returned with take-out dinner for all of them from a nearby chicken joint.

When he returned, he saw a woman wearing a business suit standing outside her car parked in front of his motel unit. He noticed she was a tall brunette, attractive, despite her cold intense expression. Worried that she might be a cop, he parked five spaces away. As he stepped out of the van, he saw her walking toward him. He pulled his knife and held it out where she could see it. She continued walking straight toward him. Her steps did not falter.

Bernadette watched him shake and tremble. His eyes rolled back into his head. His skin quivered and shriveled, falling away in red flakes until his muscles and tendons and veins and arteries were exposed. His vibrations steadily increased and his physical presence began to fade, then accelerated to a high-pitched hum. Then he was gone.

***

"This is an outrage!" Hiram Bean stormed about his First World Corporation office. "She keeps terminating the very people we put out there to do our work. We have to find a way to stop her. There must be something in her programming. Blum, there has to be some way you can get inside her and turn her off."

"The only way is to terminate her," said Blum.

"Which means we have to kill the woman who's hiding her."

"You've talked to Mars Livingston."

"I have, but so far he can't find her."

"Like I said before, Simonetta has created her own world. She has any number of ways to escape us," said Blum.

But if we kill this Bernadette Garcetti, Simonetta won't have anyone to hide in when she comes out into the real world."

"I don't know, Hiram. She has developed abilities beyond what we anticipated. Remember, she's our first female prototype. She could conceivably hide in anyone who adopts her or anyone she chooses, for that matter."

"Once we capture her, we need to dissect her spiritual programming. We can't let this ever happen again."

"We will get her and with the data we extract, I'll be able to create a beta blocker that will prevent this from ever happening again."

"Time is running short, Blum. We have not completely taken over. We are not in the clear. We're only halfway there."

Chapter 24
Imprisoned

Bernadette didn't quite know what was bothering her. At first she thought her headaches were migraines. They would last a few hours, then subside, leaving her comatose for the rest of the night.

The incidents always occurred at night when she was preparing for bed. She began to fear even a hot evening shower, brushing and flossing her teeth, and applying moisturizing lotion to her hands and face, and using the toilet one last time before retiring. The ritual triggered a recurring reaction. She saw the mental image of a rising wave. The pain in her head intensified and exploded as the mountainous swell crashed over her, consuming her in a swirling miasma that forced her to her knees.

Gale Walsh, Ignatius Stroud, Father O'Herlihy, Richard Stoli, Jefferson and Candace Jergen, and Blade Maggoy were trapped in her imagination. They were no longer sentient beings, but each existed as a molecular mass in her neural system. Even subjected to torture by Simonetta, they had not completely died or dissipated into a state of nothingness. Their energy as neural impulses continued to persist, attempting to seek an escape. Bernadette's visual cortex and mental workspace in her brain would unexpectedly generate their images at their times of death, appear in her random thoughts, then vanish.

The vibratory energy of Simonetta's victims, suctioned from their physical bodies, were agitated at being imprisoned in Bernadette's imagination. She also now possessed their sensory levels, thoughts and memories without their physiological brains. Those unleashed impulses roamed in search of what had contained them and to which they would never again have access.

Their hissing, whispery accusations visited Bernadette in the chaos of her dreams repeating again and again, "You have taken us. You own us. We are part of you."

Simonetta had helped Bernadette take their lives, but she had not bargained on their recurring presence in Bernadette's mind.

Bernadette's mental workspace created devices to isolate them as neural radical forms of psychic disease and keep them unsettled and wandering. Without a living purpose, they mutated into the dark spirits she had unsuccessfully attempted to conjure as a teenage girl and now appeared as festering scars within her mind.

"I don't want them there inside me," she told Simonetta through her thoughts. "They're haunting me. How can I get rid of them? I don't know what to do."

"Turn them into your dreams and together we will remove them from your mind forever and send them to the dark energy realm where they belong."

Gale Walsh's voice encouraged her to transfer large sums of money from one of his private accounts into her own. "You have access. You know the codes. You will have enough money to retire as a millionaire. In her dream, she made the transfers. Simonetta turned the mountain of money into green powder and transformed Gale into a bank card the size of a man. Bernadette inserted it into a large ATM and he was gone. She woke from her dream.

In another dream, a large snake, an anaconda with the face of Father O'Herlihy began crushing Bernadette in its coils. Simonetta appeared and severed the head with a gleaming steel blade. The head rolled away followed by the thrashing coils trying to reattach itself until both disappeared, plunging into a sewer drain. Bernadette woke from her dream.

In another dream, Richard Stoli tried to bury her in a grave along with cans of black spray paint. Simonetta appeared and raised a hurricane force wind. He suddenly replaced Bernadette in the grave which filled with oozing black paint. He tried to escape and climb out, but the liquid churned. The paint was sucked into the earth and he disappeared. Bernadette woke from her dream.

In another dream, Ignatius Stroud was chasing her through the empty streets of a deserted city. He carried an automatic rifle, but was not able to fix her in its site to shoot and kill her. On one street, a mob of children armed with assault rifles poured out of the surrounding buildings. As Ignatius rounded the corner, they opened fire and riddled him with holes until his body was ground into bloody pulp. Bernadette woke from her dream.

In another dream, Jefferson and Candace Jergen motioned her to follow them into a desert landscape. Sneering, they moved quickly away and left her standing at the center of a mine field. The mines at her feet slowly emerged from the ground as pink mushrooms the size of a stool. She sat on one and watched as Jefferson and Candace each sat on another. A moment later, their mushrooms exploded with a roar and concussion that obliterated them. Bernadette woke from her dream.

In her sixth and final dream, Bernadette saw a mob of naked young women brandishing knives chase down Blade Maggoy and hack him to death. She woke from her dream.

Hieronymous Blum saw six impulses appear in the whirling morass of his digital dark energy reservoir. With the release of energy from the six dreams, he was able to detect and locate Bernadette and Simonetta.

Mars waited just outside the Walsh Investments building lobby in downtown Manhattan and followed Bernadette when she left her office. During her ride on the subway, she caught a glimpse of him watching her. At the next stop, she stepped off the subway with the exit crowd, walked quickly to a nearby hotel and called Berzinsky on her cell phone.

"I'm being followed by someone. I need protection. I'm afraid he'll try to kill me."

"Where are you right now?"

"The Regent Hotel about four blocks from where I work. I don't see him, but he's probably hiding. If I get back on the subway, he'll follow me home."

"Are you hidden where he can't see you?"

"I don't know. I think so. I'm in a crowd of people in the hotel lobby. I'm walking into the restaurant now where there are more people."

"Stay with me on your phone. Don't disconnect. A police unit will be there to get you in ten minutes."

"I'll watch for them. I won't move."

"Don't go out. They'll come inside to get you."

Pretending he was a customer, Mars told the hostess he would return in a moment for a table. He followed Bernadette to the restroom, but she saw him maneuvering across the dining room through the crowded tables and detoured out the back door.

When the police arrived, she had disappeared. The lead officer informed Berzinsky on a radio phone.

Talking into her cell phone, Bernadette told Berzinsky the man had seen her and was coming after her. She had left the hotel and was running down the street. He ordered her to stay connected but her phone battery died. She looked around and ran up the steps to enter St. Stephens Cathedral. She joined a tour in process. Half-listening to the tour guide telling about the architecture, she kept an eye on the front entrance and saw Mars enter the church.

Bernadette split off from the tour group and rushed to the rectory. She noticed a nun's habit hanging on a rack and hurriedly pulled on the habit, coif and wimple. Through a side door, she went back out to the main street and entered a deli. She told the counterman she needed to use the phone to report an emergency, and contacted Berzinsky again. This time, she waited for him and Leon to come to her along with five police officers.

As the police units sped along back streets to confuse whoever might be following, Bernadette asked, "Where are you taking me?"

Mars hailed a cab and ordered the driver to follow the three police units, but they out distanced the cab. Through his cell phone, he reported the situation to Hiram.

"They're too far ahead. I don't see them. They're gone."

"I've got them located and I'm tracking them," said Hieronymous Blum. "Wait a minute. The image is breaking up. It's not clear where they are. There's a force shield blocking our signal. We've encountered a barrier," he said. "There's an invisible counterforce. I can't get through it."

"This has to be Simonetta's gateway to escape and hide in one of her simulated worlds," said Hiram. "It has to be. It's the only way she can disappear."

Chapter 25
Fourth Dimension

Unknown to Hiram and Hieronymous, they were competing with the magician. Max Schultz detected the attempts by Hieronymous Blum to hack into Simonetta's world by drawing her out in the guise of Bernadette, who had become a spiritual warrioress in the simulation. Through Bernadette, she possessed the magical fourth dimension powers of time and space.

Max explained to her, "You have taken Simonetta away from them and made her your own. That is why they want to kill you. You have recreated her in your own imaginary and real world. She exists as a product of your imagination and now you control her. She no longer controls you. In the world of imagination, dark energy forces influence and control the dark side of humanity. You are their opposite. You have challenged and confronted them and now they are trying to destroy you. What we are going to see happening in the SIM is happening in our own real world."

Max took digital videos of Bernadette and Bram and inserted them as characters in the SIM. The special camera had the technology to include psychological, as well as physiological features of their personae through the injection of a chip smaller than a grain of rice that was transmitted through the bloodstream to the brain. The risk was that they now carried a live link to their avatar existence in the SIM and if their avatars were killed, they in reality would die.

With Berzinsky and Leon watching the scenarios, Max directed and manipulated Bernadette's and Bram's SIM characters, (including duplicating and creating multiple versions used to confuse and deter Hieronymous and Mars, if necessary). He took them down blind alleys that would disorient them in their search for the one true Bernadette who concealed Simonetta's warrioress spirit.

Bram and Bernadette were about to embark on a journey. Bram's discovery would be used to intervene with a DNA antidote that would spread and eradicate the black spiral DNA. Bernadette's objective was to take down and destroy the First World Corporation.

In the First World Corporation command center, Hiram Bean and Hieronymous Blum watched Mars Livingston walk away from the waterfront harbor where Bernadette had disappeared without a trace. She could be concealed in any one of a long line of warehouses. He wasn't aware that he had encountered an invisible impenetrable shield that allowed him to pass through as he walked the length of the dock, but to see nothing out of the ordinary, longshoremen loading and unloading tankers, and acres of stacked containers.

"Here's what I have on her," Hieronymous Blum projected the wall-sized static image of an empty arid plain stretching to a pale blue horizon that morphed into the planet earth slowly rotating in space. "Simonetta can create anything she wants in that four dimensional digital canvas. We only see this image, because it is the link we established when we created her. She somehow managed to sever that link, but that location is where she must return to dispose of her victims. I don't have any way to access where she is beyond it, because she has imagined herself into other scenarios, other worlds. We are essentially locked out by her mental and spiritual barriers hidden deep within the imagination of Bernadette Garcetti. We cannot just hack in to her worlds, as the case may be. They come from her mind."

"We have to find an opening, an access, a way for Mars to infiltrate and break through to get to her," said Hiram. "We have to create a reality SIM model for Mars that we operate and control.

That image we see, the planet earth, is our playing field, our battle ground."

Now inside their SIM, Bernadette and Bram left their jeep parked at the same trail head in Vermont where Bernadette had visited years ago following her graduation from college. They walked along the same worn dirt path and heard the same voices ahead of unseen children laughing and calling to each other that merged with a bubbling stream through the woods and sounded like they could have been spirits.

They followed the stream to where it flowed into a clear lake that caught the refracted rays of the mid-morning sun.

"Where are we?" Bram looked down the grassy hill that bordered the shore of a lake until it merged with deciduous broad leaf trees, oaks and maples and elms.

"I'm not sure," said Bernadette. "But I've been here once before, many years ago, just after I graduated from college. I think we're in a memory."

"It's a peaceful place, calm and beautiful."

"I feel safe and secure here," she said.

A warm breeze caressed the surface of the water that stretched three miles across to the far shore.

They paused to sit for a while among a field of wildflowers. The voices of the children faded as they moved on accompanied by their mother and father. She spotted them briefly coming into view and passing from sight among the dense forest on the curve of the opposite shore.

A medley of bird song rippled from the tall meadow grass and surrounded them with cadenzas of warbling notes. "They could be spirits," she said, "if I want them to be."

They returned to their jeep at the trail head and drove on into the countryside along narrow back roads through rolling maple tree forested hills and fields punctuated by occasional farms and signature landmark white church steeples of small towns until they came to the house. She remembered the house being a warm solid place built of stone near a faded red barn and silo and a few sheds bordered by fenced enclosures that used to contain pigs and chickens.

They saw the skeletons of the old woman sitting on her chair and her dog crumpled on the wooden front porch, and the scattered bones of a flock of sheep.

"What we see here is from my memory," said Bernadette, "but the images have changed over time. I had a wonderful visit with the old woman and her dog when they were alive. Her name was Maggie Bischoff. Her dog's name was Jasper. He herded the sheep in that pasture." Bernadette described her chance encounter. "At that time, she wore those silver bracelets and hoop earrings we see that reminded me of a gypsy. She said that by her living out here the darkness couldn't find her."

I remember saying to her, "You'll probably laugh, but I came out here looking for spirits."

"Not a laughing matter," she had said, "except what tickles your fancy."

"I remember our conversation," said Bernadette. "I can recreate it in my mind."

"So you believe in their existence?" I had asked.

"I know they exist," she said. "They're all around us. I'm in touch with 'em daily."

I said, "I tried to find them out in the woods, but I didn't see any."

"Depends on what spirits yer lookin' for."

I had asked her, "What did you mean when you said the darkness can't find you here?"

"The dark spirits hunt for those of us who live in the light. They inhabit humans who never know they are there."

"And you truly believe that."

"I do."

"I wanted to believe that, but I was told it's just my imagination," I had said. "They don't really exist except in my mind."

"It's not just imagination. They are there. The evidence is what you see, how they

turn people and manipulate them to perform acts large and small that will bring about our downfall. We have to be vigilant to stop them."

"How do you mean vigilant?"

"We have to defend ourselves from the destruction they bring to life."

"You mean when they break the law."

"Yes, and to stop them from continuing."

"How do we do that?" I had asked.

"You see signs of it with young people and others who've suffered loss, the violent sacrifice in the name of hate, greed, and corruption and lies committed by those with twisted minds who lead twisted lives."

"There are people trying to change things," I had said. "They're in the news everyday."

"They meet with resistance," said Maggie. "Those who resist the betterment of lives stop the efforts to change, because they have power. They have money. Money is their god."

"I'm only one person. What can I possibly do against them?"

"You have to discover that in yourself, in who you are. That is where your spirit lives."

"In who I am?"

"Yes."

"I gave up on spirits a long time ago," I told her.

"You gave up on dark spirits. That's a good thing. Now you are open to what you came here on your search to find."

"But I haven't really found anything."

"She will come to you."

"She?"

"You are a woman."

"But I'm not a spirit. I'm flesh and blood."

"Your spirit lives in you. She has not yet come fully alive. You will know when she does."

"I don't understand. How will I know?"

"By your deeds, the acts you perform," she said.

"I'm just going back to New York and try to find a job."

"That is a step along the way. Your journey began when you were a child."

"You mean going to the bookstore?"

"What did you find in the bookstore? You talked to a woman there."

"It was about a book I bought, The Dark Arts."

"That was the beginning. Until you recognize the dark spirits, you will not recognize the spirit in you that will fight against them."

"Are you saying I should join some protest movement?"

"You already have, Dear. You already have."

Bernadette turned to Bram. "And now here I am. Here we are. I became what she predicted."

"We're being hunted," said Bram. "We can't stay long. I have a plan. It's dangerous, but it's our only way to fight back. For now, we need to keep moving."

Bram turned the jeep around. They bumped along over the ruts of the washed out gravel driveway to the road.

"Where are we going?" asked Bernadette.

"To see a friend of mine. We did research together at Unicell. He left a year before I did when he saw the intended use of black spiral DNA by the First World Corporation. I stayed on until I created the antidote and took it with me when I left a year later. They've been hunting me ever since."

"Who is your friend?"

"Tom Davenport. He's a micro-biologist who specializes in genetics and entomology. He did leading research on insect reproduction and evolution that contributed to my research."

"Where can we find him?"

"We have to leave the SIM to get to him."

"Go back outside? Can't we bring him in?"

"Not to do what we have to in the real world."

"Max said what we do inside can be transferred to the outside world."

"I understand we coexist, but we're going to have to cross the boundary between here and there to set the process in motion. When we reenter the SIM, we can bring the technology and the process with us and incrementally spread it in different regions of the world. We have to go outside to trigger it and put it in motion though. That's the dangerous part, working outside the SIM. In here, we can hide and move around nearly undetected. The SIM is open cyber territory, fair game. Someone at First World will be scanning it for evidence of where we are, what we're doing, and how to find us."

Chapter 26
Exit

"You're coming out," said Max. "You're exiting the SIM. If you have some other way to meet Tom Davenport, I'd recommend it. Outside the SIM, you are the most vulnerable to being detected." He swiveled around in his chair to face Bram and Bernadette who had emerged from the SIM and now stood before him in the warehouse studio.

"There isn't any other way," said Bram. "We have to start the process out here."

"Do you know where to find him or is he in hiding from First World, as well?"

"He lives in California, the Central Coast. He left the company a year before I made my discovery of the antidote. He provided experimental input for my research, but we didn't stay in contact after he left. I need him to help us take the next step.

"You'll have to keep a low profile," said Berzinsky. "How do you plan to get there? You need to stay clear of public places where it's easier for First World's satellite to locate you."

"How about a private jet out of a small regional airport?"

"We can help you with that," said Berzinsky. "What about protection?"

Bram looked at Bernadette. "Simonetta exists in her mind. If we're threatened, she'll protect us."

"An imaginary psychic force may not be consistent, not a sufficiently strong impulse," said Leon. "I'm still having a difficult time accepting the idea."

"We've seen what she's capable of," said Max. "And now that you've witnessed the dynamics of the SIM, you should be convinced that what we are doing here is more than an illusion."

"I don't disbelieve it," said Leon. "I never thought illusion and reality could become so integrated that they are one and the same."

"Not for everyone. It depends on the individual. Bernadette is one of the unique ones. Her brain receptors function way beyond those of an average person."

"I understand that. I see what is happening and I have to believe what I see. It's just beyond the realm of my medical and scientific experience."

"I don't think any of us here believe in religious faith," said Max. "For what is happening, you have to believe in and have faith in magic which is just as real or no more real than religious faith. First World has turned that corner and created a new paradigm through dark energy. We're living in a psychic world."

***

Amidst a cloud of bees filling the air with a high-pitched whining buzz, Tom Davenport opened the top of the hive. Defending drones swarmed up and coated his arms protected by thick elbow length gloves and clung to his mesh mask and white beekeeper's suit rendering him the appearance of some extraterrestrial being.

He lifted the top bar of one of a dozen frames from which hung wax combs constructed of hexagonal cells filled with honey, small white larvae, and pollen.

He inspected the lowest box section of the hive, the brood box, and observed the queen bee was continuing to lay eggs. The hive was healthy and she would be able to produce for her third and final year.

He moved on to the next pink painted box hive identified with the black number twenty on one side. Set out in a fenced pasture among grassy foothills facing a backdrop of the dark chaparral green Santa Ynez Mountains, the hives provided Tom not only with honey, but genetic information.

His bees gathered nectar from purple sage, manzanita, ceanothus, and wind swept fields carpeted with golden wild mustard, orange and red poppies, blue lupines, and a range of wildflowers that added fragrant aromas to the honey they produced. Sacs of a variety of microscopic pollens adhering to the bee's spiny legs and antennae provided food to the colonies and the material for Tom's independent genetic research in agricultural production.

The pollen was a microscopic fine coarse powder containing male gametophytes which produced the sperm cells in seed plants. The hard coat of the pollen grains protected the sperm cells as they were moved on the legs and appendages of bees and other insects from the stamens to the pistils of flowering plants. The sperm was transferred to the ovule, female gametophyte which became the new seed.

A large male Golden Retriever leaped up from where he had been waiting a respectable distance from the hives and pranced beside him, as Tom carried thirteen combs in a wooden crate to a white Toyota Tundra pickup truck. Tom removed and stored his protective bee suit along with the crate in the truck bed.

Furiously wagging his banner tail, the dog waited patiently for Tom to open the cab door, then bounded up to occupy the passenger seat.

As he drove slowly along the rutted dirt road across the pasture, sun rays sliced through the receding coastal fog casting variegated moving shadows over the landscape. He had selected the location for its Mediterranean climate and proliferation of natural plants, live oaks, pines, and wildflowers that provided abundant food sources for bees. He had bought the ranch nine years ago, and within the past year had quit his job at the Unicell Laboratories in the Silicon Valley south of San Francisco and moved to his ranch near the small Central Coastal town of Buellton.

Through the truck windshield, Tom saw a black suburban turn off the distant backcountry road and progress at a crawl through several vineyard covered acres along the half mile gravel driveway. He slightly increased the truck's speed on a downward slope, as the suburban stopped near the modest stucco and tile house and four passengers stepped out, three men and a woman. He saw his wife come out onto the front porch to greet them. Her long blonde hair whipped in the wind as she gestured back up the hill behind the house at his approaching truck.

Drawing closer he recognized Bram Vernon among the visitors. He drove past the barn and corral and parked next to a tractor in the open yard. The dog slipped past Tom exiting the cab and filled the air with thunderous enthusiastic barks as he bounded over to the group.

His wife waved her hand at the dog. "Tuck, hush, quiet. It's okay. He's friendly, just loud," her lilting laugh reassured them. He sniffed their shoes with aggressive snorts.

"Is it okay to pet him?" asked Bernadette.

"Wait 'til he's done checking you out. He'll love to have you pet him." She turned as Tom joined her, his curiosity raised by the two men in black suits standing next to the car.

Bram offered a broad smile of recognition. "Sorry I couldn't call you in advance, but we're keeping a low profile. Tom, this is Bernadette Garcetti. Tom Davenport."

He shook her extended hand. "Very nice to meet you, Bernadette."

"Nice to meet you, Tom. Bram has told me a little about you."

"Hope it wasn't all bad."

"Not in the least."

"I guess you've met my wife, sort of. Mindy."

"Yes, Bram introduced us."

"So why are you keeping a low profile? Running from the cops? On the lam?" He chuckled.

"These two gentlemen with us are cops, FBI agents. No, trying to avoid a killer. He doesn't know we're here, but he's trying to find us. We can't stay long. I have a favor to ask."

"I'll do anything I can for you, but can you explain about the killer?"

Bram motioned the two agents to come forward. "These are Agents Berzinsky and Saffulo from New York."

They nodded, but did not offer to shake hands. Tom raised his in greeting. "Witness Protection?"

"Yes, I guess you could call it that. Whistle blower protection is closer to it."

"From First World and Unicell," said Tom.

"Yes, you still have your lab out back?"

Tom nodded. "Independent research." The expression in his brown eyes intensified. "You must be here because of the black spiral."

Bram studied his friends longish features, a slightly crooked nose and strong jaw. "A year after you left, I discovered the antidote."

Tom's boyish grin revealed a flash of perfect white teeth against his weathered tan. "And you never called me?" He pushed back an unruly lock of blonde hair. Bram remembered that both their son and daughter were blonde.

"Couldn't. Had to go underground. I took everything with me I could. All the research documentation, the software, everything. They didn't have the final results. I had to keep moving, destroy my credit cards, encrypt all my messages. Change cities, locations. No mail box. No cell phone. Slowed me down, but they couldn't find me until now. They found Bernadette and she unknowingly led them to me. I'll tell you about it in the lab. She's at the center of my plan."

"We don't have to stand around out here," said Mindy. "Why don't we go inside." She removed the green apron loosely tied over her snug-fitting jeans and dark blue polo shirt that matched her husband's.

"This is a quick stop," said Bram. "Don't even have time for a beer."

"Follow me," Tom started walking toward a gray wood framed outbuilding attached to the back wall of the three car garage.

"How are your kids?" Bram asked as he matched Tom's stride.

"Jeff's started his third year in pre-med at Standford and Samantha's in law school."

"You and Mindy are lucky. You have it all."

"Don't really know what that means. We're fortunate, grateful. You and Bernadette – ah – together?"

Bram glanced back over his shoulder at Bernadette, who was petting and talking to the dog a short distance behind. "Don't know yet. We're together in one sense. We need each other to survive. I think I need her more than she needs me."

Leon and Berzinsky remained standing by the car. Mindy had gone back inside the house.

"Sounds like a winning combination. How did you meet?"

"You probably won't believe when I tell you."

"Let me grab the combs from the back of my truck." Tom returned with the box containing the honeycombs. "I was out harvesting. I'm a scientist, but I'll give you the benefit of the doubt."

"There's a paranormal side to this."

"You mean the dark energy theory you always talked about?"

"It's more than a theory."

"A theory nevertheless, unproven."

"I have the proof and Bernadette is the other part of the proof."

Tom smiled. "She's a brunette. Does that mean she's from the dark side?"

"It's not a laughing matter. The First World Corporation is only a front. It's a gateway to the existence and phenomena of dark energy forces, quantum physics, not fictitious spirits. Black Spiral DNA is the source of dark energy beings in the form of humans. One of them is hunting us with the intent to kill us."

"Which accounts for your escorts, I take it. Obviously, they're convinced."

Bram nodded. "We wouldn't be here without them."

They reached the lab building and Tom balanced the box between his body and the wall so he could open the door. "Judging from the fact you have two Federal agents with you, there must be something real going on. I acknowledge there's more out there than we know about. I'm open-minded to that."

Bernadette and the dog followed them into the lab fully resourced with a library of glassware neatly arranged on wall hooks and in cabinets, a variety of labeled buffer solutions, a manometer, calibrated balance scales, a hood to vent toxic chemical fumes to the outside, a dozen microscopes, petrie dishes, a hotplate, refrigerator, and an oven.

Tom set the box on a stainless steel side table, then individually removed the honeycombs and hung them in radial baskets in a large cylindrical extractor that applied centrifugal force to the upper end of the combs and ejected the honey from the hexagonal wax cells. The honey dripped and flowed to the bottom of the extractor for collection.

"Tell me about your antidote," said Tom. "Do you have a sample with you?"

Bram removed a small insulated wooden box containing a sealed vial of the antidote in a viscous solution.

"We need to introduce this into bee pollen to distribute through the food chain. It's one of many ways I'm planning to do this, not just seed plants, but in sources and bodies of water, wells, aquifers, filters and air dispersal systems. First World is producing seed contaminated with black spiral DNA that is being planted in agricultural regions of different countries. I'm trying to be one step ahead of them."

"How are you going to do that?"

Bram looked at Bernadette. "With her."

"What can she do?"

"She's a spiritual medium, an envoy into that other world."

"I'd like to say I believe you, Bram, but I do have doubts. Regardless, I'm going to help you. Those two Federal agents somehow lend credence to what you're telling me."

"Thank you. I didn't think you'd tell me I'd lost it and should check in to a mental institution."

"Even if I thought you were bonkers, which you're not, I'd support you, knowing your research and knowing how disreputable and corrupt First World is. That's why I left Unicell. I'm open to phenomena and possibilities beyond the limited use of the human brain. I just hope your antidote works."

"It works at the laboratory level. Now comes the field test. I need bees and other insects, animals, all kinds of biodiversity to spread it throughout the planet. Once it becomes part of the human organism, the act of reproduction will supplant the black spiral DNA. The reproduction of plants is only the beginning."

Bram briefly explained features of the antidote's genetic structure recounting how he had cut the DNA fragments and separated them by electrophoresis. He had applied an external electric field to the electric surface charge of the particles suspended in a solution. The DNA migration pattern created a genetic fingerprint from which he could identify overlapping DNA stretches in clones and sequence the clones to reveal the DNA sequence of the organism.

"The black spiral didn't have any relationship and I couldn't trace it to a biological form. That's when I began exploring what I suspected was a missing branch of the evolutionary tree.

There's an unexplained branch linked to the black spiral helix. The research you and I conducted at Unicell was for new synthetic pharmaceutical drugs and nutritional substances and genetic hormones that could be introduced into the human food chain. Of course, we weren't told about that. It was management's secret.

I discovered the black spiral helix during the physical mapping of a DNA sample in a substance First World planned to introduce into seeds and plant forms, fertilizers and water tables. They intended to distribute it through ocean currents and have it assimilated into the food chain of marine life forms, and consumed by species of fowl and mammals from grains and grasses. The harvested and processed food sources would then be consumed by humans and assimilated into their genetic DNA and passed along to their children and grandchildren."

"What you're describing fits in to the First World global seed management plan some call a conspiracy."

"Turns out it is a conspiracy."

Both Tom and Bram knew of the attempt of agricultural breeders to establish plant variety rights issued at the national level that gave the breeder exclusive ownership and marketing control over the seed material and the harvested material, including all plants that demonstrated the unique botanical characteristics. The varieties were stabilized by genetically arranging the characteristics so they did not change from one generation to the next.

Tom delicately gripped the small glass vial that Bram handed to him. "It will take me about an hour to prepare the pollen for you. The others are welcome to wait at the house."

"Thank you, we'll stay," said Leon.

Tom pulled on a white lab coat and handed a second one to Bram, who opened the polyethylene bag and removed it. Wearing latex gloves, Tom began selecting a variety of pollens from small jars stored in a particle and temperature controlled glass front cabinet. He placed tiny samples in Petri dishes under three different microscopes and motioned for Bram to view them. Using an eye dropper, he then applied one drop of the antidote solution to each of the pollen samples and invited Bram to observe the chemical interaction through the scopes. He repeated the process sixty-seven more times to complete a set of seventy-two glass vials containing different pollen varieties. He arranged sixty in slots of protective foam packaging inside a wooden crate and enclosed the remaining twelve in an aluminum carrying case.

"I don't know how well this is going to work," said Tom, "but I'll send samples to research labs I exchange data with in several foreign countries."

"Which ones?"

"Most prominently, Central and South America, South Africa, India, Australia, and Southeast Asia. They can seed plants with the treated pollen and infuse the DNA antidote in ecological plant systems and work it into the food chain. I don't know what their level of interest will be, except for Raul Cortez in Argentina. We did research together at Stanford. He's the most open-minded, especially about stopping plant variety rights. He says it's a corrupt scheme to control the world-wide seed market. "

"So you believe this is possible?"

"I believe it's worth trying. I believe you."

"Thanks." Bram gave him five.

With Berzinsky at the wheel of the suburban, Leon Safullo, Bram, and Bernadette drove in silence to the Santa Maria regional airport where they boarded the Government Lear Jet for their return to New York.

The hypothetical nature of what they were undertaking continued to disturb Leon, since there was no concrete evidence that would allow them to investigate the First World Corporation. The Attorney General in Washington had said there was no indication from IRS records and the financial history and operations of the company that it engaged in political corruption and tax evasion schemes like other major U.S. corporations.

Leon's and Berzinsky's involvement with Bernadette and Bram had plunged them into an unknown paradigm outside the reality in which they lived and functioned. Although they continued to search for some pragmatic condition to anchor their investigation, they had come up with nothing but the pressure to accept a paranormal phenomena in which they did not want to believe, but now had no alternative but to acknowledge.

With the Suburban lights on low beam, Leon and Berzinsky drove slowly along a deserted back street that paralleled the waterfront dock until they came to the warehouse. They had dozed on the return flight from California and were on the alert from the moment their private Jet had hit the tarmac at Kennedy International Airport and taxied over to the secure remote terminal.

Berzinsky had phoned ahead to Max to let them know they were on the way and called again when they arrived for Max to open a garage access door so they could drive into the warehouse and keep the vehicle hidden.

Overcome with anxiety, Bram and Bernadette had not rested well during the flight. They did not relax until they were inside the warehouse and greeted by Max, who escorted the four of them upstairs to his studio. His news ratcheted up their fears. They sat in a semi-circle and viewed Max's large screen.

"We are seeing a preview of what First World has begun in the real world and the campaign and onslaught of what is to come. The SIM provides a mirror of what is beginning to happen. I suspect the events are also an attempt to draw you out, Bernadette, so they can excise and capture Simonetta from your mind, from your imagination, and destroy her by killing you. And, Bram, they will do everything they can to stop you from putting the black spiral DNA conversion into effect."

In the distance, a coal fire plant spewed nitrous oxide into the atmosphere while in the foreground, sporadic explosions of flame from subterranean toxic chemicals dotted the arid landscape. The view shifted following the clouds of toxic gases into a thinning shredded ozone layer and swirled into a maelstrom of storms, hurricanes destroying shoreline cities and tornadoes roaring across prairie land ripping up trees like bones from sockets of the earth, shattering homes like so much kindling and reducing buildings to rubble.

Street fighting, suddenly filled the screen, rock throwing citizens in a Middle-Eastern city bludgeoned by paramilitary police, exploding vehicles, a helicopter wheeling overhead strafing the crowd with automatic gunfire, people running and screaming in pain and anguish as their limbs were torn apart spurting gouts of blood.

The view panned across a body of ocean water where millions of dead fish carpeted the surface clear to the horizon.

An oil pipeline bisected a tract of denuded forest and snaked across thousands of acres of once fertile, now dead, farmland dotted with ponds of toxic waste left behind from hydraulic fracturing.

The momentum of the view pulled them along tributaries to the Mississippi River and down to the Gulf of Mexico, now a dead sea in which plants and marine life no longer flourished.

Brandishing rifles, handguns, and knives, marauding gangs roamed deserted city streets lined with shards of broken glass from windowless store fronts. Controlled by drug lords, harems of women and girls were kept imprisoned for sex in what had once been high end hotels.

Nomadic tribes of modern citizens roamed the countryside hunting game and foraging for food through forests and across farmlands fallen into disintegration and decay. Pets and small animals were killed and butchered, cooked over fires and eaten. Suburban dwellers lived in neighborhoods sectioned off by barriers of steel concertina wire and fortified with militia guards armed with assault rifles. Residents were bused daily to work in government controlled factories and on government farms.

The communities of the wealthy elite had become armed fortresses behind steel walls scanned by surveillance cameras and protected by Government soldiers who maintained a steady stream of food and supplies flown in daily on military aircraft from the government farms. Masses of men, women, and children survived in military controlled FEMA camps for displaced populations.

Fractured roads and highways pocked with holes and jagged trenches and collapsed bridges sagged into polluted rivers.

In third world countries, dictators waged brutal bloody wars against their citizens to suppress uprisings.

The waves of rising seas eroded waterfront land masses and washed away coastal cities and towns tossing their floating debris and drowned bodies in an incremental steady assault.

"The world doesn't entirely fit that picture and the conditions of what we are watching. If the political oligarchy seizes power, what we see will become the new reality. If you can reverse what First World is moving into position through their covert dark energy invasion, you might not stop the destruction and collapse, but you might be able to prevent it from consuming and changing the existence of humanity and the environment of the planet."

"Where will you send us?" asked Bram. "How will we begin?"

Chapter 27
Seeding

The Mid-west summer heat and humidity left them feeling displaced and unfamiliar with the hundreds of acres of corn fields, dense armies of green stalks taller than a man, occasionally interrupted by sweeping vistas of hay and grain fields and pastures dotted with grazing herds of black and white spotted dairy cattle.

A hot wind rushed through the open window enveloping them with the sweet greenish scent of freshly turned loamy soil and new mown hay. A ring-necked pheasant rose up out of the cornfield ahead of them in an explosion of variegated rust and gold plumage tipped with black extending into its long trailing tail feathers. The bird lifted in a graceful arc high over the moving jeep and descended into the wall of corn stalks on the other side of the road.

Bram steered the jeep around a large pothole in the narrow two lane country road.

"It's beautiful out here," said Bernadette. "So quiet and peaceful. I could live in that little town we passed through a few miles back."

"If we didn't have to travel so far and cover so many places, we could take a few days." Bram and Max had brought up different regions of the planet with concentrated agricultural resources and riparian wilderness and windswept desert terrains that supported natural populations of bees. The dispersion of Bram's DNA treated pollen had to be strategically global so that its influence in botanical reproduction cycles could not be reversed or destroyed by chemical plant killers and pesticides.

Bram noticed a cluster of beehives in a pasture adjacent to a farmhouse set back from the road. Miles of flowers commingled with vast acres of hay and wheat dotted the surrounding fields. He pulled the jeep over to the side of the road and turned off the engine.

Stepping out of the jeep, he reached back to the driver's seat and opened the aluminum brief case containing the first twelve of the pollen vials. The wooden crate rode concealed under a tarp in the back section of the jeep. He smiled up at Bernadette.

"Like to join me?"

She got out on the passenger side and walked around the jeep.

"Hold out your hand. Be careful. It's precious stuff, worth more than gold." He tipped the vial and sifted a small pile of pollen dust into her open palm. She gently closed her hand around it.

They each walked several steps in opposite directions along the shoulder of the road and gently scattered the minute pollen grain particles from the tips of their fingers into the wind that lifted and carried them across the landscape and randomly deposited them floating down on the warm currents to cling to plants and settle into the open blooms of flowers where the small yellow and black bodies of bees clambered over the pistils and stamens depositing the new generation of pollen and disseminating it clinging to their spiny legs in their lazy drift from flower to flower.

Bram and Bernadette returned to the jeep. Bram closed up the aluminum case and tucked it away on the floor of the back seat. "It's a beginning," he said, as he started the engine. "Want to get some pie and coffee at that café back in town?"

"Sounds good. Do you think it will all be this easy?"

"At least until we're discovered. Max said First World doesn't know we've re-entered the SIM and we have the ability to stay one step ahead of them, as long as we keep moving." Bram executed a tight U-turn. There was no traffic to be seen.

"What's your favorite kind of pie?" Bernadette draped her elbow out her open window.

"Apple, what's yours?"

"Custard. I'm a real sucker for custard. I used to help my mother make it when I was a little girl. I did most of the stirring until my arm got tired. I got to scrape the bowl and lick the spoon."

"Where did you grow up?"

"New York City, The Bronx."

"You talk like a New Yorker."

"What is that supposed to mean?"

"Your accent."

"Do you like it?"

Bram grinned. "Yeah, I like it. It's cute."

"Cute, I never thought of myself as cute."

"Well, actually, you're beautiful," he paused, "sexy."

"Hoo – whoa, watch what you say."

"Did I offend you?"

"Not at all. No one has ever said that to me before."

Bram glanced at her. "You're joking. I would have thought you had lots of boyfriends, guys stumbling all over themselves just to ask you out on a date."

"I never dated much, once or twice."

"Once or twice. I can't believe it."

"It's true. I've never been comfortable with men."

"Are you saying?"

"No, I'm not a lesbian. I mean socially comfortable."

"Well, I hope I'm not threatening or intimidating."

"No, you're the first man I've met in years I'm okay with. Maybe it's because we've been thrown into this together, but I feel all right with you," the corner of her mouth curled up in a sidewise grin, "kinda like pals."

"Pals?"

"Maybe more than pals," Bernadette smiled. "Just give it time."

"That sounds promising. You're not like anyone I've ever met."

"I'm not like anyone you've ever met or will ever meet."

"Makes me feel special," said Bram. "By the way, who is Simonetta? Max kept bringing up her name."

"She sometimes lives with me, in my head, my mind. She's a powerful force who inhabits my mind and body when I want her to, when I call on her."

"You are different." Bram laughed. "Remind me never to cross you."

"It's not a good idea, but don't worry. I activate her only for big important reasons. She's an executioner. Through me, she brings consequences to people infected with the dark influences. She dispenses justice."

"I don't see you carrying any lethal weapons."

"Simonetta is my weapon. She crossed over from the First World. She's a vigilante, a rogue spirit on the good side. She's like you, only your weapon is science. Hers is punishment and revenge."

"Will I ever meet her?"

"I can't say."

"That's okay. Only if you want me to."

"Only if she wants me to."

"Understood. No further questions, except, where did she come from? Where did you find her?"

"My imagination. I saw her in a painting in an art museum. Her image stayed with me. That's all I can tell you. I don't have any more of an understanding than that, myself. I've never been able to explain her to myself. I just accept the fact that I have her gift. What about you? Where did you come from? How did you get here?"

"Not from someone's imagination, that's for sure. The old fashion way. I had a mom and dad. They had sex and got me."

"That explains it. Where did you live?"

"Southern California."

"How did you come by your interest in science?"

"I was strongly influenced by my mom, who was a biology teacher, and my dad, who was a math teacher in the same high school."

"Were you a nerd? You don't look like one."

"No, not a physical nerd. Both my parents were athletic. They swam, ran, and played tennis and they didn't let me spend a lot of time sitting at a computer. I had to swim, run, and play tennis with them. So I inherited their physical attributes, as well."

"You don't seem to have a problem with what we've gotten into."

"Dark energy and quantum physics are a scientific reality. I don't know how the people at First World, if they are a human cross-over, attached themselves to it, or however they came into being except that my research discovered them as an evolutionary anomaly, a psycho-spiritual mutation that goes back millions of years and is embedded in many segments of human populations today. The creators of the First World Universe, I call them, are setting about germinating and awakening that black spiral DNA potential in humans who are the most susceptible to it. It's an insidious plot that is unstoppable unless my antidote can counteract it."

***

"I've located an antiviral impulse." Hieronymous Bloom pointed to a tiny blinking yellow blip on the global projection in the First World command center.

"Where is it coming from?"

"Argentina." Bloom maneuvered through a maze of floating touch controls. "It's near one of our seed factories."

"That can only be happening if the DNA antidote has been seeded. How did it get down there? We have to stop it. Put all the factories on alert. Contact Jaime at the plant. See if he has any information on who might be doing this in Argentina."

Several moments later, the three dimensional image of the middle-aged plant manager, Jaime Guerrero, appeared in Bloom's holographic sphere.

"Jaimie," we have a problem in your sector."

"Whatever it is, I'm not aware of it. Production has been running smoothly. We're making our quotas and seed shipments are going out on schedule."

"It has nothing to do with production. It's a competitive DNA antidote being introduced into the global food chain."

"I didn't know there was an antidote."

"We were aware of it and thought we had buried it. But it's active and we have to stop it. The effects are irreversible."

"And you say this is happening here. How?" Jaime broke into a sweat. "Our security systems and procedures are impregnable. Nothing can be smuggled into the plant, let alone into the process."

"I'm not blaming you. I'm just saying we've detected the presence of the antidote in your area. It may not be in the plant, but it's certainly nearby."

"How near?"

"About a one hundred mile radius," said Bloom.

"That covers a lot of agricultural land, mostly grains."

"Do you have any suspects?" asked Hiram.

After a thoughtful pause, Jaime spoke. "There is one, probably the only one. We employ a lot of local people here, about three hundred. They haven't raised any complaints, but there is one who has in the past. Raul Cortez. He's a scientist at the university."

"What kind of scientist?"

"Genetic research. When we first built the plant here, he spoke out against us in the media."

"But you took care of that," said Hiram.

"We did. He stood to lose his funding if he didn't keep his mouth shut."

"So he's been quiet until now."

"He hasn't said anything recently, and we keep him under tight surveillance."

"You need to take a closer look. See what he's up to, if he's the one."

"How would he come across this antidote?"

"It was invented here. What it is and how it happened is proprietary. We know of only one source here in the States and we're tracking it. Have security make an unannounced visit at his home. He needs to feel some pressure."

"I'll get on it."

"And by the way, you're doing a fine job."

"Gracias, I appreciate hearing that from you." Jaime's image pixilated and disappeared from the room.

When the UHL package arrived, Raul Cortez hesitated to respond to Tom Davenport in California. Argentina was nearly two continents away. Raul had cut off his email and phone communications one year ago when he realized the seed company had hired private investigators to spy on him. He had also received a threat to pull his research funding provided through a private bank linked to the seed company, even though the money was wire transferred to him from a medical nonprofit research organization in the United States.

He had not been surprised at the contents of Tom Davenport's letter. He was intrigued at the discovery of the DNA antidote to black spiral, whose existence he had always suspected, but of which he had never seen the conclusive evidence. He knew that black spiral had been a factor in Tom's leaving Unicell to do independent research. Tom didn't mention in the letter who had made the discovery of the antidote. He only asked that Raul strategically disseminate the pollen vials contained in the package for maximum coverage and exposure to bees and other entomological forms indigenous to the Argentine agricultural lands, forests, and grasslands, the *pampas.*

Knowing he was being watched, but unaware of the surveillance technology being used, he had to devise a distribution method that would minimize detection and not draw attention to himself.

Insistent dark eyes expressed Pia's love for Raul and Gianna, tempered with a clear intelligence inherited from her mother and father, who had migrated from Italy as children with their parents during World War II to escape Mussolini's fascist regime. She had been raised in Buenos Aires where her father taught mathematics in a university and her mother worked as a nurse.

She and Raul met as classmates attending the *educación secundaria.* They maintained a written correspondence while he was studying for a degree in micro-biology at Stanford University in California and she underwent training to become a nurse like her own mother.

Raul did not open the package inside the house, but went out to the barn where Pia and Gianna were grooming their horses after returning from an early evening ride. They were both ardent horsewomen, their compact athletic bodies suited to the rugged Gaucho style of riding *criollo* horses.

Wearing matching boots, leather chaps, *pampeano* hats, and red bandanas, they could have been taken for sisters, sharing the same high cheek bones and smooth olive complexion. Both wore their sleek dark hair tied back in a bun.

Pia noticed him standing at the open barn access to the adjacent paddock where she and Gianna had tied and unsaddled their horses. Brown dust rose in small explosive clouds as hard hoofs stamped to rid their legs of flies. The smell of fresh dung permeated the air. A flock of hens scratched and pecked for particles of wind blown chaff around the riders' boots.

"How was it?" Raul's wide grin underscored the twinkle of appreciation in his muddy blue eyes. A slightly bent nose injured during a soccer match as a youth lent an aura of amusement and sophistication on what would otherwise be a mischievous face crowned by tight curly dark hair.

"Good as always," Pia tossed a brush and curry comb into a nearby box hanging from a paddock cross bar.

"We saw a herd of deer, two foxes, and an armadillo," said Gianna.

"What have you been up to?" asked Pia. "You're holding a large package."

"Delivered an hour ago."

"From where?"

"My research friend in California."

"Thomas Davenport?"

"Thomas."

"What is it?"

"I'm going to show you. Then I'm going to ask you and Gianna to help me out."

"What's it about?"

"Bee pollen."

"Bee pollen?"

"Yes, our little friends."

"Are we discussing it over dinner?"

"No, out here in the barn. Want to keep it from prying ears."

Pia's expression hardened. "I wish there was something we could do about them."

"What's contained in this package is a step in that direction."

"You've got my attention. Gianna." Pia and her daughter followed Raul into the barn. Raul scattered more grain about for the hens to encourage their clucking.

To maximize the effect of the pollen distribution, Raul instructed his wife and daughter to discreetly disseminate the grains on different outings in different ecological terrains, some in the drier *pampas*, but a larger concentration in the humid zone in outlying areas in Buenos Aires province. For three successive weeks, they rode undetected through the back country, making periodic stops to let the pollen sift through their fingers and be scattered by the prevailing winds to settle among the indigenous plants and flowers, and skim the surface of streams that flowed into rivers and estuaries.

Raul hoped that the intended purpose of the pollen would turn out to be true.

Chapter 28
The Shield

"Another impulse is showing," said Blum. "This time, it's here in the States. That would have to be Bram Vernon and Bernadette Garcetti.

"Do you have a link?" asked Hiram.

"If I can pinpoint where it's coming from, I can get a fix on them and we can send Mars in after them."

"Can you detect what they're doing?" Hiram Bean left his chair and walked across the cavernous, subdued blue-glowing room to Blum.

"Not precisely, but judging from their location in the American heartland, Bram Vernon could be initiating his plan to counter the black spiral DNA. Why else would he be out there with Bernadette, which leads to the question, how did they meet? Who or what coordinated their partnership? Who is supporting and guiding them?"

"Can you find out?"

"I can't seem to lock in on them. Something is blocking our signal. Other than identifying their location, I can't track back to their source. Someone or some force is shielding and protecting them."

"Do you have enough information so Mars can find them?"

" We have only a weak signal, barely enough to send Mars to the general area. He'll have to track them on the ground from there."

"Do it then. We don't have time to waste. We have to stop them."

"We have another option that can help us."

"What is it?"

"We flood the digital media and airwaves with their photos as identified eco-terrorists who are polluting food and water sources with a toxic virus. If they are recognized, they can be arrested and incarcerated. If that happens, most of our task is done."

"Except the destruction of Simonetta and Bram Vernon and his antidote."

"Finding the source of the antidote is problematic. Once he starts disseminating it, its existence is irreversible."

"We can't let that happen. We have to block it."

"Send a communication to Mars. Give him the general location. He can take it from there."

***

Blum had given him little to go on. On the pretext of making a promotional visit to GRA clubs in the state of Iowa, he had been flown on a GRA private Lear jet from Washington, D.C. to Cedar Rapids where a black Mercedes Benz rental car awaited him. As soon as Mars drove out of the lot, Blum connected with him through the car's remote satellite phone and navigation system. Blum's voice directed his attention to highways and roads that took him out into the countryside. Two hours later, he passed the farm where Bram and Bernadette had stopped to scatter pollen.

"I'm here," he said. "Now what? There's nothing to see but cornfields and pastures in both directions. Do you have anything more?"

"There's a small town about ten miles up the road," said Blum. "I can't be certain they are there, but they were moving in that direction. It's a start."

Barney Hodgeson always took an interest when travelers passing through the small farm town stopped at his café, a breakfast, lunch, and supper mecca for regulars. He and his wife specialized in serving a variety of eggs, pancakes, ham, bacon, sausage, chicken fried steak, biscuits and gravy, hot open-faced sliced turkey and pork sandwiches and gravy mashed potatoes for lunch, and meat loaf, pot roast, beef stew, and thick juicy sirloin steaks with baked potatoes, peas, beans, and sweet corn for dinner. The draw of home cooked comfort food was only surpassed by Marie's pies.

He didn't recognize the man and woman wearing cargo pants and tan shirts bearing the insignia of the Iowa Department of Natural Resources as they parked their jeep in front of the café. Most other park and forestry officers serving the area he knew by name. As they entered, he welcomed them with a smile and directed them to the nearest unoccupied table. Only a few mid-morning customers, an elderly man and wife, and two farm laborers seated at the counter watching a local cable news channel were eating late breakfasts.

Barney pointed out the specials and stepped away for a few minutes to let them peruse their menus. They focused on the list of pies.

A news story about Barney's Café was prominently displayed in a glass frame hanging on the wall next to the door. The faded two column print captioned a photo of the heavy-set, gray-bearded Barney and his plump rosy-cheeked wife wearing aprons imprinted with the café name.

"See what you want?" asked Bram.

"I do. I do."

Bram waved Barney over to the table and they ordered.

Bernadette's fork sliced into the thick yellow custard filling of a large wedge of pie coated with whipped cream. Bram watched her lift it to her mouth and insert it. He chuckled as her eyes rolled with culinary pleasure. "That good, huh?"

She nodded and mumbled, "That good."

"My turn." He sampled a forkful of hot apple pie ensconced in aromatic vapors of cinnamon and brown sugar. He looked at Bernadette and nodded.

"That good?'

"That good." He wiped away a slight drool of the golden pie filling from the corner of his lips.

Max alerted Bram and Bernadette that Mars was in the area, still some distance away, but approaching rapidly. They quickly left the small town café and headed east to the Mississippi River.

Barney figured that anyone wearing a business suit and driving a black Mercedes was from the Federal Government. They had come to this small rural town many times in the past to talk to local farmers about farm subsidies and harvesting corn to be processed into fuel. This guy was different. He didn't look like a salesman or a bureaucrat, more like a military type, and Barney detected the slight bulge of a handgun under his coat. He also projected a nervous lethal energy. The television program on in the café was interrupted by a news announcer showing photos of Bram and Bernadette as eco-terrorists. Mars flashed an FBI badge and questioned the café owner. With a surge of patriotic emotion, Barney said they had been there and left about an hour ago.

"What direction?"

"Headed east."

Bram and Bernadette were at the center of a long bridge crossing the Mississippi when Max's voice shouted out, "He's closing fast. You need an evasive maneuver, now. I can't do it for you from here."

As Mars increased his speed and approached the bridge spanning the river, the bridge suddenly disappeared.

Mars spoke to the disembodied presence of Blum. "They disappeared. They're gone. I've lost them. The whole bridge is gone."

Blum could see the Mercedes stopped at the approach. "It's an illusion. The bridge is still there, only you can't see it."

"You must be joking. The bridge is gone. The highway ends at the river."

"Do you see other vehicles? Other cars?"

"There are no other vehicles. No trucks, no cars. The highway is deserted."

"Were there cars and trucks before the bridge disappeared?"

"Yes, going in both directions. What do you see?"

"We see you in your car with only the river ahead of you. Simonetta has blocked us and she has isolated you."

"I thought you had control of her."

"Not until we capture and reprogram her. But because she conceals herself in the imagination of that woman, Bernadette, you have to capture her. But you have to kill Bram Vernon to stop what he is doing with the black spiral antidote."

"Well, I'm stranded here in the middle of god damn nowhere. What was real to me is now gone. What do you want me to do?"

"I have to discover where she went, then I can tell you and you can travel there. For now, turn around and drive back the way you came. Follow the river north."

"How far?"

"Until you come to the next bridge."

"So you think they crossed the river or did they just disappear?"

"I don't know yet," said Blum. "Simonetta is very clever. They disappeared into a void, perhaps a time warp, and could come out anywhere. When they do, we have the means to find them again and track them. Only next time we insert you into Simonetta's world, we'll have a tracking device that will give you the ability to follow her no matter where she goes, even if she disappears."

"I guess you never told me this would be easy."

"The black spiral is established but we are still in our infancy. So we are vulnerable."

"I'll keep that in mind."

"Also keep in mind that not only do we control you, we support you."

Mars floored the accelerator and the black Mercedes roared down the deserted highway.

After an hour, Blum spoke to him again. "Do you see a bridge yet?"

"Not yet."

"You'll be coming up on it in about five minutes."

"Thanks for keeping me informed."

"Attitude, Mars. Attitude. Stay focused."

"I am focused, very focused."

Chapter 29
Tracking

When they emerged from a blinding fog, Bram shouted, "What happened? Where are we?"

"I don't know," said Bernadette. "I have no idea. We'll have to figure it out."

"I thought you had an arrangement with Simonetta. She lives or hides inside you."

"She's in my imagination, but she's also separate and independent when she chooses to be. Just to make things clear, I am not Simonetta. I'm flesh and blood. She's a spirit."

"What about Max? What can he tell us? Max, are you there? Can you help us?"

"I've lost connection with him," said Bernadette. "We're on our own."

"Not good," said Bram. "Not good."

In the SIM, Max picked up transmissions of the eco-terrorist alert identifying Bram and Bernadette. He witnessed Mars showing his badge to the café owner and saw Mars rush outside, get into his car, and drive at a high speed east out of town.

"He's impersonating an FBI agent," said Berzinsky.

"I can't tell what's real and what isn't anymore," said Leon.

"A cross-over has occurred," said Max. "The SIM and reality have crossed over. Whatever is causing it is contained in the First World satellite signal. They are operating outside of our limited definition of the physical world. They've created their own parameters, their own forces, their own world. The antidote is the only way we can stop them."

A news anchor appeared on one of the adjacent screens in Max's media command center. What he was saying and the projection of Bram's and Bernadette's photos drew the attention of Leon and Berzinsky, especially the message that the FBI was now looking for them as eco-terrorists.

"Is what we're seeing and hearing real?" asked Leon. "Or just something that is being imagined in the SIM."

"Unfortunately, it's real. Not only do they have Mars trying to hunt them down, but the FBI is trying to find them."

"We need to notify headquarters," said Berzinsky. "Tell them to back off. Let them know."

"Actually, they could be safer, at least protected, if the FBI does find them," said Leon.

"FBI agents might identify them, but they won't capture them," said Max. "Through Simonetta, Bernadette can escape them, just like she did Mars."

"We need to let her know," said Berzinsky. "It's one more situation she has to deal with."

"She and Bram disappeared from the SIM. I can't seem to find them, let alone warn them."

"Well, let's hope you find them before Mars does."

"I think Bernadette will have to find us."

"Keep trying," said Berzinsky. "Just keep trying."

Concealed by tall dense spruce and pine forest, they followed a two lane paved road that wound along the shoreline of Lake Itasca in north central Minnesota.

Near a remote trail head at the edge of the lake, Bram deposited a vial of black spiral antidote serum in the water. It would replicate itself by trillions as the current carried it into the headwaters of the Mississippi to begin its long journey southward to the Gulf of Mexico infusing aquatic plants and algae with DNA that would be ingested by fish and waterfowl and land and aquatic mammals and proliferate and drift with sea currents to enter the global food chain of sea life that became a food source for man.

That they continued to be out of contact with Max worried Bram and he wondered why Bernadette didn't seem to share his concern.

"How did you know about this place?" he asked.

"When I was a little girl in elementary school, the class read about it and the teacher showed us on a wall map. I remembered it and that's what happened back at the bridge. Simonetta brought us here."

Other than the squawking of a jay and the distant rattle of a woodpecker mining for grubs in the protective bark of a tree, silence ruled the sunlit serenity of the lake's surface interrupted from time to time by the dimpling concentric whorls of rising trout feeding on floating insects.

"We're safe for the moment," said Bram, "but we can't stay. I'm depending on you to take us wherever we need to be."

"Simonetta is our guardian."

"Only if she's with you. You said yourself. Sometimes she isn't."

"She's with us when we need her."

"That sounds convenient, but don't you think we need her most of the time?"

"She's with us when I call on her."

"Don't you think that's a bit dicey, considering what's at stake and what could happen to us. The odds against us are more than fifty-fifty."

"We can't escape the killer. But I want to confront him on my terms."

"Your terms?"

"Simonetta's terms become my terms."

"So you're saying that at some point in time, we have to place ourselves at risk."

"Yes."

"Do you know what he's capable of?"

"I know what he's capable of. What he doesn't know is what Simonetta and I are capable of."

"It might help if I have a better idea. Your unexpected surprises leave me hanging."

"I'll get us to where we want to go."

"What about Max? We can't do this without him."

"We need Max to keep us informed where Mars is and what he's doing."

"It sounds like you can't do that yourself, or you and Simonetta."

"I don't know any more than you how close Mars is to finding us."

"Back at the bridge was too close."

"All I can do is react unless we can lure him into a trap."

"A trap? What kind of trap? He's a professional killer."

"I'll know when the time comes," said Bernadette.

"So everything you do is based on your intuition."

"Call it what you want."

"Like I said. This is all dicey. I'd like to know how well we're being protected, guaranteed security we can count on."

"There are no guarantees, Bram. We both know that. That's why we're here. That's why you're doing what you do and I'm doing what I do."

"You're saying there's a chance we won't succeed."

"You know the opposition as well as I do. You're closer to it on the science side. I'm closer on the spiritual side. We share the same goal."

"I guess that makes us well suited for each other."

Bernadette grinned. "You could say we balance each other out."

"Yeah, we have something in common."

"Without me, you'd still be hiding in some dark cellar in downtown New York City."

"Instead, I could be anywhere in the world with my life in danger."

"That's the spirit."

"You're really strange, but I can get used to that."

"You don't have a choice. We're partners." She paused, "for the duration."

He looked up from dabbling his fingers in the cold clear shallow water. "You mean for life?"

"At least for this SIM life."

Bram's eyes widened. "Is that a proposal?"

"Of sorts."

"Of sorts?"

Bram walked a few steps away, then turned and came back. "Can I think about it?"

"If I said no, you'd think about it anyway."

"But there are too many unknowns," said Bram. "We're in the middle of a war. We have a way to stop First World or at least hold them off, and in time, your DNA antidote will destroy the black spiral DNA."

"That could take centuries."

"At least you've started to reverse the black spiral influence and that reversal will continue. We have Simonetta to protect us. She's our shield."

"For how long? I'd like to live another sixty years or so. Dark energy is permanent in the universe. It doesn't go away. Hiram Bean will always be coming after us. What if Simonetta leaves you?"

"That will never happen."

"How can you be sure?"

"Because I'm a woman. I know. Simonetta is a part of who I am. I'm a daughter of Venus."

"Is that just something you're saying because we're inside a SIM?"

"I'm saying it because I am a reality, just as you are. Any more questions or are you done being skeptical?"

"I'll always be skeptical. That's my nature. That's who I am. I'm a scientist. I look for proof."

"Well, living proof is standing right before you, Mr. Scientist. You have to accept it. You have to accept me."

"I do."

"Good. We have to stay focused, on target, on task. You can't let your mind wander off being a doubting Thomas. It makes our situation more dangerous when you do that."

"How so?"

"When you question or doubt me, you weaken Simonetta's power. You have to believe in her without reservation, one hundred percent. Can you agree to do that?"

"Yes."

"Good, then we have a pact."

They watched the pollen powder sift away through their fingers. Picked up by the high winds they floated over the billowing prairie grasslands of Nebraska and Kansas and Oklahoma and joined the diaspora of the alpine meadows and forests of Colorado where they were further carried and spread by swarms of bees and insects. The grasses would be ingested by livestock and, eventually, the harvested grains by commercially raised fowl to become implanted and enter the food chain of man.

Since leaving the source waters of the Mississippi River, they drove undetected by the tracking system of Hieronymous Blum for ten days, crisscrossing the Great Plains region, spreading their precious supply of pollen over the land and DNA serum into rivers, lakes, and streams.

On a southbound highway from Utah into Southern Nevada, their situation changed.

Daphne DeBrunh's cascading leonine blonde streaked hair was her most important fashion feature followed closely by her physically augmented breasts, enlarged two cup sizes six months ago to celebrate her fourth divorce. Lacking the fine Aryan skin tone of the Orange County housewives, she tried her best to emulate their curvaceous figures by shedding thirty pounds, which increased the uplift of her breasts. She had also undergone a face lift to smooth out the appearance of telltale wrinkles at the corners of her eyes so that her expression was alluring rather than harsh and irritable, a condition she attributed to surviving her last four marriages.

She changed her name from Daphne to Kirsten, because it sounded Scandinavian and blonde. She had to constantly remind her friends and relatives that her name was no longer Daphne, but Kirsten. She started over, again, beginning anew with marriage number five as her latest conquest. Conquest in the sense that she had seduced the Southern California Orange County scion, Karl Kristofferson, out of his faltering second marriage for which he blamed his wife and six children for ruining his life and taking most of his money earned from real estate investments (flipping foreclosures).

He considered himself an expert in five card stud poker. A number of dealers and players disagreed with him and let him know by winning large sums of his money. He and Daphne/Kirsten were on their way to Vegas with a grand plan to recoup his losses before Daphne/Kirsten found out he was nearly broke. Assuming he was wealthy, a multi-millionaire, she was more interested in the alliteration of their Scandinavian names, Karl and Kirsten Kristofferson, and that they lived in Orange County. Her secret ambition was to become a star on the reality television show, The Housewives of Orange County.

The endless monotony of the Nevada desert had lulled Kirsten to sleep. Her head lolled to one side and came to rest against the passenger window. A light snore escaped her open mouth.

Her snoring irritated Karl. It spoiled her image of being an elite Orange County housewife sans children. She had no excuse but to maintain herself at all times of the day and night, be picture perfect. She did an excellent job of being sexy and photogenic, except for the small snore. He had had enough of exhausted wives who didn't keep up their sexual energy and interest and physical appearance. He had decided the time had come in his life and career to have a trophy wife. Although he would have preferred that Daphne/Kirsten (He had a hard time thinking of her as Kirsten, since he had met her as Daphne.) was ten years younger than forty, he had to admit she was a looker, and sexually charged. After all he was fifty-five and didn't want to be sleeping with someone who looked like his twenty-something daughters from his first marriage.

A sudden clanking noise under the car hood and an engine failure warning icon on the display reminded him he had not taken the vehicle in for maintenance service in over two years and he had added one-hundred-twenty-thousand miles since the last service. The sudden rapid loss of power alarmed him and he quickly pulled off onto the shoulder of the highway.

The loss of momentum woke Kirsten from her nap. "I fell asleep. Are we there?" Her view through the windshield and side windows told her otherwise. "We aren't there. Why are we stopping? What happened to the air conditioning? It's getting hot."

"I think it's the water pump," Karl snipped.

"The water pump?"

"It sounded like it broke."

"What do you mean broke? Cadillacs don't break down, at least not out here in the middle of nowhere."

Karl pulled out his cell phone. "Shit, the battery's dead."

"Here, use mine." She fished her phone out of her purse and handed it to him.

"Yours is dead too."

"Well, what the hell, Karl. What are we going to do? We're stranded in the middle of the god damn desert. You can't run the air conditioning. It's a hundred and twenty degrees. We're going to cook sitting here. We're going to die, Karl. Instead of going to Vegas and getting married, we're going to die. They're going to read about us in the Orange County Register."

"Don't get hysterical. You're overacting. We're not going to die. Someone will stop and help us. We'll get a ride to Henderson and I'll send a tow truck back for the car."

"Looks like someone's having car trouble," said Bram. "He shouldn't be standing out in the middle of the highway though. He could get run down."

As their jeep approached and slowed, the tall paunchy man with the desert wind whipping his thin blonde hair askew stopped wildly waving his bare arms and motioned them over behind his car with the passenger doors standing open. He removed his dark sunglasses. The tension in the man's body and the anxious expression rolling from his blue eyes caused Bram to think more than car trouble might be happening there. He saw the back of the woman's head in the car..

"Thank you for stopping. Thank God you stopped. My fiancée is really suffering."

"Should I call paramedics?" asked Bram.

"Another hour out here and we'd need paramedics. My car broke down and we're cooking alive in this heat. We're about an hour from Henderson. Could you give us a ride in?"

"Do you have a cell phone? You could have called Triple A or the highway patrol."

"Both our phones are dead. Not smart about that, or about the car. I ignored the service sign."

"Sure, we'll give you a ride."

"Thanks, you're a life saver. Be right back." Karl strode to his car and leaned in on the driver's side. "They'll give us a ride. I have to lock up."

"I need to get my bags out of the trunk."

"I'll have to ask about that. It doesn't look like they have a lot of extra room."

"At least one of my suitcases goes with me. I don't want to be stuck in the hotel without a change of clothes, and, of course, I need my bridal gown."

"You may have to wait for that until the car is towed in."

"How long you talking about?"

"Until the car gets towed. Later today. Our wedding isn't scheduled until tomorrow afternoon anyway."

"All right, but if anything happens to that dress, you're buying me a new one, on the spot. They have a bridal store right there in the hotel."

"Nothing will happen to your dress. Get out of the car. We don't want to keep them waiting."

"I'm getting. I'm getting. This is so frustrating, Karl. You don't know how frustrated I am."

"I know. I know. I'm frustrated too. Let's just deal with it."

"When we get there, I want a good stiff drink."

"So do I. So do I."

"Two or three. Open the trunk so I can get my suitcase." Kirsten lunged out of the car.

Bram and Bernadette watched the Cadillac trunk pop open and Karl haul out an oversize pink Samsonite suitcase and carry it back to Bram's side of the jeep.

"Do you think we could pack this in? My fiancé doesn't want to leave it out here."

"You can try," said Bram. "It'll have to fit between you. There's no room in storage."

Bernadette opened her passenger door and stepped out as Kirsten wobbled up on her heels.

"Thank you. Thank you," Kirsten flashed her perfect white crowns with a wide mouth smile. "You are so kind. You are both so kind. You never know when you're going to depend on the kindness of strangers."

Bernadette supported her elbow and heavy purse into the back seat, while Karl closed and locked the Cadillac doors and trunk, then returned to squeeze in behind Bram.

"God damn, it's hot," he said.

Bernadette handed them two Gatorades, as Bram pulled the jeep out onto the highway.

"Thanks." Karl twisted off one cap for Kirsten, who chugged half the bottle.

"God, I didn't know I was so thirsty," she gasped. "Your little jeep is cute, but you don't have air conditioning. You're just open to the hot air."

"We like fresh air," said Bernadette.

"That's easy for you to say wearing a tank top and no bra. But you've got a nice set, so nothing to be ashamed of."

Karl reached behind the pink suitcase between them and poked her arm.

"Of course, when we get to the hotel, I'll put on a tank top. Better yet, I'll wear a bikini and go out to the pool and have a triple mai tai. It's my favorite drink, even if we aren't in Hawaii."

"You goin' for the casinos?" asked Karl.

"Actually, we're just passing through."

"Oh, you look like outdoor types, boots and all. Hiking, camping, roughing it, sleeping out under the stars and all that."

"We do a lot of all that," said Bram.

"I'll take silk sheets and a posture pedic mattress and room service any day. How can you stand to sleep on the ground. I mean bugs and snakes. Aren't you afraid?"

"No," said Bernadette, "we're not afraid." She smiled sardonically at Kirsten's image in the rearview mirror. "We're one with nature and all that."

"You mean environmentalists and tree huggers and all that?"

"All that. We love all that," said Bernadette.

"Well, to each his own," said Karl. "It takes all kinds to make the world go 'round."

"It takes all kinds just to keep the world round," said Bram.

"What do you mean? The world is round. Always has been."

"It's getting flatter every day," said Bram.

"It is? How do you know that? I never heard anything about that."

"Not in the geophysical sense, in the digital sense."

"You must be a techy. I don't understand that kind of talk."

"In terms of how rapidly communication takes place and advances technology."

"You talk like a techy, so I won't ask."

"You two look kind of familiar," said Kirsten. "Are you from Hollywood? Maybe I saw you on television or in a movie."

"No," said Bernadette, "not famous at all. Nobody knows us."

"Where are you from?" asked Karl.

"New Yawk," Bernadette thickened her accent.

"Did you drive all the way across the country?" Kirsten asked.

"Every mile," said Bram. "Beautiful scenery. Interesting people, interesting places."

"I never traveled that much before. Raising kids and all that. But that's all going to change after tomorrow. Karl and I are getting married."

"Congratulations," said Bram. "Second marriage."

"Third for Karl. Fifth for me."

"Sounds like you've finally found true love," said Bernadette.

"It's amazing that something like that takes a while."

"Experience," said Karl, "life experience. You don't know what you're getting into in your twenties. Takes a few tries, if you know what I mean."

"We're still on our first," said Bram.

"You're not married yet?" asked Kirsten.

"We are in a manner of speaking."

"You have one of those modern relationships," said Kirsten.

"Yeah, pretty modern," said Bram. "Different."

"You really should get married, you know. You don't know what you're missing." Kirsten patted at her windblown hair. "I'll have to have my hair done all over again when we get to the hotel. This wind. It's awful. Your short haircut looks good on you," she said to Bernadette. "I don't have the face for it, but you do. But I like being blonde anyway. Being a brunette just isn't my personality. We're from Orange County, in Southern California. You've heard of it."

"We have," said Bram. "I have friends in California."

"Orange County?" asked Kirsten.

"Central Coast, wine country."

"Oh, I love wine," bubbled Kirsten. "Especially pinot grigio and chardonnay and champagne. Champagne is so festival."

"You like the sweet stuff," said Karl. "Me, I like the dark heavy reds, the cabs and zins and Jack Daniels."

"Sounds compatible," said Bram. "I like Glenn Fiddich and Glenn Mourangie."

"Never heard of 'em. They friends of yours?"

Bram grinned. "Yes, definitely, good friends."

Kirsten kept staring at Bram and Bernadette in the rearview mirror until Bram caught her eye and she quickly looked away.

As they approached the outskirts of Henderson, Kirsten moaned, "Oh, I really have to use the rest room. Could we stop at that minimart gas station?"

"Sure." Bram took the next off ramp which brought them to the gas pumps and minimart parking lot. He pulled the jeep into the nearest empty parking space and left the engine idling.

"You have to go too, don't you Karl?" Kirsten kicked at his leg to signal him, then stepped out of the jeep past Bernadette holding the door open for her. "Karl!"

"Yeah, yeah, I have to go. Excuse me." He tapped Bram on the shoulder. Bram stepped out to let him get past.

"We'll hurry," shouted Kirsten. "We'll be right back."

"Take your time," said Bram. "We're not in a hurry."

When they were out of earshot and entering the minimart, Bernadette said, "They recognize us."

"Yeah, I know," said Bram. "Probably saw us on the news."

Once they were inside the minimart, Kirsten grabbed Karl's arm at the restroom doors. "Don't you recognize them? They were that couple on the news last night. The ecoterrorists. There's a million dollar reward out for them. They're wanted by the FBI."

"No shit, I wasn't paying attention. If we turn them in, we'll get that reward money."

"Our cell phones don't work."

"Tell the cashier we have an emergency and need to use her phone."

Bram and Bernadette could see them through the store front window, as Karl and Kirsten cast surreptitious glances at them while scurrying over to the cashier.

"Time to move on," said Bram. "Kick that damn suitcase out of the back."

Bernadette reached into the back seat and pulled out the pink suitcase which she unceremoniously dropped in the empty parking space next to the jeep. She and Bram climbed back into the jeep and sped away as Karl was making his call to the FBI.

Impersonating the FBI agency contact, Hieronymous Bloom listened to the tense voice of Karl Kristofferson at the other end of the line describe his location at the minimart until Karl shouted, "They're driving away. They're leaving us and driving away. But I still want credit for identifying them and calling you. I'm entitled to that reward."

"Give me your address, Mr. Kristofferson, and I'll send you a check."

Ignoring Karl's rapid-fire response, he beamed in on Mars Livingston, who had been following the highway routes taken by Bram and Bernadette based on Bloom's satellite sightings. But the tracking signals had not been long enough or consistent enough and the jeep always eluded him. Despite his complaints to Blum, the situation didn't improve until the identification and call were made from Henderson, Nevada. Mars was driving across Arizona when Blum routed him to Las Vegas.

As they continued up the highway from Henderson into the city of Las Vegas, Bram and Bernadette picked up Max's voice.

"I have some bad news," he said. "You're not in the clear. The television and Internet media announcements have made it easy for anyone to identify you. And it's happened, only not the way we thought. Since you're in a SIM, First World is using the FBI as a front. The call-in number goes directly to First World and makes it easy for them to locate you. Mars Livingston will not be far behind you. Given that, what's your next move?"

"We're going to check in to a hotel for a couple of nights for a little well deserved R&R and get married," said Bram.

"Get married? Are you joking? You must be joking. You have to stay ahead of Mars. You can lose him again, but you have to keep on moving. You don't have a choice."

"You put us in this SIM. We want to take the situation into our own hands."

"Big mistake, Bram. There are too many unknowns. Your situation is going to be like that until you destroy First World."

"We can't destroy dark energy, Max. You know that. It will always be there to some extent no matter what we do. History bears that out. People don't change that fast. They just keep repeating themselves. We don't want to be stuck in this SIM forever."

"Not forever, but as long as you're there, you can accelerate the evolutionary process."

"By how much?"

"A few thousand years."

Bram guffawed. "Aren't you being a little overly optimistic?"

"Considering the pace of technology and medical advances, not at all."

"We're not going to be here in a few thousand years. We wouldn't want to be here in a few thousand years."

"Anything's possible in a SIM, Bram."

"So you think you can make all this happen?"

"I couldn't do it without you and Bernadette. You are my instruments."

"So you're playing God."

"God is only a product of the imagination. God is nothing more than an illusionist, a magician."

"And you're that magician."

"Yes, I am that magician."

"Bernadette and I are still going to get married, Max, tonight. We're coming into Vegas."

"I know. I can see you on my screen."

"Are Agents Safullo and Berzinsky still there with you?"

"They went home to their families. They'll be back in the morning."

"What do they think about all that's happening?"

"It has opened their minds and given them a new perspective of the world."

"We'd like to ask a favor of you, Max."

"What is it?"

"Don't spy on us when we're having sex. We value our privacy."

There was a long pause.

"Are you still there, Max, or did we lose you again."

"No, I'm here. I won't look at you. I'll just hover."

"Something like a guardian angel."

"Something like that."

"You're a dirty old man, Max."

"That's the nature of The Almighty. Remember, The Bible is filled with stories of sex and pornography."

"If we put you out of our minds, maybe you'll go away. We can do that, can't we? We're in a SIM after all."

"That's at your discretion, but you don't want to sever your connection with me. You're going to need me to bail you out when you get in trouble."

"We have Simonetta."

"She won't always be there for you."

"She's with us," said Bernadette.

"She's a free spirit. She can come and go. If you lose her, you might not be able to get out of the SIM and return to real life."

"She came to me in real life," said Bernadette. "She'll be with me always."

"Being chased by an assassin is not my idea of a happy honeymoon," said Max. "But congratulations on your impending marriage, nevertheless. Stay in touch."

"Thanks, Max. We will. You're a great guy."

"I know. It's my nature."

As they drove past the smaller hotels, motels, and fast food and service station franchises leading in to the strip, Bernadette posed a question to Bram.

"Why did you tell Max we're getting married?"

"I didn't think we should surprise him."

"Why? He's not a close relative. He's not even a relative. What we do is really none of his business."

"He seems to think everything we do is his business."

"Only because we're in his SIM."

"We have to complete the mission before we ever get out of the SIM."

"You mean before he lets us out."

"I guess that's what I mean."

"Did you get a sense that he really doesn't want to let us out? He likes controlling us. He called us his instruments."

"I don't think he would prevent us from returning to the real world when this is all over."

"I'm not so sure I feel the same way. He likes to be in charge. He likes to play God, even though God is only an imagined concept, as he puts it."

"I guess when you think about it," said Bram, "life is a kind of SIM. We all live and play out our roles. Some are more fictitious and imaginary than others. Look at all the media entertainment that tries to emulate life, movies, plays, reality shows, social networks, books. Even a wedding," said Bram. "Even though we're in a SIM and it's kind of a charade, a wedding would give us legal closure, clinch the relationship, made up or not."

"All weddings are charades. Just like that screwed up couple we tried to help out back there and they double-crossed us."

"Great view," said Bram.

"Beautiful, like having our own light show." Bernadette's nude body stood framed against the backdrop of the Vegas strip at night in all its megawatts of flashing glory.

Bram sipped the effervescent wine from his champagne flute. "Great champagne. Three hundred dollar bottle."

Bernadette threw back a long swallow that accentuated her stunning Celtic/Italian profile. "It's festival." They both laughed.

"You're festival," said Bram. "You're beautiful."

"Thank you, dear. I never thought you'd notice. You've been so preoccupied with your pollen."

"I'd like to create a little pollen of my own."

"Do you have the right DNA?"

"The best. You know, we could have brilliant and beautiful children. The best of both worlds. And I did notice you, from the first time we met. I haven't stopped noticing you since."

Bernadette crossed the penthouse suite to the super king size bed.

"Do you think Max is watching?"

"No," Bernadette drained her glass and gently set it on the side table. "Max is kind-hearted. He's a nice guy. He'll respect our privacy."

"Actually, I think he could be a voyeur," said Bram.

"No, be nice. Remember, he lost his wife. He's still in love with her."

"I'm in love with you."

"I know. It shows." She slid onto the silk sheets and touched his blood gorged erection.

"And do you love me?"

She flashed a wicked grin. "Haven't made up my mind yet. You have to convince me." She pressed her firm breasts against his side causing him to drop his empty champagne glass on the floor. His pulse pounded in his head as she swung her lean muscled leg over his torso and mounted him.

When their act of love was over and they lay exhausted side by side, Bram said, "If Max wasn't watching, he didn't know what he missed."

"Hush. By the way, I do love you."

"I 'm so glad."

"What time is it?"

"Who cares," said Bram. "The earth moved. Time just stood still."

"Our wedding is in a half hour. We have to shower and get down to the chapel."

"Get us to the church on time, is it? Can we come back up and make love again afterwards?"

"We can make love all night, sweetheart, as long as you can stay awake."

"I have every reason to stay awake. And you're it."

"Shower," she hopped out of bed.

"Together?"

"Together, it's faster."

Bram and Bernadette waited for the young couple ahead of them to finish. The receptionist led them into the chapel and along a maroon carpet to the altar where the minister wearing a white ice cream suit waited. His pencil mustached grin faltered and his expression intensified as he recognized them.

"Welcome to the chapel," his mellifluous voice swept over them as the canned musical accompaniment faded. "You are Mister Bram Vernon and Ms. Bernadette Garcetti," he glanced at his prompt cards on the altar.

"Yes, Yes."

"Are you prepared to state your vows?"

"We are," said Bram.

"Would you excuse me for just one moment," said the minister. "I have to take care of one small matter, and then we'll get right on with the ceremony."

"Okay," said Bram.

"Don't go away. I'll be right back." The minister stepped around them and walked quickly out to the front office. He closed the door shut behind him.

"Quick, call the FBI. I thought I recognized these two. I saw their pictures on the television news. They're the eco-terrorists. They're wanted by the FBI. Hurry. If I keep them waiting too long, they'll get suspicious."

But Bram and Bernadette were already suspicious and slipping out through the back exit of the chapel. They were gone when the minister returned.

"They were having a Vegas wedding," said Hieronymous Bloom. "At least they're still in town. Mars should be able to catch up to them."

"Do you know what hotel?" asked Hiram.

"The Wynn."

"Can you track them on the satellite?"

"Not in the casino. Too much interference."

"How about once they leave the hotel? They'll be on the run again."

"I'll be able to pick up their vehicle."

"Let Mars know."

"He's receiving my communication as we speak."

Bram and Bernadette rushed through the jangling casino and crowded hotel mall to the parking lot. Fifteen minutes later, they joined the heavy traffic on the strip and accessed the freeway south out of the city.

"What a pisser," said Bram. "I was looking forward to a night of ecstasy and instead, we're on the run again."

"Well, they say love has its obstacles."

"Max," Bram spoke into the warm desert night air, "you with us?"

"I'm with you."

"You know what happened?"

"Same as with that couple you gave a ride to. The minister recognized you and tried to call the FBI."

"Are we in the clear?"

"So far. Just keep heading southeast."

"What's southeast?"

"The Hoover Dam. You'll be turning off before you get there."

"What are we going to do there?"

"I'll tell you when you arrive."

***

With the help of Blum's tracking system, Mars had located the jeep headed west out of Las Vegas. Maximilian picked up Mars's black Mercedes in the SIM and warned Bram and Bernadette they were being followed and needed to execute a diversionary maneuver to lose him.

"He's about five miles behind you and closing fast," Max's voice came to Bram and Bernadette in the jeep. "Go off road at your first opportunity. It will be harder for him to catch up to you in rough desert terrain. He doesn't have the car or the tires for it. At some point, I'm going to have you disappear from his vision. Don't be afraid to follow my directions and do what I tell you. You won't be in danger."

"Is that your way of telling us we will be?" asked Bram.

"Nothing is going to happen to you, but Mars will believe what he sees."

Max directed them to drive to a high plateau overlooking the Colorado River gorge. Bram stopped the jeep.

"You can't be serious," said Bram. "Drive over the edge? This is not like crossing a bridge. There's nothing in front of us. There's nothing out there."

"Just stay where you are until Mars comes into sight. I want him to envision you going over the rim."

"But we don't really have to do that."

"I have perfect control of you. Remember that in the SIM, you exist as an illusion in an illusion as far as Mars is concerned."

"But we don't have to drive over the edge."

"No, you don't, but I'm going to make it appear that you are driving over the edge. At that moment, you will disappear."

"And by look you mean we can sit here in park with my foot on the brake."

"You can keep your foot on the brake. You can turn off the engine if you want."

"You're going to move the jeep with us still in it."

"You will still be in it."

"Where will we come out?"

"You'll know when you get there. I don't want you to be concerned with too much advance information."

"Hey, Max, don't do us any favors. Just get us back alive."

"You're not alive now. You're an illusion."

"I don't know what an illusion is supposed to feel like, but I feel like my old alive self."

"Keep on thinking that and you'll do fine."

"That is not encouraging, Max. Not encouraging." Bram looked over at Bernadette. "You okay with this?"

"Simonetta is here with us. We'll be all right."

"I'd feel better if I could see her."

"You're looking at her."

"I'm looking at her."

"Yes."

"You're her."

"Yes."

Bram glanced at the side view mirror. "Oh shit, I see his car. He'll coming up behind us."

"How far back?"

"A few hundred yards. All right, Max, don't keep us waiting. Work your magic. Do your stuff."

Mars stepped out of his car and walked to the edge of the chasm and looked down at the one thousand foot drop to the Colorado River, a shiny ribbon on the canyon floor.

"They're gone again," said Mars. "They just drove over a cliff and disappeared. You need a better plan to get them, Blum. What you're doing isn't working."

"Your point is dissatisfying, but well-taken, Mars. I get the message. Hiram and I have been discussing the situation. She will have to come after you outside of the SIM. Once Bernadette

Garcetti is a real person again, she has no way to escape. We can take her."

"I'm listening."

"Simonetta exists in Garcetti's mind. Once you kill her, Simonetta becomes a rogue dark spirit without a home. She'll be vulnerable and we can capture her."

Chapter 30
The Return

"Max, where have you sent us?" Bram looked ahead as the jeep careened along, then slowed to comply with the speed limit in the suburban neighborhood.

"You're back in New York."

"The real New York?" asked Bernadette.

"The real New York," said Max. "Drive directly here to the warehouse. You're not safe out there on the streets. I had to take you out of the SIM. Until you terminate Livingston, you won't succeed in taking down First World."

"Where is he now?"

"As soon as First World picks up your new location, he'll be after you again. You can't escape Livingston. You have to kill him before he kills you. The problem is, since you're no longer inside the SIM, you can't escape from him by disappearing. You and Bram are just like every other person, except for one weapon."

"Simonetta."

"Yes."

Bernadette left the warehouse and walked out among the throngs on the crowded streets. Hieronymous Blum tracked her movement and alerted Mars. He went to her location and stalked her among the surge of pedestrians and the rush of city traffic.

Max's voice spoke in her head. "He found you. He's following you now."

The crowd was too dense for Bernadette to run. She turned up the steps into St. Stephens Cathedral. Mars forced his way through a group at the entrance and went inside. He looked about for her, but she was nowhere to be seen.

As he approached a crowd of Chinese vacationers on tour, he noticed a nun emerge from a side door, but paid no attention to her. She walked across the front row of pews and with head bowed, turned toward him coming along the aisle to the altar. Her hand rose up from under her cloak like a striking snake and plunged a hypodermic needle containing the DNA antidote into his mid-section thrusting upward under his ribs directly into his heart. He cried out as his body shook and trembled. He turned and ran out of the cathedral into the traffic. Rending the air with the crunch of metal and braying of horns, cars and trucks and buses swerve to avoid him and piled up in multiple collisions.

Stunned bystanders watched him vibrate and physically disintegrate to a core of incandescent flesh, leaving a small pile of ash. A sudden rising wind scattered the ashes down the street.

Dressed as a nun, Bernadette stood on the steps of the cathedral. Simonetta left Bernadette's human form and walked steadily forward in the direction of the First World Corporation building at the central block of Wall Street.

She entered the building. A moment later, a violent explosion toppled the black glass tower reducing it to a pile of dust and debris. From the cathedral steps, Bernadette watched the crowd of people cowering in the street, believing another Jihad attack was happening. They heard a deafening roaring sound and saw the long tail of a tornado descend from a massive black cloud, vacuum up the remains of the building and carry them away out over the ocean where it rose into the atmosphere and vanished.

Epilogue

When Bram and Bernadette went back to see Maximilian, they discovered the magician, and all that the warehouse had contained were gone, as though the man and his props had never existed. Their footsteps echoed along the deserted floors.

Maximillian's disappearance did not confound them. They had both experienced the paranormal world, Bernadette with spiritual possession and Bram with the discovery of a parallel existence to humans. They believed Maximillian still existed somewhere and they would encounter him again.

Bram and Bernadette were no longer two separate individuals struggling against the overwhelming forces of dark energy. They had come together to survive and, in so doing, had discovered their connection of love.

They bought a house in an outlying New York suburb and began living normal lives. Shopping together at the supermarket was a more valued shared experience than escaping from an assassin in a virtual world. Jogging in the park was part of their daily routine. Sharing a bottle of wine and having dinner on the patio became a ritual.

But the greatest happening in their life was becoming the parents of two children, a boy, they named Max, and a girl they named Simone.

Bernadette went to work for a progressive think tank, New Millennium.

Bram was hired as a genetic researcher in a prominent laboratory where he further investigated the existence, evolution, and influences of the triple helix Black Spiral DNA.

The spiritual invasion had advanced too far to stop it from spreading like a cosmic cancer into every facet of life. It existed on a parallel plane and was consuming and taking over the original physiological genetic phenomenon of biological evolution. Individuals and groups, and whole societies could only react to it.

The world could not escape it.

About the Author

Author and retired business and management consultant in a wide range of industries throughout the country, Rob resides with his wife in Southern California.

He is a graduate of the University of California, Santa Barbara and of the University of California, Los Angeles with Bachelor's and Masters of Fine Arts Degrees. He is a recipient of the Samuel Goldwyn and Donald Davis Literary Awards and has also worked in advertising, corporate communications, and media production.

An affinity for family and generations pervades his novels.

His works are literary and genre fiction that address the nature and importance of personal integrity.

***

Tell-Tale would like to thank you for your purchase. If you enjoyed this work of fiction, please let the author know by leaving a favorable online review. If you would like to read other works by this or other fine TT authors, please visit our website:

www.ingramcontent.com/pod-product-compliance
Lightning Source LLC
Chambersburg PA
CBHW030624310726
48979CB00003B/861